D1606210

A Forever

Home

GREY'S RANCH TRILOGY

A Novel

Pamela J. Roe

PAGE PUBLISHING, INC.
Conneaut Lake, PA

First originally published by Page Publishing 2020

ISBN 978-1-6624-0664-5 (pbk)
ISBN 978-1-6624-0665-2 (digital)

Printed in the United States of America

To my remarkable husband, Jeffrey, and our family, John, Ryan, Michael, and Katelin. Dreams really do come true.

Map of Kosovo

Maroon Bells and Maroon Lake

Colorado Mountains

Preface, January 1998

ALESSANDRA PETROVICH IS forced to leave her home, caught in a struggle between ethnic groups and terrified by the father she loved. She and her mother hide among hundreds of thousands of refugees seeking asylum to escape Kosovo. Their journey ends in the United States, where the women find solace in a small midwestern town, rebuilding their lives and creating a home. After fifteen years, Alessandra finds out the father she has chosen to forget, is desperate to find her. Forced to flee the safety of her home, once again, she's on the run. This time, alone.

Orion Grey returns to the small village of Hideaway Canyon, near his family's ranch in Colorado, to recuperate from his latest mission. Striving to understand the sacrifices required of him, Orion struggles to rectify his idealistic childhood filled with love from his family and his mother's belief in the stars, with a deep darkness that haunts him from his job.

Orion does what any man would after finding an unconscious woman along the roadside during a winter storm. Alessandra and Orion's worlds are thrust together. Will Orion be able to help the woman find out where she came from? Does the woman really want to know? What kinds of dangers will Alessandra bring to the peaceful mountain village?

Kosovo, January 1, 1998

KNOWING IT WAS safest to keep her identity a secret, Alessandra remained quiet as she sat in the back seat of the car with her mother. Her mind wandered, thinking about the many miles they had walked, with little food or water. Their shoes were now shredded by the rough terrain and their clothes dirty and soiled as they struggled among strangers to survive. Afraid, as she lay on the hard ground in the darkness, her eyes searched for hope as she saw the bright stars in the sky. Always walking, always moving, the days passed slowly. Alessandra and her mother hid among thousands of families, escaping the violence in their own country—refugees fleeing their home in search of another. Throughout the long drive, Alessandra watched out the window from the back seat of the car, at surroundings she had never seen before. She knew her journey would be long; they had already been driving for hours. Her sixteenth birthday would be celebrated in a strange country without her friends. Tears pooled in her eyes as the memories floating through her mind took her to the place she was forced to leave behind. Would she ever see the beautiful mountains and valleys of her home in Kosovo again? She knew she would never see Milena or her father again. Alessandra remembered the wonderful days spent with her father and mother, on picnics at Mount Gjeravica, where they would spend the day hiking, picking flowers and searching for chamois, deer, and foxes. Many days she and her father would ride horseback through the rolling hills along the river. Tall grass and oak trees blanketed the rolling hills, and pine trees covered the surrounding mountains. On special occasions, Anton Petrovich would take his wife and daughter into Pristina, the capital, for a long weekend of shopping. Alessandra's father would surprise the two women before ending their vacation with a visit to the ballet, her mother's favorite part of the trip, and an exquisite dinner at a fine restaurant. Her mother would always weep at the end of the weekend; tears of happiness, she would lie to her husband.

A deep cough caught Alessandra's attention. Recognizing it as her mother's, she looked over to check on the woman, knowing her mother, sitting next to her in the back seat of the driver's car, had been sleeping for the past two hours. Koysta had hired the man to drive them to the coast. She had never seen the man before, and she and her mother had been instructed by her uncle not to speak a word during their trip. Koysta would do the talking. Gazing at Alina Ulanova Petrovich, Alessandra saw the beautiful woman that still lie under the layers of soiled clothing. As she studied her mother, sadness enveloped her, disheartened by the woman's slight build and deep, dark, sunken eyes. Alina Ulanova had been a premier ballerina with the Mariinsky Ballet in St. Petersburg, Russia until she, by happenstance, met a handsome young officer in the Yugoslav People's Army, Anton Petrovich, Alessandra's father. Alina and Anton fell in love. Anton was mesmerized by the beautiful ballerina, impressing her into marriage, and moving her to Gjakova, Kosovo, a small village in his home country. Alessandra's mother left the ballet company shortly after marrying her father, happily joining him for what was promised to be a beautiful life. Petrovich had already established himself as an up and coming leader in the Yugoslav People's Army. The couple made a happy life for themselves in the small community of Gjakova, enjoying the rewards of hard work and a life filled with their love for one another. It wasn't long before the young couple was blessed with the birth of Alessandra. Life could not have been better, until one day, when it turned so ugly—the day she left home forever.

Alessandra paused, once more, to look out the window at the unfamiliar land, glancing back to her mother. Her eyes gazed upon the woman she loved so much. She had rebelled against the thought of leaving her home, arguing with her mother refusing to leave. But now, looking at her mother and the coat she was wearing, she knew differently. Alessandra knew the quality of the coat her mother wore, and that of her own. She noticed how shabby and tattered and dirty they were now, causing her heart to leap in anguish. Gently reaching for Alina's scarf, Alessandra pulled it closer around her mother's neck, protecting her from the cold. She glanced at the driver and her uncle, Koysta, sitting in the front seat of the car before letting her mind wander once again.

It wasn't long before the car she now road in, pulled off the road to stop. Alessandra woke her mother aware they would have only a few minutes to take care of necessities. After pulling the scarf over her head to remain hidden, she helped her mother out of the car, signaling to her uncle they would only be a few minutes. Koysta stepped out of the car and pulled out a cigarette, after paying the driver for gas. When Alina and Alessandra walked back to the car, Koysta joined them, telling them they would be at their destination within the hour. Once they arrived, there would be no time to waste. Alina and Alessandra would make haste boarding a ship crossing the Adriatic Sea that would take them into Italy. When they landed, Koysta's guide would locate the women and transport them by car to Rome. Throughout the drive, they must remain quiet and keep their faces covered. The driver will believe the women couldn't speak his language. When they arrived in Rome, Alina and Alessandra would be dropped off at the airport. At the end of their journey to Rome, the driver would hand them a package with airline tickets and directions. They would catch a flight to Paris where they would wait until Koysta contacted them. He would not contact them until he knew it was safe.

Signaling it was time to leave, the passengers got into the car and drove off. It wasn't long before Alessandra saw the glistening blue waters of the Adriatic Sea. The beauty of the sea and the excitement she felt could not prevent her eyes from filling with tears.

Alessandra's uncle wrapped his arms around her, pulling her into his huge body. "Kroshka," he said, kissing both cheeks, "take care of your mother," and released her. Koysta hugged his sister as they exchanged a few quiet words. He handed her an envelope containing new passports and money to use until they arrived in Paris. In Paris, they were to go to the airport lockbox, with the number that Koysta gave them, and take out the envelope enclosed. At that time, they would destroy their old passports and cell phones, using only the ones in the envelope. Taking one final look at her uncle, Alessandra took her mother's hand in hers, each picked up one small piece of luggage, and the two women boarded the ship. Alessandra knew she wouldn't look back.

After a week of traveling, Alina and Alessandra had arrived in Paris. Both were exhausted and dirty. As instructed, Alina and Alessandra went to the lockbox and took out the envelope. They remembered to destroy their old passports and dispose of the cell phone they had been using in their escape. Alina called her friend. Maria McBride and Alina had met during a performance at Moscow's Bolshoi Theatre years before and had struck up a friendship. Anton Petrovich had always refused to allow Alina to keep in touch with her friends from ballet. However, Alina knew through newspapers that Maria remained in Paris, and she was sure her friend would help them out. Alina and Alessandra remained with Maria for almost three months in Paris, anticipating word from Koysta. Refusing to accept charity, mother and daughter cleaned the apartment and cooked meals to earn their keep. Alina earned money with the little bit of laundry and mending Maria would bring home to her from company ballerinas. Alessandra spent her days reading and studying French and English at her mother's assistance. They couldn't afford a tutor, nor could Alessandra attend school, but between Maria's help and books from the library, Alessandra began to understand both languages. Mother and daughter settled into their short-lived life in Paris, becoming part of an invisible community of refugees whose only wish was to escape and survive. As a small reprieve from the trauma of their exodus from Kosovo, Maria would gather mother and daughter and lead them up to the rooftop of her flat, where the three women would drink wine and dance under the stars. For its short duration, life in Paris was a safe and simple one.

Finally, a small package arrived from Koysta with instructions for the final leg of their journey. Following the enclosed instructions, Alina and Alessandra bought a disposable phone, memorizing the phone numbers and instructions within the package. Tears ran down Alina's face as she whispered a 'thank you' to her brother, then hid the money Koysta had sent in her luggage. She opened a small white envelope holding a single sheet of paper inside, with the words "Petrovich searches." The words terrified the women. Already packed, the mother and daughter hastened to the airport for the rest of their journey after thanking Maria and saying their goodbyes, knowing they would never see her again. Their immediate departure was critical to Maria's safety; Anton Petrovich would be ruthless in his search.

Alina and Alessandra took a taxi to the Paris Charles de Gaulle Airport, arriving in time to catch their flight to Montreal, Canada. Alessandra had never seen anything like it. Her mother ushered her through the security checkpoint, instructing her not to speak. Alina answered questions from the security officers, explaining her daughter wasn't fluent in the language. She explained she was accompanying her young daughter into Canada, for college.

The crowds of people, all hurrying and talking at the same time, mesmerized Alessandra. She'd never seen so many restaurants or smelled so many wonderful smells in one place. Alina, recognizing the wonder in her daughter's face, and smiled. "Alessandra, let's treat ourselves to breakfast before our flight leaves." Hugging her mother for the kind gesture, the two women sat down in a little cafe, sharing strawberry crepes with fresh cream, laughing and enjoying the moment.

Upon their arrival in Montreal, the mother and daughter were met by a man hired by Koysta, who would take them across the border from Canada and into the United States. Seeing the two beautiful women, the driver smiled; he would drive them as far as they wanted to go, as long as they had money to pay him. Sickened by the wicked smile the man was giving her daughter, Alina asked the man to stop at a bus stop when they arrived in Chicago. Alina recognized this kind of man. The bus stop hadn't been part of Koysta's plan, but Alina feared for her daughter's safety. After the women got out, Alina approached the ticket counter, asking when the next bus left. The attendant told her in thirteen minutes. She bought two one-way tickets. "By the way, where is the bus going?" she asked.

"The final stop is Seatonville, Illinois," the ticket attendant answered.

"Perfect, thank you."

Fifteen years later, Illinois, April 19, 2013

The road had become a familiar one for Alessandra. Once she was out of the city, she would hit the highway heading out of Illinois through Iowa. It was a main corridor through an area she grew to love and one she had wanted to call her forever home—until now. Heartbroken, she realized, forever was nothing she could ever wish for. Forever was only in fairy tales. Once again, she was being forced to flee, escaping her past, searching for safety. She'd been on this drive countless times, leaving Chicago every weekend to visit her mother. For Alessandra, Seatonville was the last bus stop, a small Midwestern town, halfway between Chicago and the Iowa-Illinois state border. Seatonville had been the women's hiding place for over a decade. It had become home; Alessandra had even begun to feel safe.

But this morning, as she drove from her apartment in Chicago, the familiarity of Interstate 80 should have been calming; however, the further she drove, the louder and quicker her heartbeat. Alessandra wouldn't be turning off the road on her usual path to her mother's. She was forced to leave her home, a place she grew to love, and her mother. Alessandra's head pounded.

Driving through the acres and acres of corn and hay fields had grown to be comforting and ordinary, always noneventful, always familiar and safe. Rolling hills with beautiful hues of long verdant leaves whispering in the wind and rows and rows of plants, each perfectly aligned. When she first arrived, she missed the beauty of the mountains that had surrounded her home in Kosovo, but that seemed so very long ago. Having frequently driven this corridor, Alessandra didn't need to put any thought into watching for road signs, knowing it would be hours until she needed to look at her Google Maps app for further directions. Her memories took her back in time, fifteen years ago, when she and her mother fled their home in Kosovo. She never imagined she would be fleeing again. She thought she was safe, but she wasn't.

As so many times before, Alessandra's citrine eyes collected with tears reflecting the deepest depths of the oceans, overflowing and streaking down her cheeks and drenching her lap. Her body quivered. She was bolted from a half-conscious state by what she recognized as vociferous sobbing. Where was this crying coming from? She looked around inside her jeep, but no one was there. Alessandra recognized two old and scuffed suitcases used by the two women when they left Kosovo and a back seat filled with the only few personal items, she allowed herself to bring. She knew the black plastic garbage bags were filled with a set of sheets, some old towels, and a couple of blankets her mother had insisted on packing. And of course, the box filled with books, photos, and mementos, most from her life in the Midwest, only a few photos from her childhood. Once again, Alessandra would run for her life, this time forced to leave the mother she loved, forced to leave another home. Her mother had insisted she take the photos and her jewelry. Jewelry Alessandra's father had given his wife during a time when things were happy for her family, before the mother and child left Kosovo, before Milena's death. Alessandra had pressed her mother to keep the items, knowing they were the only few things the woman had left, fearing she might not see her mother again.

Alessandra's uncle Koysta had prepared her well for the responsibility that lay ahead, hiding in a strange land. When they settled in the small town, Alina continued to clean homes and mend clothes of wealthier people, while Alessandra finished her education. Koysta would send money when he could and even surprised his sister and niece with a visit once. But as they all knew, it was safest for Alessandra and Alina if he stayed away; Petrovich could have him followed. For the past five years, and without telling her mother, Alessandra had cashed and set aside every paycheck she received from her job in Chicago, fearing this day would come. She thought she saw the man in a dark suit across the street from her apartment. But when she recognized the same man near her office, walking to lunch with her boss, she knew the time had come.

As the years passed, Alessandra's life in Kosovo had turned into a distant memory. It had become harder and harder to remember that time; however, she would never forget her father, the man she had loved as a child, the man she now feared. The simple life the mother and daughter had found in the small Midwest town had been enough, their refuge, their home. Now, once again, Alessandra was forced to flee for her life, this time leaving the frail, sick woman she loved, her mother.

There wasn't another person in the car. Stunned, Alessandra realized it was her own cries that she heard. Clouds had gathered, and the light rain turned into a downpour. She inched her way into the right-hand lane of traffic, as cautiously as she had always done, pulling onto the side of the road without going too close to the edge, knowing how soft the shoulder of the road could become during a Midwest rainstorm and fearful that she might drop into the ditch, if she wasn't careful. Her hands were shaking; sweat was collecting on a forehead that was throbbing in pain. For what seemed like hours, Alessandra sat in her car, giving in to the pain, shivering and sobbing, her heart palpitating as the car idled along the side of the road, rain gently tapping on the windows as her windshield wipers tried to clear the way. The speed of cars and trucks driving by created a gentle rhythm that rocked her car and might have put her to sleep, had her fears and emotions not been heightened. Tears continued to flow as her mind wandered back in time.

Kosovo, January 1, 1998

Plans for Alessandra and Alina's escape had been prearranged by Koysta. Her mother had insisted weeks before, that both the women have their luggage packed, hidden away from her father, enabling them to leave at a moment's notice. If he knew, her father would never allow them to leave. Petrovich's job in the army required him to be gone for days, weeks, and sometimes months at a time. Her father would be angry finding out her uncle Koysta had visited his sister and niece while he was away. Most times, after her uncle's visit, Anton would shout at her mother, before storming out of their home. The older Alessandra became, the more she began to understand the fear she would see in her mother's eyes when her husband returned home. The father she loved so much could be a very cruel man. He was one of Yugoslav's top commanding generals, and his job was to extinguish the radical movement at all costs, notwithstanding the use of oppressive tactics and violence. Mother and daughter hid their plans to leave Anton Petrovich, knowing the danger they would be in. Alessandra did not speak of their plans of escape to anyone, not even her best friend, Milena. She knew her mother lived in fear that Petrovich would find out Koysta was planning their escape, both knowing the man's anger could lead to unspeakable things. Alessandra had seen a number of students dwindle in her classroom, until finally, one day, the school was closed entirely. Actions credited too Mikozavich's tyranny. No one was safe anymore. Even Alessandra's friends seemed to whisper behind her back, knowing the position her father held in Mikozavich's army. Alessandra had always wanted to believe the innocence of her father; he was only following orders.

It was a beautiful morning for a horseback ride. The sun was out, and the cool air from the fall day chilled the girls' faces as they raced around the trees on their horses. It was Alessandra's idea to follow her father when she saw him mount his horse and head into the woods. It was a day she didn't want to remember, a day she lost her friend, her father, and her home.

Not long after, on a night when the moon was nothing more than a sliver, Alina and Alessandra waited quietly in their home in the dark, expecting a signal. Hours seemed to pass, and nothing happened. Just as Alessandra began to dose off, her mother called her name out sharply, commanding her to grab her bag and quickly follow her out the back door. As her mother held onto her daughter's hand and pulled her hurriedly toward the edge of the trees, Alessandra was alerted to faint cries she heard coming from the other side of town. Looking back, she saw a huge glow in the sky—the town was on fire. Without words, Alina and Alessandra ran into the forest behind their home, never stopping to catch their breath. When they arrived at the bank of the river, the women recognized Koysta and quietly followed his instructions to get into the boat. Covering their heads with their scarves, they huddled silently together, conscious of any motion that could threaten their three lives. Koysta rowed for several miles to a cove along the river, where he helped the women onto the bank. In the moonlight, Alessandra saw thousands of people hiding, waiting silently to begin their journey. They walked for hours in the dark. Stumbling and picking themselves up. Never complaining about the need to rest. Soon, the sun began to rise, and Koysta pointed to a man standing near a car on the road ahead, indicating what was to be their passage to the coast. Overwhelmed by exhaustion and relief, tears stung Alessandra's eyes. Would she ever have a home?

Illinois, April 19, 2013

"Why am I crying?" she asked anyone listening. She knew the possibility had always been there, that she might be forced to leave; however, she hadn't expected it to be so soon. And not without her mother. Now was not a good time. Her mother had been ill for months and wasn't seeming to get better. Her mother needed Alessandra's care. Knowing her daughter's safety was at stake, her mother insisted Alessandra flee, refusing to go with her. She was too weak to travel, and her medical needs would prevent them from being able to completely disappear. Alessandra would flee, and when she knew it was safe, she would send for her mother. It would be too much of a risk for Alina and Alessandra to remain together.

Alessandra sat on the side of the road, lost in her memories. Koysta had warned the mother and daughter, many times, a day might come when their survival would require Alina and Alessandra to part ways. Alessandra had always dismissed what her uncle said, knowing she was strong enough to care for them both. But now, she wasn't given a choice in the matter. Alina made the decision—Alessandra must leave, alone. Was she strong enough to do this? To move across yet another country, walk away from her mother, begin again in a place she didn't know. For over ten years, she felt safe. She had a home. Her dreams had grown up to include this place she called home, where her mother brought her so many years ago, to the anonymity of a small town in the Midwest. But now, this couldn't be home for her anymore. Even though years had passed, Alessandra recognized her father's men. The very men she and her mother had run from so many years ago. Before long, Alessandra and her mother knew Anton Petrovich would come for them, knowing his anger would not diminish with time. If he didn't order their deaths, he would have them brought to him, where they would be forced to live a life in captivity. Knowing her father as she did, Alessandra believed her mother's illness would keep her safe. He might demand she return to Kosovo, but he would provide her with the best medical care possible. Despite everything, Anton always held a great love for Alina Ulanova Petrovich, even after she and her daughter defied him and fled. Her mother would be safe; for now, she wouldn't know where Alessandra was. The decision had been made to keep them both alive. Tucking old memories as far back in her memory as possible, Alessandra would once again, flee her home. She was determined to make a new life for herself, to find a home. One far away from an old life filled with heartbreak. A place where heartbreak and her father couldn't find her.

Scattered cumulus clouds floated in the sky, shedding a shadowy haze on the road ahead. Was this a foretelling of what lay ahead? she thought. After what seemed like hours, with feelings of fear, self-doubt, and anxiety, and the weather—a gloomy rain-filled day, typical for the Midwest, what she was used to—Alessandra swiped her sleeve across her face to wipe away her tears and commanded out loud, "Okay, quit crying. You have to do this. You are going to survive! You are brave and strong. You have generations of Ulanova and Petrovich blood in you. Be proud." This was a new beginning, a chance to see the world, a chance for opportunities you would never have been able to realize, and a chance to find out what you want, a chance to escape. A chance to be content, find happiness and a home," Alessandra said out loud to the only person listening. She could never go back. She would send for her mother. Seatonville wasn't her home anymore.

After clearing her thoughts and regaining her composure enough to drive safely, Alessandra sat up straight, inhaled deeply, took a final swipe across her eyes with her sleeve, and cautiously, like always, inched her way back onto the interstate in her old jeep. She would have used her left blinker; however, before starting her trip, her mechanic indicated it would cost sixty-nine dollars to replace the light, and Alessandra knew she needed every dime in her pocket for when she arrived at her final destination. It wasn't something essential for her to make the trip. She would need to find a job immediately and a place to live. It didn't need to be fancy, just a bed and a shower. And there was nothing she wasn't willing to do to survive.

Her side-of-the-road breakdown must have worked because, before long, she crossed the state border, her tears were a memory, and the sun began to break through the clouds. Her headache was gone, and the pounding in Alessandra's chest had submerged into her chest and was only slightly noticeable. The "Welcome to Colorado" sign in her rearview mirror made her smile, but she was only passing through.

Colorado, April 19, 2013

Sitting in his usual spot, back to the wall, Orion did not shine brightly, like his namesake constellation. It only took one glance to know the man wanted to be left alone, deep in his own thoughts. Memories growing up on his parent's ranch near Hideaway Canyon brought a small curve to the corners of Orion's lips, one of the reasons he'd decided to visit the area. He loved his mother and father; he couldn't have asked for a better family or better childhood. Oaklin always allowed the stars in the sky to guide her life, making important life decisions only when the stars aligned. How many times had she entertained her family with stories of Greek gods and mythology and the formation of the constellations she chose to name her children after? All Oaklin's children, including her youngest son, were proudly told they had celestial beginnings. According to his mother and his father, Orion was a special gift granted to the Greys from the heavens above. Of course, he knew all parents thought of their children as special gifts. Despite his refusal to allow the stars to control anything in his life, he loved his mother and respected her choice to believe. He was a skeptic of Greek lore; he never saw himself as a giant hunter placed in the sky by Zeus to defend himself against Taurus. Orion was a pragmatic, his head was not up in the clouds, nor embedded in Greek mythology. Orion had no desire to shine bright; however, without a doubt, Orion was noticeable.

Taking a draw on his beer and trying to forget his last assignment, Orion was comforted by the darkness he found in the corner of this desolate tavern, nursing his wounds, wounds covered by his clothing and tucked away in his mind. He relaxed as much as any paid mercenary could, replaying the events leading up to his arrival in the small western town of Hideaway Canyon. He had arrived three months ago looking for a place to disappear and a place to clear his head, from the horrors he saw on the job. At the prodding of his sister, Lyra, Orion accepted her offer to return to the place he grew up and sought solace among his family and in the familiar canyon. He never meant to stay longer than a week. However, the stars began to align, as Oaklin would say. Orion was finding peace and contentment in the small, unassuming community he grew up in and began to thrive as he accepted the slow rhythm of life at Hideaway Canyon. The ranch lifestyle was one he had never considered, his job took him all over the world, oftentimes to dark places. He liked the travel, to see the world, and meet new faces. Now, more than ever, the faces returned at night during the darkest of his dreams. Of course, having Lyra and her family living in Hideaway Canyon and Crux, on the family ranch outside of town, gave Orion incentive to extend his stay.

Orion stretched his long muscular legs out, tension visibly leaving his shoulders while he devoured the last of his beer and signaled the bartender, Jess, for another. Orion had golden shoulder-length locks curled at the nape of his neck, peeking out from under his collar in its usual disarray. Ignoring his western disguise appropriate for the inclement weather—a thick Carhartt sheepskin lined coat thrown haphazardly over an extra chair at his table, the worn jeans, dusty and stained cowboy boots, and a faded and frayed flannel shirt—he looked more like a surfer after a day catching waves along the California coast. What would a California surfer be doing at a dark, isolated, cold mountain town far away from a more cosmopolitan beach population, where he looked like he should be relaxing on the pier with a beautiful girl, or catching waves on the beach until sunset? Deceptive in looks to all but those who didn't know him or those who hadn't been close enough to read the signs in his penetrating dark eyes, any passerby wouldn't have given him more than a glance. Locals had learned to keep their distance when Orion occupied the corner table at The Rip at the end of the day, especially when he showed no signs of offering an invitation to join him.

The weathered lines drawn in Orion's face would have made anyone entering the tavern think he was a local rancher dropping by at the end of the day for dinner and a beer. But he wasn't a local rancher. He didn't want companionship or conversation with anyone, especially today, not even with Lyra, whom he was known to make time for. He was only a patron with a yearning for a cold beer and privacy.

Jess—who, more often than not, assumed the role of bartender, sometimes cook and custodian, and always proprietor of this dark, out-of-the-way establishment—approached his brother-in-law sitting in the corner with his usually long strides, dropped off another cold, tall one, gave a quick glance at Orion, picked up the empty, and returned to the bar. He'd had enough experience to know when a man needed to be left alone, needed some solitude. Suspecting that Lyra had been pressing for more information from her brother, Jess decided now wasn't the time to interrupt the man's thoughts. He would hear soon enough, what was transpiring between brother and sister, even though he already had a pretty good idea what brought Orion's mood out. Jess loved Lyra, and there was no one who would say otherwise; however, Jess knew that once Lyra had created a plan in her head, her tenacity would prevent her from seeing any other way. And Jess knew, Lyra had a plan for her older brother. Picking up the phone when it rang, and recognizing the voice at the other end, Jess replied, "Yes, he's in his corner." He knew the reason Lyra was interested in her brother's whereabouts. He suspected Orion was here only because he didn't feel like facing the beautiful green eyes, he himself, had fallen in love with. "Listen, why don't you give the man a little more time. Pushing him will only keep him in his corner, and you won't get what you really want. We both know Orion needs to make his own choices, and right now, he's still in Hideaway Canyon. If you push, you could push him to another part of the world, where you won't know if he's dead or alive." Jess knew the sacrifices the job required and knew the torment each soldier went through after every operation. Right now, he was well aware that Orion was still struggling from his last mission; making it out alive when others didn't lay heavy on any soldier's mind. Jess also knew Micah was pressing Orion for an answer: Was he ready to accept another mission, and would he ever return for duty? He knew, no matter what decision his brother-in-law would make, returning to the job or leaving it behind, Orion was deeply afraid. No man liked to admit it, particularly the type of man Orion was. Pausing to listen, Jess continued, "I think you are making the right decision. Give it more time. How's my baby?"

Lyra conveyed her frustration in Orion, stopping midsentence when realizing Jess was talking about their one-year-old daughter, Skye. "I guess I'll have to adjust to a new normal. When you said 'baby,' you were referring to our baby, weren't you?" she said.

With all his heart, Jess responded, "You will always be my baby, and that, my dear Lyra, will never change. Now, how's our baby, my little Skye?"

After hanging up the phone, Jess checked his watch for the time, surveyed The Rip, and glanced at the corner, realizing Orion had somehow slipped out of the bar. He must have used the back stairs while he was talking to Lyra on his phone because he would have seen him walk toward the front door. *Good choice.* Jess smiled, knowing Orion must have anticipated an invitation for dinner tonight, and not wanting to decline by making up a lie that Jess would have to share with his wife. *I owe you yet again, brother*, Jess thought, knowing he couldn't lie to his wife. As bartender, Jess asked the last two patrons if they needed topped off before he retired to the kitchen to clean and prep for the next day.

He had sent his staff home early tonight. It was already nine o'clock, and that was a late night for midweek at the bar, especially when the forecast indicated the usual spring storm moving into the mountains. By midnight tomorrow, visibility was expected to be down to a foot or two, and roads would be closed. No one should be out in that kind of weather, not even him. All the locals knew it was important to prepare for the weather, it was too much of a risk to think the weatherman might be wrong or the storm would pass further south of their mountains. He needed to make sure his own family had enough wood chopped and stacked on the front porch for easy access and that the animals were tucked away in the barn with enough food and water to last a couple of days. Some of the worst storms created whiteouts, and he might not be able to see his way to the sheds. Jess planned to be home; he wanted to be home, keeping the fire stoked and making sure Lyra and Skye were safe and warm. Watching over and protecting them was second nature to him.

Jess was sure Orion slipped up the back stairs to the apartment above The Rip. Lyra and Jess had suggested Orion use the apartment as his home during his stay in Hideaway Canyon. He could always stay with the oldest Grey brother, Crux, at the ranch, but Orion seemed to need more privacy than what the family home would offer. Jess understood the demands placed on a man with Orion's job. He also knew the side effects—the sleepless nights, the terror of reliving each moment of the last mission. He knew the nightmares, the sounds of mortar and cries for help, never went away. Jess could see Orion's physical wounds were healing, his limp was only slight; however, he knew the other wounds would take a lot longer to heal. Jess would check on Orion tomorrow; before the storm hit, making sure he had supplies to last a couple of days and to offer him one of their rooms for the duration of the storm, knowing good and well Orion would decline, preferring the solitude and privacy the apartment offered, hiding above The Rip.

Lyra was average in size, with long chocolate-brown hair, mostly worn in a ponytail for comfort and to alleviate any need for attention throughout the day. Even though she was the younger sister to

Orion and Crux, she never needed either of them to run interference for her. Her warm green eyes and smile emitted a kindness that drew people to her; however, once one got to know her, the depth of her wisdom and authority stood out. From the time she was three years old, her family knew she was gifted in ways the world would one day come to appreciate. As the story was told to her when she was older, Lyra's adoptive parents, Oaklin and Abel Grey, rescued her from the riverbank. Oaklin loved to tell Lyra how the stars in the sky watched out for her until Abel arrived to cherish and protect her. The Grey family welcomed her into their family with open arms. Orion and Crux adored their little sister and would do anything for her. But as life happens, it was the brothers who were most often the ones to lean on Lyra for the most challenging moments in their lives.

Crux was the oldest and the heart of the Grey siblings. He was rock solid in what was expected of him. His role had been ingrained in him since birth; he would inherit the family ranch outside Hideaway Canyon, along with Orion and Lyra. But it was Crux's birthright and responsibility to manage the property and see its prosperity continued for generations of Grey's to come. Crux took his responsibility to heart. His love of the land and his love for Orion and Lyra never wavered. Along with his family, only a few select friends of Crux's knew the struggles he had endured to keep the family's kingdom from crumbling. Like Lyra, Crux's destiny was predetermined, and he had inevitably followed in the footsteps of the family patriarch, overseeing the vast ranching lands and business investments of the Grey's. Like Orion and his California surfer look, Crux could have been his twin. However, Crux kept his hair short and trimmed. Always attired in a suit and tie, he was polished and professional when leaving the ranch, revealing the educated man he was. The tanned, weathered lines in Crux's face, acquired through the long, hard hours working the ranch and riding the range, revealed the man's devotion to the family empire and his life as a rancher.

Oaklin and Abel Grey had been the best parents any child could have asked for. Oaklin was a wild, untamed beauty who always knew what she wanted, a simple life on her father's ranch outside of Hideaway Canyon. She spent her days exploring the ranch and nursing stray animals or any tramp brought to her by local villagers. Much to the chagrin of Oaklin's father, ranchers from adjoining counties drove out the long dusty road leading to the ranch, searching for Oaklin and her renowned nursing skills. When she wasn't caring for the earth's creatures, she was riding the range on her stallion, Galaxy. Oaklin spent her nights under the stars, identifying constellations, dreaming of places beyond the stars, and sleeping under the moonlight. Only after she experienced boarding school and college in the big city, did her father allow her to return to the canyon and join him, once again, on the family ranch. Dreaming about places beyond the stars was enough for her; she wanted no part of the cosmopolitan life her father had forced her to endure. When Oaklin was quite young, the stars revealed themselves to her, bestowing upon her a gift, the love of a generous man. She and that man would be blessed with remarkable children, cultivating a family saturated in love. Oaklin knew that her heart would relish any children she would have and that those born from her womb would not want for love or attention from their parents. Meeting Abel and becoming a family fulfilled her celestial dreams. The Grey children were encouraged to seek adventure and dream a life beyond the stars, searching for their ultimate love.

As Orion hid in the living room of the apartment above The Rip, he thought fondly of his childhood on the ranch, of his parents and his siblings. He didn't begrudge his mother for her stories or his parents for love. He would never have wanted any other childhood. He was happy Lyra found love with Jess and was proud seeing Crux fulfill his destiny as family patriarch, managing the Grey empire. But his life and beliefs were different. His job had taken him to some of the darkest, most destitute places in the world, places where pure evil flourished, places no one should go. From what he had experienced and seen, there wasn't a star in the sky that would convince him he would find happiness and love for himself. He wasn't destined for love, nor did he want it. The kind of love that occurred having a wife and family would never exist for him; however, knowing Lyra and Crux found love, Orion knew that would be enough for him.

Midwest, April 20, 2013

Using her cell phone to check directions on her Google Maps app for her location and the time, Alessandra realized she would be able to make it into Denver by late morning tomorrow, or actually today? Time had passed quickly. The sun had gone down hours ago; she needed to get some rest. She hadn't realized it was almost midnight, adrenaline still flowing in her veins from the excitement of her trip and the constant companionship of other cars and semitrucks, not allowing her to feel alone. She was making good time traveling to an unknown place. Alessandra left her fear, and pain, and anger behind when she crossed the state's border. She couldn't remember the last road sign she saw to let her know just how far the next town was, however, spending the money on a hotel room tonight was just not an option. It would be too late by the time she found a place to stop to get full use out of a room, and her priority was to get across the country as quickly as possible. She had canceled her one credit card before leaving Chicago, knowing it could be easily traced. She didn't want to leave a path of breadcrumbs for her father's men to follow. The sooner she made it to the coast, the sooner she could get lost in the crowd. The sooner she found a job and place to live, the sooner she could be joined by her mother. Once again, they would build a home. With a population of over fourteen million people, Alessandra was confident the two refugees could hide in Los Angeles.

Pulling off on the side of the road to sleep would be illegal and dangerous. A dark country road might be quiet; however, it didn't sound inviting. It actually sounded frightening. Who knew what could happen in the middle of nowhere, no lights, no other person, no help, if needed. She'd watch too many CSI and FBI movies and read too many stories from headline news; abject fear crossed her mind. Alessandra was not about to become a headline story. As she continued on the road, she soon saw a familiar blue and white rectangle sign indicating a rest area was eighteen miles down the road. She could make it that far. She would pull over and spend the night in her car. She would have access to a bathroom and water so she could wash up in the morning before hitting the road again. She didn't need to bother putting on makeup or washing her hair. Comfort was her only priority as she drove. If for some reason she needed help, she was sure people would be coming and going from the rest area throughout the night.

It wasn't long before she saw the sign again, directing her to take the next exit for the rest area stop. Cautiously, Alessandra inched onto the exit ramp, drove past several parked cars, a row of semitrucks, and a large building with dim lighting. She chose a place to park at the far end of the rest stop so she wouldn't be disturbed by the lights on the building and ramada or traffic coming and going throughout the night. Semitrucks were pretty loud, and even now, as late as it was, trucks were pulling in and out of the area. Her parking spot was located under several large trees. Alessandra had selected the spot, knowing her car would be shaded from the early morning sun. She needed to sleep as long as she could. She was tired. It was already past midnight. She would spend the night sleeping in the back seat of her jeep. She had pulled out her sleeping bag, a pillow, a comforter, and a couple of blankets to make the softest, warmest bed possible, suspecting that the temperatures would drop during the night, and it would get much colder by morning. Alessandra realized shortly after stopping and jumping into the back seat, her jeep wasn't made to lie down in, stretching out across the back seat wasn't the most comfortable, but it would have to do. Even though it was late, she sent a quick text to her mother, letting her know she had stopped for the night, then turned the phone off. She knew she shouldn't use the phone more than a couple of times since it would be traceable, always turning it off when she didn't need it. She would dispose of the phone tomorrow, knowing that the hotel she spent the night in would have a phone for her to use. She took one more glance around the pitch-black area outside her car, and as uncomfortable as it was in the back seat, she fell asleep almost instantly.

Seeming like minutes later, Alessandra was alerted by what sounded like a scratching noise and feeling like her jeep was rocking. What time was it? Glancing at her phone, she saw she had slept for four hours. It was windy. She could see the tree branches swaying in the wind. Could that have been the scratching sound or cause of the rocking? Looking through the windows, she thought she saw some tree branches. Maybe the branches were loosened in the wind and had blown by, scratching the jeep. The wind could be the cause of the rocking, she thought. Rubbing her eyes and neck, trying to clear her head of sleep, Alessandra was startled by a large dark shadow scurrying beside her jeep. Afraid, she glanced at the locks on both doors, not being able to see clearly because it was dark. Panic began to strike her as she desperately tried to remember if she had locked both doors before falling asleep. Out of her peripheral vision, the shadow seemed to move away, then suddenly it was gone. Was that a person? she thought, trying to shake herself awake. The shadow had passed by the passenger side of the jeep. Whatever or whomever it was, was too close for Alessandra's comfort. Could one of her father's men have followed her from Chicago? Was someone trying to break into her jeep? Alessandra maneuvered her body into the front seat and unlocked the driver's side door, looking carefully around all sides of her car, as she slowly got out of the jeep. Examining the area around her car, even though the sun had not risen, she could see no one was around, but multiple small tree branches and leaves were wedged up underneath the jeep near the wheels. Knowing she wouldn't be able to go back to sleep, Alessandra packed up her bedding, rearranging her few possessions, deciding to get back on the road. Trying to deter her fear, she decided it was best to drive down the highway a bit further rather than use the facilities. She needed to fill up with gas and could use a good strong cup of black coffee. The shadow was probably her imagination. Alessandra knew scars from her past left her suspicious and wary, deciding to shake it off and leave that life behind. The wind was strong, blowing lots of leaves and twigs across the road. The sun would rise soon. As she pulled out of her parking space to drive away, she gave a quick glance through her rearview window. Under the faint light of the building, she saw a large shadow disappear around the corner. It wasn't her imagination. Alessandra realized she hadn't left her fear at home.

Hideaway Canyon, April 20, 2013

Orion jolted awake, sweat soaked, blond locks matted to his head and in complete disarray, throbbing in his left shoulder and right ankle—all remnants of the job. His night, as usual, had been filled with deafening explosions, cries in the dark, shots fired from what he recognized as M16s and grenades exploding. That part of his restless sleep didn't bother him so much; it was the endless eyes looking back at him, blood-stained faces, all pleading to him for help, yet there was never the sound of anyone's voice. Eyes didn't talk. What was he thinking? he thought as he lay in his bed. He was in bed and not on the floor, which told him he must have slept part of the night. He threw off the down comforter Lyra bought him. After deciding to stay another week in Hideaway Canyon, Lyra insisted they go shopping for supplies for his apartment. He told her he didn't need supplies since he wasn't staying long, but she convinced him the apartment would need to be furnished when he left, so why not have a few comforts while he was there. Besides, he would be doing her a favor by purchasing the items, which his nomadic lifestyle would require him to leave, allowing her to keep for the apartment's next occupant. Still, the apartment was sparsely appropriated, only furnished with the bare necessities anyone would need. But it was enough for Orion. The apartment had been as close to a home as he'd ever had, not counting his childhood home. The life he had chosen denied him such things.

His apartment was cold, so Orion quickly slipped on his torn jeans and a well-used hoodie to grab some wood off the deck. The woodstove needed to be stoked. By the time the stove would warm the apartment, he would have a pot of coffee warming and be able to take a quick shower. As he stepped out onto the deck, the sun was beginning to rise. In the sky, above the woods off to his right, he could see clouds forming, reminding him that a winter storm warning was in effect for later tonight. Turning back toward his apartment, a cold breeze swept past him, encouraging him to grab an extra couple logs for the fire. Orion knew the night would be a cold one. After stoking the fire, he finished his first cup of coffee and jumped into the shower. He would head over to Lyra and Jess's to see what supplies they needed before he went down the mountain and into town to get supplies of his own. And of course, take time to play with his beautiful, sweet niece, Skye.

Orion spent the next half hour bringing wood in off the deck and stacking it next to the woodstove. He knew he would be busy the remainder of the day and not knowing exactly what time the storm would move into the area, he wanted to be prepared. Heavy snow could down power lines, a familiar consequence of storms passing through, so he filled up a couple five-gallon water jugs he had sitting on the deck. They would freeze up on the deck, so he placed them inside the door. He would be able to keep warm with the stove and a good supply of wood. He had extra water for emergencies and candles for light should the power go out. He didn't mind the dark; oftentimes he preferred it.

After a nice long hot shower, he wiped the fog from the small mirror in his bathroom and took a quick glance at his face. He rubbed the dark stubble on his face. *No.* He paused. *I don't want to waste any time shaving. I might need a little extra growth to keep warm.* After rummaging in his closet for nice thick socks, a sweater, and his winter boots, he dressed and surveyed his room. Grabbing his coat, gulping down the last of his coffee, he was out the door and down the steps. If the storm hit hard, he would be stuck inside for a day or two, and he would have plenty of time to clean up this mess. You would think his military training forced him to keep an organized, clean house. What he saw made him exit the room and close the door. Smoke was coming out of the chimney at The Rip, signaling to Orion that Jess was already at work. Orion decided to stop by to see if there was anything Jess needed in the bar before heading over to meet Lyra's inquisition. Pushing open the front door, he yelled, "Good morning," trying to determine what part of The Rip Jess was in. He didn't see him behind the bar, nor at any tables. Orion knew he must be in the kitchen or office.

Working his way to the back, he heard a crash. "Damn it all to hell" He recognized Jess's voice.

Another "good morning" was offered by Orion as he entered the kitchen. He saw Jess on his knees next to the dishwasher, attempting to wipe up what looked to be a water leak.

"Is it?" Jess replied without looking up. "The last two days I've been having trouble with this machine and need to get it fixed before the lunch and dinner crowd," he said.

"Well, with the storm closing in, you might just have a couple of days to work on it. Everyone will be snowed in and business might be slow," Orion responded.

"I can't count on that. I know you haven't been around Hideaway Canyon long, but once the locals or anyone else staying at the Inn can get out after a winter storm, they all head to The Rip," Jess said. He continued explaining to Orion that Hideaway Canyon may get snowed in from the outside world, but that didn't stop people from gathering before the storm hit and after the worst of the storm passed through. Residents would shovel their way out of their homes, offering help to those who needed help, and wander into The Rip for food, drink, cards, and camaraderie. The community would find a way to move about their little village, but it could be days, or a week, before snowplows would filter their way up the mountain, enabling residents to get into town.

"Listen, I'm pretty handy with plumbing, so why don't you let me take a look at it. Hopefully, it's something simple. I stopped by to see if there was anything you needed. I was planning on stopping by the house to check to see if Lyra and Skye need anything before I head down the mountain to pick up supplies. Might as well stock up on things, the storms due to hit tonight," Orion offered. "Go do what you've got to do while I take a look at this. And make me a list of things you need. After I return from town, I'll help you with any crowd in the bar," he said.

Jess gave him a look he knew. "Okay, okay, I know I'm not the best with customer service. I'll wash dishes or something. Just stick me in the back room. I know my skill set is lacking when it comes to conversation with the locals."

"Or the best at mixing a drink," Jess grumbled. "Didn't you throw one of my paying customers out of the bar when he suggested you mixed his drink wrong the last time, every time you helped me out before?"

With a frown, Orion answered, "That was months ago, when I first arrived and hadn't made friends. Plus, no one grabs my sister and pulls her down on their lap when she's singing. That time wasn't my fault."

"It was Marco. He's been a member of both our ops teams in South America and Kosovo, he saved Lyra's life, and he's eighty-three years old. His wife was sitting right next to him," Jess replied in disbelief. "Besides, Lyra loves the old man, and she was laughing."

The front door of The Rip opened, catching Jess's attention. By the time he turned back to hear what other excuse Orion had to offer, Orion's head was inside the dishwasher; apparently there was no need for any further conversation on the matter. By ten o'clock, Orion had figured out the problem with the dishwasher, letting his brother-in-law know he would buy a piece for the machine from the hardware store when he went to pick up supplies. He'd fix it when he returned to the mountain later this afternoon. He grabbed Jess's list and stuck it in his pocket while heading out the door to Lyra's house to see what she might need.

Knowing by sounds coming from inside the house, his sister and niece were in the kitchen. Without knocking, he entered the house through the back door. The familiar smells reminded him of his own mother's kitchen. Oaklin Grey's kitchen was always filled with warmth and mouth-watering aromas. Recognizing the footsteps of her brother as he entered the mudroom on the way to the kitchen, Lyra turned away from the oven with a sheet of baked cookies in her hand, smiled at her brother, and pointed at the table without saying a word. The soft giggles coming from underneath the table brought a smile to his face. Orion, unable to resist the opportunity, crouched down on all fours and immediately saw sweet little Skye, with her back to him. Her long golden curls dancing on her shoulders, he reached out to tug on one of them. Before he could let go of the curl, Skye whipped around, screaming, "Unca O, Unca O, Unca O." Tall enough to stand up under the table, she jumped to her feet and ran to her Uncle Orion, hands raised as a signal to be picked up.

He knew how to follow orders, like anyone trained in special operations, and immediately complied. Little Skye always brought a smile to his face and the depth of love he held for her in his heart was undeniable. Laughing and hugging Skye as she tried to wiggle out of his grip, Orion looked at his sister, giving her his knowing smile. As he released Skye from his grip before she managed to cause more of a commotion, he sat down at the table and grabbed a cookie. Lyra poured him a cup of coffee and joined him at the table, while Skye ran in and out of the kitchen, bringing her toys in one at a time for him to see. Orion spent the next ten minutes indulging his niece and taking interest in everything she had to say and show, while indicating to Lyra that he was headed down the mountain for supplies and wanted to know if she needed anything. She, too, like Jess, made a quick list for her brother while watching the interaction between Orion and her daughter.

"Skye, how would you like to watch *Frozen*?" Lyra asked. Stopping dead in her tracks, Skye bobbed her head up and down at a speed not possible by most humans and ran into the great room. Completely forgetting her uncle Orion, she grabbed her favorite blanket and pillow, on her way to the floor in front of the television.

Lyra glanced at her brother with a slight smile. "She loves Elsa." The entire family knew Elsa was an important character in the toddler's mind; however, Orion wasn't tricked into thinking Lyra's motivation was to please her daughter. He knew she wanted Skye occupied, so she could be alone with him. Lyra wanted to talk to Orion, and he knew he could no longer escape the words of his sister.

Lyra disappeared for a few minutes, making sure her daughter was occupied, returning to the kitchen where Orion sat eating his second cookie. She topped off her brother's cup with fresh coffee and sat down next to him. "Orion, I want you to stay," Lyra said. Orion reached over and took his sister's hand and squeezed it, without saying a word. He had never been able to resist his sister's emerald eyes. She continued, "I know that your wounds are healing. Your physical one's anyway. Even I hardly notice your limp, and when you just picked up Skye, you didn't wince in pain like you used to. I know you are expected to make a decision soon on whether or not you will accept the next job." She paused when she saw Orion's eyebrow raise. "Micah called Jess."

Orion wasn't surprised by what his sister said. Micah was his boss who'd managed The Firm since Jess's promise to Lyra not to return to the field. He also knew that although Jess remained behind the scene and didn't do fieldwork anymore, he had a hand in each operation from his office in Hideaway Canyon. Orion also knew that Micah was concerned for him, sending him away with orders requiring Orion to take a minimum three-month furlough. Orion had already spent a year out of the field, recovering at an army hospital in Germany and completing physical therapy in the states. Micah said the three-month furlough was an opportunity for Orion to rest and fully recover from his last job. Micah needed Orion to be in top physical and mental form if he was headed back into the field to command the Firm's next operation. Micah wanted him back for the next operation but only if he was in top form.

Moving his hand from his sister's and wrapping his arm around her shoulder, he pulled her in close, "Micah needs me. But I don't need to go now. I need to get down the mountain for supplies and return before the storm hits. Your husband needs me to replace a part in his dishwasher before the evening dinner rush, and I told him I would help with the crowd."

Lyra snickered in disbelief. "You can't wait tables! We lose customers every time you do. And I know you just don't want to have this conversation with me!"

Orion pulled his sister to him, giving her another warm hug, releasing her as he stood up, stating, "You're right...I don't." He walked into the great room where Skye was still engrossed in *Frozen*. He leaned over and kissed the top of the little girl's head and walked out the front door, never looking back at Lyra. Lyra glanced in the room to make sure her daughter was happy and content and turned back to her baking. She knew Orion would be deep in thought all the way down the mountain.

Colorado, April 20, 2013

Alessandra made her way into Denver before noon. A light snow was falling, but not enough to make the roads hazardous or to keep traffic off them. The sun was shining, and off in the distance to the west, Alessandra could see the beautiful snow-capped mountains of the Rockies. She had planned to make them her one and only stop. A hotel for the night in the splendor of the Rocky Mountains. The mountains would remind her of her home in Kosovo. She had seen so many pictures and read so many books. She couldn't pass up the opportunity to enjoy them for a day, knowing her arrival on the coast would not allow her time, nor afford her the opportunity to take a vacation in the near future. As much as she wanted to make it to California and get settled, she was too awestruck with the Colorado Rockies not to spend an extra day enjoying the beautiful outdoors. She knew that a hike in the mountains would be good for her. She was looking forward to getting out of the jeep for a few hours, stretching her legs, taking a nice warm shower, and having a home-cooked dinner. Knowing she'd be exhausted enough to fall quickly asleep with the luxury of a bed for the night, she would find a diner early in the morning to indulge in one of her favorite dishes of warm biscuits and gravy before hitting the road for the final stretch of her journey.

She took an exit off Interstate 70 to fill up with gas. The stop was busy. As she waited her turn in line for gas, she turned on her phone to text her mother and let her know her progress. Alessandra messaged that she was all right and that she would call tonight after finding a hotel and settling in for the night. When her gas was pumped, she went into the convenience store where she picked out a couple of snacks for the road and paid for her gas. When she inquired, the nice lady at the cash register told her it would be another two and one half to three-hour drive into the mountains. The older woman told her the weatherman was predicting a storm to hit the area later tonight. "Honey, there will be a lot of places along the highway that you can stop and find a hotel room for the night. But the weatherman is predicting a record-setting snowstorm heading that way, so the sooner you get into the mountains, find a hotel, and get settled, the better. No one wants to be caught out in the storm like what they are predicting for tonight. It's going to be a doozy," the wise woman said. "You've got a good coat, gloves, and some nice warm clothes with you, don't you?" the woman asked.

Alessandra smiled, "Yes, thank you for asking. You make me feel at home, you sound like my mother." After collecting her purchases, she glanced at the lady with a smile and returned to her jeep. She knew her jeep had four-wheel drive, and she was used to Chicago's weather, so Alessandra relaxed and turned up the volume on the radio. The next three hours would be an easy drive. She jumped into her jeep, excited at the prospect of seeing the mountains up close and spending the night in a nice warm bed! She also knew she would wake up to her final leg of her journey. She was startled by a slight pang of fear; however, the discomfort was washed away quickly by the excitement she was feeling about her new life and new home.

The further Alessandra drove west, the closer she came to the mountains, the more her thoughts drifted to Kosovo. Growing up, Alessandra had occasionally heard her parents talk at the dinner table about religious or political fighting in other towns around them; however, she paid little attention. It didn't affect her. Usually the fighting was somewhere else, not in Gjakova. Alessandra's best friend was Serb. She and Milena were like sisters. And in school, she had many friends, some Serb, some Bosniak, some Croat and Montenegrin. She and her friends had nothing to worry about. Their carefree life allowed them to have adventures in the grasslands and roam the mountains filled with pine trees. Never did it cross their minds to worry about the fighting taking place in their country and how life might change. Their families always managed to work things out. The residents of Gjakova helped one another regardless of religion; it was a community filled with love. At home, Anton often brought news from other parts of Kosovo. Conversations centered around the fighting that was occurring among the religious groups in other small villages became more frequent between her mother and father at the dinner table. More often than not, these conversations led to fights between her mother and father. Anton often became enraged, storming out of the house angry and not returning for days. When he finally did return, for a time, everything would return to normal. Her father's job in the army took him away for weeks and months. The more time passed, when Anton did return on furlough, the Petrovich family could never seem to regain their early days of bliss as a family. More stories of fighting ensued.

Koysta would bring news that the government was not only forcing people from their homes, but people were being massacred, and entire villages were destroyed. Alessandra's friends and neighbors were beginning to scatter too. There seemed to be a steady stream of villagers walking from town. Stories continued of people being threatened and disappearing, leading to a massive flight of civilians seeking refuge in other counties. Slobodan Mikozavich had been in power for years; however, he began taking steps to strip Kosovo of its autonomy, taking direct control of its administration. For years, her country had endured religious and political strife. Alessandra refused to believe that the stories she was hearing would change her life until Mikozavich began to close all schools teaching in the Albanian language. Her school would be closed. She was no longer able to attend school, nor see Milena and her other friends. She and her mother stayed in their home, rarely leaving for the market or to visit friends. On rare occasions she would beg her mother to let her and Milena go horseback riding in the mountains. Alina feared those times would be gone for her daughter forever. They no longer left the house to attend church, nor did neighbors visit them. A weekend vacation in Pristina was only a memory. One day while Anton was at work, Koysta arrived to visit his sister and her daughter. After he said his goodbye's, Alina called her daughter to her. Mother and daughter needed to pack and be ready for flight.

The snowfall continued, getting heavier and heavier the further west into the mountains she drove. Alessandra adjusted her speed, although traffic was beginning to get lighter, snow was starting to accumulate on the roads and made them slippery. Her windshield wipers worked desperately to clear large snowflakes turning to ice. Clouds took over the sky, making it difficult to believe there would be enough daylight left to get her to her destination for the night. She remembered what the nice lady said, "Another three hours and a doozy of a storm.' She looked at her cell phone—no service. She wasn't exactly sure, but she'd been driving close to three hours. Alessandra knew she needed to pull off the main road and find a room for the night. The snow was getting deeper and deeper, and visibility was almost gone. Inching her way down the road, Alessandra saw flashing, bright lights ahead. The few cars out on the road now slowed down to a complete stop. The road ahead was barricaded. Several uniformed individuals were approaching the stopped cars one at a time, and a uniformed woman approached hers. She rolled down her window, and the officer told her no one was allowed passage tonight. The road was blocked for fear an avalanche might occur along the highway due to snow accumulation, and all vehicles were being diverted off the highway. After identifying her name and having a short conversation with the officer about the services in the area and the weather, Officer Stokes gave Alessandra directions off the road and onto a street that would lead her to a couple of mountain communities with hotels, restaurants, and shops. Hideaway Canyon was the next town on the road, not more than three miles up the mountain. The officer told Alessandra she suspected the weather would be bad for a couple of days, but to keep checking the weather stations to find out when the roads would be cleared and ready for traffic. Officer Stokes also told Alessandra to get her headlight fixed before she got back on the road. The news station was saying the storm was going to last a few days, but you never could predict these storms. Alessandra knew she might not be able to get back on the road tomorrow, but that was okay. She'd have fun exploring in the mountains.

It wasn't late, but the weather had darkened the sky. Alessandra knew she was following the directions that Officer Stokes had given her; she kept slowly driving for what seemed to be miles and miles. The wind was picking up, the snow was about a foot deep on the road, with no snowplows in sight. Three miles seemed like a long way as she inched along. She was grateful for her jeep and its four-wheel drive. Alessandra's headlights were on, at least her one headlight was on, but the tall pine trees left no sky to be seen and the road was dark. Out of nowhere, a big buck and four does, one with a fawn, leaped onto the road. Horrified at the thought of hitting the animals, Alessandra slammed on her brakes and swerved to her right.

Reaching for her forehead and feeling wetness, Alessandra lifted her head off the steering wheel, realizing she must have been knocked out. As she looked around, she wasn't sure where she was. Looking out the front windshield, she saw tree after tree, covered with beautiful soft white snow, and a deep, deep ravine. Panic erupted inside her. She had to get out. As she reached to open her door, it stuck. She started pushing as hard as she could; the wind had picked up enough to slightly rock her jeep. She desperately tried again to push her door open. "Don't move," a deep loud voice commanded. She froze. *Am I hearing things? There's no one out here.* Looking out her front windshield, she could see the ravine and what looked like a river below. There was no one in sight. She slowly turned her head to look out her driver's side window, so frightened she felt like vomiting. As she turned, she saw what looked like a big black shadow. She passed out.

Orion made his way down the mountain. He picked up the supplies he, Jess, and Lyra needed, as well as a few other items for some of the locals who overheard he was making the trip and asked him to run some errands for them. Orion didn't mind helping out his new friends from Hideaway Canyon. He owed them. Lyra and Jess's friends had opened their hearts and home to him when he first arrived. He owed many of them for their kindness and patience as he healed and recovered from the nightmare leftover from his last assignments. He knew that the terrors and night sweats were all part of PTSD, and he knew some of his paranoia and overreactions to some of the simplest situations were part of it. The first month in Hideaway Canyon had been extremely difficult for him, unable to let down his guard, he held a gun to one local man's head, thinking he was still on a mission and the guy was an assassin. Of course, there were other times that he overreacted to an incident or something said in jest, which now, he understood, were symptoms of PTSD.

He didn't waste a lot of time shopping, knowing the weather forecast predicted a turn for the worse and knowing he needed to get back up the mountain, fix Jess' dishwasher, and help out at The Rip. By 7:00 p.m., the bar would be packed with people gathering to eat, drink, play cards, or just talk, regardless of how bad the weather was. As Orion walked down the street to find his truck and load all the supplies in the back, he passed a little shop with the cutest stuffed puppy in the window. Checking his watch, and knowing he was running out of time, he couldn't resist stopping in. He grabbed the toy out of the window, checked the price tag, and took it to the counter. He dropped a twenty-dollar bill on the counter, telling the cashier to keep the change. She looked up at him and smiled. Orion hurried out of the shop, jumped in his truck, and started his trek back up the mountain. He was glad he had accomplished all his errands and was able to find supplies everyone had asked him to get. The storm was moving in quickly, and he knew his drive up the mountain into Hideaway Canyon would be a treacherous one, regardless of the truck he drove.

It wasn't even five o'clock, and the roads were almost a foot deep with snow, and the snow had just begun to fall. At this rate, throughout the night, no one would be going in or out of Hideaway Canyon tonight or for the next couple of days. Orion was confident that his lifted four-wheel-drive truck could make it anywhere and wouldn't have any trouble making it back up the mountain. He could see faint tire tracks as he drove on; however, the snow was coming down so hard, and the wind was blowing that the tracks were being covered up quickly. Someone else must have come down the mountain for supplies. Then he saw the spot where the tracks stopped all of a sudden; that was odd. "Damn!" he said, horrified. The tracks led right over the edge of the shoulder, and he could see that a car—no, a jeep, now a snow-covered jeep—veered off the road into some trees and was prevented from plunging into the river below by a few strong pine tree branches. He struggled to keep his truck on the road as he slammed on his brakes. Not recognizing the vehicle and not being able to see if anyone was inside, he jumped out of his truck and cautiously looked around. At first, he thought he saw movement, but as he moved closer, he could see someone slumped over the steering wheel, clearly unconscious. Realizing the instability of the jeep, he knew he didn't have a lot of time. Hurrying back to his truck for the chain he always carried in the back, he knew he would need to secure the vehicle to prevent a strong wind or snow slide from toppling the jeep over and into the ravine. After he secured the chain to his truck and made sure it would hold, he pried the door open to find what looked like an unconscious teenage boy. Orion didn't take time to find out who it was. It must have been one of the locals trying to get down and back up the mountain for supplies before the storm hit; hopefully, he was still alive. He knew no one would survive the evening out in temperatures like this.

The music and laughter in The Rip permeated through the walls as Orion skidded to an immediate stop at the front door. Within moments he had made it out and around his truck to the passenger side, made one quick cautious jerk, and had the boy in his arms heading inside. He was out cold. Orion could hardly see the boy's face; however, the young man was dressed for the weather with a warm jacket, ski hat, and scarf. Blood continued to flow from a cut he could see on the young man's forehead. Two men standing outside The Rip, smoking cigarettes, could see Orion was in no mood for a conversation and that his hands were full. With silent questioning looks to each other, one grabbed the door handle to the bar and held it open for Orion as he bounded into the room.

Orion began shouting orders, "Jess, I need you to get Doc Sterling over here now." The bar was half-filled to capacity, the music and laughter were loud, and curious patrons were straining their necks trying to figure out what was going on. People began jumping out of the chairs, moving tables, and clearing a path for Orion and the boy in his arms.

Jess looked up from his place as bartender to see Orion rush in holding a limp body in his arms. Throwing down a towel, heading toward Orion, he shouted, "Josie, get Lyra from the kitchen and call Doc!" As he crossed the bar to assist Orion, his eyes met Iker.

Witnessing the commotion, Iker jumped up from his table of friends and headed to the bar saying, "I've got it covered." Jess had reached Orion in time to open the door leading to the inside stairs of the apartment. Jess ran ahead into Orion's bedroom, seeing the mess, clearing as much as he could, to make room for the motionless body to be laid on Orion's bed. As Orion made it across his room in three long strides, he placed the young man gently on his bed. Jess ran into the bathroom, grabbing wash clothes and towels and whatever he could get his hands on, handing them to Orion as he tried to find out where the bleeding was coming from and getting it stopped. Jess continued his search in the kitchen, looking for a pan and filling it with water just as Lyra came through the door. Glancing at her husband, who nodded toward the bedroom, she crossed into the bedroom.

Without words, Lyra began assisting her brother as he was slipping off the young man's boots, getting rid of his scarf, coat, and mittens. At least the boy was prepared for the weather. He was cold to the touch, and brother and sister knew they needed to get him undressed and under the warm blankets as soon as possible. As they continued to undress the boy, Orion instructed Lyra, "He's got a pulse, the blood's coming from a deep cut on his forehead, and his wrist might be broken. It's red and swollen pretty good. Haven't checked the rest of him out, he might have broken ribs. We'll leave that up to Doc when he gets here. He's been unconscious since I found him," Orion relayed to anyone listening. Orion stopped abruptly, staring at a bra. It was a bra. Why was the boy wearing a bra? Unable to move or look at his sister or Jess, looking around the room, more puzzled than they, he said, "It's a girl!"

With a slight smile on her lips, Lyra turned to her husband. Jess smiled. "My words exactly, when Skye was born!" Both stifled their laugh seeing Orion's face. The three could hear footsteps advancing up the stairs, as Doc Sterling and several bar patrons entered Orion's apartment. Stepping aside, Orion reiterated the information he had just given Jess and Lyra and got out of Doc's way. He could feel his temperature rise and felt dizzy. Maybe he was coming down with something.

He stepped back into his living room planning to check the stove and cut back the heat, he found an audience wanting answers, "I found him—I mean her on my way back up the mountain. She made it halfway up the mountain and veered off the road into some trees. I had to chain his—I mean her jeep onto my truck before I forced his—damn—her door open, I didn't want her falling into the ravine. No one else was with her, but her car was packed, as if moving."

"What's her name?" someone asked.

"I have no idea. I just found out he was a girl," Orion responded, "he—I mean she wasn't there when I went down the mountain. I couldn't have missed the jeep off the side of the road. With the wind and snow, it's almost impossible to tell how long she would have been there…could have been up to two hours."

Jess added while watching Lyra enter the room, "In the morning, weather permitting, we'll take the truck and collect her stuff and see if we can find some identification. If we can, we'll pull the jeep out. With the potential for a snow slide, we might need to leave it there until it's safer to pull it out." After nodding in agreement, Lyra left the men and headed back into the bedroom to check on the woman and hear what the doctor had to say. Jess said he was heading back to the bar, while Orion stood alone, wondering what a woman, all alone, would be doing in Hideaway Canyon in the middle of a snowstorm.

Orion stood in the doorway of his bedroom, hearing Doc Sterling talking to Lyra and telling her that the woman needed a hospital, but the weather wasn't going to permit it. The woman had a concussion, and he couldn't determine when she would regain consciousness. Without the use of an x-ray machine, he guessed that she had a couple of broken ribs; in addition, he knew from experience, her wrist was broken. He stitched up the gash on her forehead, which was quite deep and attributed to all the blood, he wrapped her ribs and splinted her wrist, indicating he would stay with her until she regained consciousness. He couldn't say how long that would take, maybe days. Although she was a slight thing, overall, she was in good health. He quietly mentioned the woman had some scars that couldn't have been caused by her accident. He could only imagine what the woman had endured resulting in the scars. Orion's eyes darkened as he overheard the conversation, looking at the unconscious woman lying in his bed. Heat began to rise in his body; anger was about to take over him. He swiftly turned and left the doorway, leaving neither the doctor nor his sister to miss his presence.

Lyra told Doc she would bath the woman and find something clean for her to wear. Looking around Orion's room, she suspected he must have a clean pair of sweatpants and a T-shirt somewhere. "While I'm doing that, why don't you run downstairs and get a bite to eat before relieving me as a nursemaid. Between you, me, Jess, and Orion, we can make sure someone is with her when she wakes up. I'm sure she will be disoriented and afraid," Lyra instructed. Doc took advantage of the offer and headed downstairs, not seeing Orion in his living room, staring out the window looking for stars.

Orion didn't know how long he had been standing at the window, but he felt the warmth of Lyra's hands softly touch his back as she began to wrap her arm around him. She joined him, looking out the window, "We need to take care of her, Orion." With an almost unnoticeable nod, Orion agreed. Blizzard conditions were upon the residents of Hideaway Canyon. Orion knew he and Jess would be lucky if they could dig the woman's car out tomorrow. However, maybe they could find some identification in her possessions. If not, they would have to wait until she regained consciousness to know who she was and to notify anyone about her accident. Someone had to be looking for her.

"Why don't you go grab something to eat too, Orion. I'll stay with her while you go downstairs, there's nothing anyone can do now. As Doc says, we just have to wait," Lyra said.

"I need to fix Jess's dishwasher. Will you be all right for another hour? I'm sure Jess is up to his elbows in dirty dishes, and I did promise to get his machine fixed for tonight's rush. Guess I'm a little late on that," Orion replied.

"I'll be fine. Maybe I'll even pick up your room," Lyra said, glancing around. "This is a real mess!" Lyra hadn't seen her brother blush since he was a teenager when she caught him kissing the neighbor girl, Summer Thompson. Lyra smiled at her brother.

Feeling more embarrassed than he should, Orion gave his sister a quick hug and headed out the door, saying, "I'll be back as soon as I can."

It was a lively crowd at The Rip tonight; music and laughter abound. The locals knew they could be snowed in for the next couple of days, nothing not to be expected from a winter season in the mountains, so they always made the most of it. As Orion walked down the stairway, he could hear the uncontrollable chatter throughout the bar. Who was the lady? What was she doing at Hideaway Canyon? How did she end up in the ditch? She's lucky she didn't fall into the ravine. Did Orion know her? Where did she come from? These were enough to make Orion put his head down without making eye contact with anyone and head straight into the kitchen, stopping for no one. He didn't know the lady. For crying out loud, he didn't even know she was a lady. He'd never been one to participate in idle gossip, especially when it involved him. Orion found himself strangely affected by the woman's arrival and curious himself, although he had never seen her before, there was something beckoning him to find out more. It was almost nine o'clock by the time Orion finished fixing the dishwasher, grabbing a bite to eat, and making his way back to the stairs. The bar was filled with patrons who looked and sounded like they had no intention of going home. Of course, no one was going anywhere in this weather, they had the night to enjoy. Reaching the stairs, Orion looked over his shoulder, making eye contact with Jess. He immediately knew everything was under control and he wasn't needed, so he bounded up the stairs, once again, to his apartment.

When he arrived in his bedroom, Doc was checking the woman's vital signs as Lyra looked on. "There's not much we can do tonight. The weather's not going to allow us to get her to a hospital, so the best we can do is keep her warm and comfortable, and see if we can break this fever," Doc instructed.

Orion replied, "I'll take over tonight. This is my place, and it makes most sense for me to stay up with her tonight. Doc, you and Lyra go home and get some rest. I'll send for you if she wakes up in the night and I need you. Like you said, she might not gain consciousness for a while."

Doc agreed. "Just make sure to send someone for me if you need anything. We need to keep her calm, and if I have to, I can sedate her. Keep cold compresses on her forehead throughout the night, and hopefully, her fever will break by morning. As soon as I can shovel myself out, I'll be back in the morning to check on both of you."

"I'm going to help Jess clean up, and then we'll head home. Skye's been playing in the kitchen downstairs with Josie, and we need to get her home, bathed, and in bed. You know you can send for me anytime too…right?" Lyra said with a nod to her brother.

"Don't worry, I've got this handled," Orion replied as she and Doc walked out the room.

Seeing that his sister had created three stacks of laundry, Orion grabbed a load to throw in the washing machine. After stoking the fire, Orion recalled Doc's words to keep a cold compress on the woman's forehead and check for a fever. As he quietly approached the bed, his awareness of the woman heightened. Heat rose from deep inside him, but it wasn't driven by anger. His breathing became deeper and louder. Perspiration collected on his forehead as he ordered himself to focus. The crescendo of his heartbeat caused him alarm, and he urgently placed his hand over his heart and mechanically taking long breaths, as if to stop his heart from pulsing out of his chest. Orion felt an overwhelming need to protect this woman lying in his bed that he'd never seen before. Of course, any decent person would see that she received all the medical attention she needed. He'd seen worse than this. Why did he have such a desperate need to rescue this woman? He'd rescued so many others. What was it about her that was different? He didn't know. He knew he had to keep her safe.

Lying flat on her back, even with layers of sheets and blankets surrounding her, she seemed so frail to Orion. She was pale, with dark circles around her eyes. A bandage covered most of her forehead; however, he could tell she must have a goose egg underneath the wrap. Her lips were blue; he wondered if he kissed them, would they change color? *What! What's the matter with me? Why would I even be thinking such a thing?* Orion stood aghast at himself. He needed to follow orders. Remembering the doc's words, Orion gently felt the woman's cheeks and forehead to determine if her fever was subsiding. Only allowing himself a brief touch, he knew she was burning up. He took a washcloth, rinsed it out with cold water, and gently tried to wash the heat from her face. She looked so young. Yet so unafraid. Who was this woman? What was she doing in Hideaway Canyon on a night like this? And why was she alone? He knew it would be a long night.

While doing the laundry, Orion went about his apartment, quietly picking up the place. For some unexplainable reason, he wanted it to look presentable for the woman sleeping in his bed. Orion busied himself by folding a couple of piles of clothes and cleaning up in the kitchen, loading the dishwasher and wiping down the table and countertops. *What would the woman think waking up in his apartment? Why does what the woman thinks matter?* he grumbled at himself. *She's lucky I found her before the worst of the storm hit. She would have frozen out there tonight.* Surveying his apartment, Orion praised himself for its appearance. Just as he opened the refrigerator to grab a beer, there were a couple of swift knocks at his door. Glancing at the clock on the wall, he saw it was half past midnight. Not worried about who was showing up at this hour or wanting to disturb the woman sleeping in her bedroom by calling out the door was unlocked, he quickly crossed to the door and opened it, as Jess walked in.

"Just having a beer. Want one?" Orion asked, knowing Jess had closed up the bar and was about to head home. It was a habit for him to swing by at the end of a day. Knowing where the refrigerator was and without responding, Jess walked into the kitchen, grabbed a beer from the refrigerator, and joined Orion at the other end of his couch. Neither spoke, both seemingly deep in thought, yet completely comfortable without speaking to each other, enjoying their beers as they relaxed watching flames jump in the stove.

"Weather permitting, I'll come over in the morning, and we can take a look at the lady's car, look for some identification, and load whatever she might need into the truck and bring it up here," Jess stated. "Someone must be looking for her. She's not from here, and no one in Hideaway Canyon was expecting a guest."

The lines on Orion's face deepened, "How do you know that?"

With a smile, Jess took a sip of his beer. "Haven't you learned by now? You're in Hideaway Canyon, and nothing gets past us. The Rip was packed for the night, and all conversations lead to the arrival of your woman. Words already spread that she's here." Jess stood while taking a final draw on his beer and turned to his brother-in-law.

"She's not my woman," Orion stated, giving Jess an indignant look.

With a casual glimpse at Orion, Jess placed his empty bottle on the coffee table. "She is now," he said with a smile, "I'll see you tomorrow." And he walked out the door.

After disposing of the beer bottles in the trash, Orion checked on the woman. She remained unconscious. Again, being as gentle as he could, he washed her face with the cold washcloth, checking to see if her fever was subsiding. No change. He stoked the stove one more time, knowing he needed to keep the apartment warm for the woman. He was in a habit of letting the fire go out at night. So often, his job required he sleep outside, in all kinds of weather, and the temperature dropping by morning never seemed to bother him. He grabbed a pillow and a couple of blankets from the closet and made his way to the couch, knowing this would be his bed for the next couple of nights. Orion reached for the lamp and turned off the light, settling on the couch. The couch wasn't made for his six-foot, three-inch frame, but he didn't care. He could sleep anywhere. But not tonight. Orion lay awake staring at the ceiling.

Hideaway Canyon, April 21, 2013

Throughout the evening, Orion checked on the woman. He followed the Doc's instructions and wiped the woman's face with a cool cloth every hour. Her fever hadn't broken. Worried that she wasn't regaining consciousness, he thought of sending for Doc. He didn't want to seem too alarmed, so he checked for her pulse. It was strong. He would wait. Not able to sleep and needing to keep busy, Orion walked out the door and onto the deck to collect more wood. Like many quiet nights, he searched the sky for stars. Even though the cloud cover was dense, he was able to spot the bright light of a couple of stars. He watched as the clouds moved to conceal them, wondering what his mother would say about the woman's arrival. Feeling a cold breeze blow past him, Orion gathered the wood and returned to his apartment. After adding more logs to the fire, Orion grabbed the extra blanket he'd planned to use on the couch and walked into his bedroom to place it on the woman. He knew she had several blankets on her already, but he didn't want her to be cold. He felt an almost desperate need to make sure she was warm and safe, and there was no way to ask her. Feeling helpless, a feeling he just wasn't used to, he folded the blanket gently around her, tucking the ends under her slight body. Orion could hear the storm begin to rage outside and see big fluffy snowflakes coming down through his windows. It was three in the morning, and there was no sign of the snow or wind letting up. He went back to his couch, hoping to sleep.

Jess opened the apartment door at six-thirty in the morning, finding Orion sleeping in a chair next to the woman in his bedroom. The apartment was hot, hotter than he'd ever known Orion to keep it. Tapping Orion on the shoulder to wake him, he pulled one of the blankets off the woman and grabbed a cloth, wiping her face with a damp cloth to cool her down. "What are you trying to do? She's burning up!"

Shaking himself awake, Orion defended himself, "I was only trying to keep her warm."

Jess continued, "The woman's breathing is shallow, and her pulse is slow, maybe one of us should get Doc?" Orion agreed with Jess and started pulling on his jacket to go get Doc. "Lyra's taking Skye over to Josie's house to play with the twins so she can come over here and help out. We've got two feet of snow, so no one's going anywhere. We still won't be able to get the woman to a hospital. Let's see what Doc says when he arrives," Jess informed him.

"Iker will let us use his snowmobile to go to the woman's jeep and get whatever we can from inside the vehicle, maybe find some identification," Orion added, needing to take some kind of action and knowing they could count on their friend for anything. Looking out the window, Orion said, "You're right, there's no going down the mountain in a vehicle today."

"A second storm front is expected to move into the area by noon, and weathermen are predicting another two to four feet of snow. We can at least check the jeep out and secure it, so it doesn't plunge into the ravine and gather whatever possessions the woman has from inside," Jess said.

"I'll be right back with Doc. You got things handled?" Orion nodded to Jess as he walked out the door.

Within thirty minutes, Lyra had arrived, and Orion returned to his apartment with Doc. Doc Sterling immediately entered the bedroom to check on the woman. Lyra followed to offer her assistance as Jess and Orion remained in the living room. It didn't take long before Doc called Jess and Orion into the bedroom needing their assistance. "I'd like to put her on a saline drip and need one of you to go to my office and get my equipment," Doc ordered. "Her fever's still high, and I'm concerned about dehydration. An IV should help with that. I'd feel better if she regained consciousness, but with the trauma she sustained to her forehead, I'm not surprised. We still need to keep a close watch on her."

Lyra looked at the doctor as if she might cry, "Will she ever regain consciousness? We have to help her?"

Touching Lyra's shoulder gently, Doc Sterling replied, "I've seen people regain consciousness months after a head injury, and she's got herself a doozy. Let's not worry too much before we need to. You boys get my supplies, and Lyra and I will keep watch." Jess and Orion headed out the door. Doc placed his arm around Lyra's shoulder and walked her back into the bedroom where the woman lay. "I need to change her bandages and treat her cuts. Let's give her a sponge bath and change the sheets. She's soaked with sweat. After that, I'll give her another dose of antibiotics. The boys should be back with my supplies, and I'll get her hooked up to an IV. Then we'll let her rest." Doc took charge as Lyra assisted.

Jess and Orion decided they could get more done if they split up. Orion would run to Doc Sterling's office to pick up the list of supplies the doctor had handed them before leaving his apartment. Orion would get them back to Doc without delay. Jess would walk over to Iker's cabin to borrow the snowmobile and see if he could cover the morning shift at The Rip. He'd also grabbed a couple of shovels and whatever other tools he thought they might need to dig out the woman's jeep and bundle her luggage on the back of the snowmobile so they could transport it to Orion's apartment. Twenty minutes later, Orion was back at his apartment with the supplies Doc Sterling had requested. As he entered his bedroom, he could see the woman's bandages had been changed, as well as the sheets on the bed. Lyra and Doc were gently clothing the woman in a pair of spare pajamas Lyra had brought over. Orion offered his assistance as Doc rolled the unconscious woman carefully forward, gently bracing her, so Lyra could slip the pajama top over the woman's head. Orion saw the scar on the woman's shoulder. He stood staring at what he knew was a gunshot wound. His mind began to spin out of control. Orion knew what a healed gunshot wound looked like. He'd seen many, even had his own. *How could this woman possibly have a gunshot wound? The scar didn't look that old. Who would shoot her? Why would anyone shoot her? Who is this person? Why did she come to Hideaway Canyon?* Orion seemed to be unable to control the questions swirling through his mind. Doc and Lyra stood looking at Orion as he finally realized someone had been talking to him.

With a questioning look of concern, Doc asked, "You all right?" Orion, as if coming out of a catatonic state, nodded in acknowledgment, unable to verbalize any words. He recalled Doc Sterling mentioning the woman's scars to Lyra the day the woman arrived; however, he had filed the information in the back of his mind. Orion knew there were many reasons any person could have scars; as a matter of fact, most people had scars. Most people didn't have scars from gunshot wounds. Unable to control his thoughts, Orion glanced toward the woman in the bed and saw Doc had the woman hooked up to the IV, with Lyra's help. The woman looked peaceful as she lay in Orion's bed. Orion thought, *She looks dead.*

"Now, we need to let the woman rest," Doc signaled the siblings to move toward the door. "There's nothing any of us can do for her now, other than letting the good Lord take over. I've done everything I can do for her. The human body is a miraculous thing, it knows what to do. Let's let her rest." Doc Sterling had other patients to check on, so he headed down the stairs, indicating he would check up on the woman later that day.

Orion could hear the snowmobile off in the distance and knew Jess would be pulling up to The Rip at any time. Lyra heard the sound too. "Orion, you and Jess need to take care of the woman's jeep and get her luggage and whatever else you can find in the vehicle. I'm sure she'll feel more comfortable knowing her possessions are safe when she wakes up. I'll stay here and watch over her. Like Doc says, there's nothing any of us can do now. Skye's tucked away safe at Josie's house playing with the twins, and I have nothing better to do. When you get back, if the bar's busy, I'll go downstairs and help Jess out. But right now, you and Jess check on the vehicle. And please see if you can find any identification. Check for a wallet, purse, or cell phone. I'm sure someone must be worried sick about her." Orion knew his sister was right. He grabbed his coat and gloves and headed out the door.

Logistics was Jess's specialty in the field, and Orion immediately saw how thorough he had been equipping the snowmobile for their trek down the mountain to the waiting jeep. At a glance, he could see Jess had everything they could possibly need to help secure the vehicle. Jumping on the back of the snowmobile, he signaled Jess with a thumbs up, and the two were off. There weren't any visible tire tracks heading down the mountain, both knowing that the locals wouldn't attempt such a dangerous trip. Hideaway Canyon would be snowed in for a couple of days, maybe more, depending on what the weather would bring this afternoon and tonight. No local would attempt coming in or out. The snow had stopped and wasn't expected to resume until sometime around noon, so Jess and Orion had a couple of hours to secure the jeep and gather its contents. With the snowmobile, it only took them a short time to arrive at the site of the accident. Taking the time to scope out the area and the position of the jeep, both men knew they would have to secure the vehicle to the trees to prevent it from plunging into the ravine before they could safely enter the vehicle to remove its contents. Working together quickly and silently, as they had done so many times before, Orion and Jess grabbed ropes, chains, and everything they needed. The two men set out to get the job done. It wasn't long before the jeep was secured.

"Looks like we have it secured," Jess noted, "but let's test it out first before we enter the vehicle." Agreeing with a nod, Orion tested all the chains and ropes twice before signaling to Jess they could enter.

As Jess started unloading the back seat of the jeep, Orion searched the front seat, seeing a purse and cell phone on a floor scattered with granola and a thirty-two-ounce Styrofoam Love's cup. *She must have been snacking.* Orion picked up a zip-lock bag partially filled with granola and the Styrofoam cup. There was still ice in the cup. *Nope, she wouldn't have survived a night in her jeep with these temperatures*, Orion thought. The mess would have to be cleaned up, but not now. That was something that could wait. Making a quick scan of the front seats and dash, he grabbed the keys from the ignition and was about to close the passenger side door when his eyes locked on the glove compartment. Seeing the lock, he wasn't sure he would be able to open it but gave it a try. He had keys in his hand that should unlock the box.

Pushing the button, immediately allowed him access to the compartment, he saw the gun. *The woman had a Glock 22? What was she doing with that gun?* Without thinking further, he used his glove to pick up the gun and placed it in his pocket. He knew how to handle evidence and didn't want to destroy any fingerprints. His training had taught him well. Shaking his head to himself, he realized there could be lots of reasons for a person to have a gun, he had one, and he had no reason to think he needed to preserve the integrity of fingerprints that might be on the gun. He was being paranoid. Orion gathered some papers he saw in the glove box, as well as a small box and a few other remaining items from the glove compartment, just as Jess was collecting the last box from the back seat. Everything from inside the vehicle was loaded on the snowmobile for their trip back to his apartment.

The jeep was as secured as they could make it for the night. Both men were sure it would hold until the weather broke, and they would be able to get back to the vehicle and pull it safely out of the ditch. Orion was grateful for the noise from the snowmobile. He didn't understand why he hadn't shared the information about finding a gun in the glove box of the jeep with Jess. It's not unusual for a person to have a gun. Many states had right-to-carry laws. For all he knew, the woman could have a carry permit.

"Why does this woman need a Glock 22?" Orion questioned out loud as they were pulling up to the side stairs of The Rip.

"Sorry, bud, couldn't hear you. What did you say?" Jess responded.

"Nothing. Let's just get this stuff unloaded and into my apartment," Orion said, dodging the question. It wasn't like him to keep anything from Jess. He never did. For reasons he couldn't explain, he wanted to keep this to himself.

It wasn't long before the two men had hauled the woman's personal items up the stairs and into the apartment. At the instruction of Lyra, the men stacked the boxes and luggage neatly in a corner of the bedroom. She thought it might help comfort the woman when she gained consciousness. She would wake up and see her possessions. Orion went back to the snowmobile to get the last load—the woman's purse, cell phone, and items he'd gathered from the jeep's glove box. When he returned, he placed everything on the kitchen table, except the gun. Jess and Lyra made a pot of coffee and hunted for coffee cups from the cupboard.

Knowing he should check on the patient lying in his bed, Orion walked into his bedroom, where he stood staring at the stranger. Without realizing he was doing so, he reached to the woman and gently began to stroke her face. *Why a gun?* he thought as he slowly moved his fingers up and down her cheek and along her jawline. Her skin felt so smooth, so soft and warm, creating a warm sensation throughout his own body. The tactile experience frightened him. Stunned by the realization that he had initiated the touch, he pulled his hand away and walked out of the room. Reaching into his coat pocket as he walked into the kitchen, he felt the gun.

Jess and Lyra sat at the kitchen table drinking coffee and staring at the items on the table, as if waiting for Orion. Neither had touched the woman's purse or cell phone or any of the other items Orion had placed on the table. Both knew they needed to find out who the woman was, but it wasn't in their nature to intrude. It didn't feel right going through a stranger's personal items. All three had to be in agreement to search through the woman's possessions, so the couple had patiently waited for Orion to join them.

When he entered the kitchen, Orion picked up the coffee pot, topping off both their cups before filling one for himself. He took a seat at the table next to Lyra. "She seems to be comfortable. Thanks for your help," Orion said, looking at his sister and brother-in-law, "Did you find anything?" He did not identify the gun he held in his pocket.

Glancing at Jess, Lyra replied, "We were waiting for you. I don't really feel comfortable going through her purse, but this is an exceptional situation," she continued. "I thought it was important that the three of us do it together."

"I agree, let's get on with it," Orion hastened. Lyra picked up the cell phone first, looking for the switch to power it up. The phone wouldn't come on. With the cold weather and passage of time, the battery was dead. The three agreed the woman probably had a phone charger packed somewhere, if they couldn't find it, they were sure someone in Hideaway Canyon would have a charger that fit and would allow them to power her phone up looking for contact information.

Jess and Orion sipped their coffee, observing Lyra picking up the woman's purse. Both men thought it seemed more respectful for Lyra to look through such a personal item. Cautiously, Lyra emptied the items from the purse onto the kitchen table. A wallet immediately caught the attention of all three. Orion was the first to pick it up. Jess and Lyra began searching through the other items to see if they could find some identification, knowing the wallet was the best bet for information.

"Alessandra Petrovich from Chicago, Illinois," Orion stated as he looked at a driver's license. "No credit cards, no bank cards, no insurance card, some cash."

While Orion searched the wallet, Jess picked up a white envelope and opened it. "Lots of cash," Jess said as he held up the envelope, "without counting, I would guess about ten thousand dollars, maybe more, all in one-hundred-dollar bills."

Lyra's eye widened. "Isn't that pretty dangerous carrying that much cash around?" The eye contact she witnessed Orion and Jess make, confirmed the answer to her question. "Wonderful, the woman has a name. We can call her Alessandra, no more referring to her as 'the woman,' calling her that seemed so sad and impersonal." Lyra felt a weight lift off her shoulders as she started to put the items back in Alessandra's purse. Barring the envelope with a large sum of cash, all the other items were normal items found in any woman's purse. The driver's license had an address on it, which could help them find the woman's family. Feeling relieved, Lyra knew Jess and Orion had resources at The Firm that could locate almost anyone, anywhere in the world. Orion asked Lyra if she would go through Alessandra's luggage to see if she could find a phone charger. They all knew it should be possible to find some telephone numbers listed in the phone's directory, that would help them locate Alessandra Petrovich's family. She was happy to help, knowing she had thoughts of dressing Alessandra in her own clothes after her bath tonight and after Doc Sterling had a chance to check on her. She knew, as any woman would feel, there was comfort in the familiarity of one's own clothes.

Orion and Jess helped Lyra carry the items from the table into the bedroom and placed them on the dresser. Jess asked the brother and sister if they would be all right. He needed to relieve Iker at The Rip and start prepping for the evening meal. He could see from Orion's window that snow was beginning to fall, and soon the locals would gather for another evening at his bar. Lyra dismissed her husband with a kiss, telling him she would pick up Skye at Josie's and be back at Orion's to search for the power chord to charge Alessandra's phone and help with her care. She knew Skye would be excited to visit her "Unca O," however, would have to curb the child's enthusiasm so as not to disturb their patient. Lyra wanted to be at Orion's apartment when Doc Sterling arrived to assist him with the woman's bandages. She also knew Orion didn't get much sleep the night before, so she was hoping to convince him to take a nap, maybe one with Skye, before she joined her husband in the bar for, what would be, another busy evening. Hugging her brother, Lyra pulled her coat on as she grabbed her hat and gloves and headed down the stairs, "I'll be back as soon as I can."

Checking for the gun in his pocket, Orion was relieved to be alone. He had so many questions, and he needed some answers. He knew he was unlikely to get any from an unconscious woman. He wasn't sure why he hadn't told Jess about the gun, other than he felt by not saying anything to his friend, he was protecting Alessandra Petrovich. Protect her from what? He didn't need to protect her from Jess; however, he knew Jess would have as many questions, if not more than Orion had, and he would demand answers. He also knew finding the weapon would open up a whole new set of questions. He didn't want to worry Lyra, but he didn't keep secrets from Jess; he could always count on his brothers from The Firm. Orion would tell Jess later when Lyra wasn't around.

Orion brought some wood inside off the deck and stoked the fire. There wasn't any wind, but light snow began to fall and was expected to continue throughout the night. Another night like last night. He decided it would be a good time to catch a hot shower and a change of clothes before Lyra returned with Skye and before Doc Sterling came back to check on his patient. Orion approached Alessandra lying in his bed before heading into the bathroom. He touched her cheek, which was still warm. He took another cool cloth and gently wiped her very beautiful face. Glancing at the IV and seeing that it was almost empty, Orion didn't waste time in the shower, knowing Doc could arrive any time.

Sensing someone was present, Orion woke to find himself sitting in the chair next to Alessandra lying in his bed. His eyes tracked to the right where he saw Lyra standing in the doorway holding Skye, neither of whom said a word. Both their eyes were fixed on Orion's hand. He was holding the woman's hand. Freeing his hand as nonchalantly and gently as possible, Orion stood and exited the room. Knowing any discussion of what she just witnessed would embarrass her brother, Lyra chose to say nothing. She could see that Alessandra had not gained consciousness and knew Orion well enough to know, her brother would offer comfort to anyone in need. Lyra also knew their patient was a beautiful woman. Was Orion attracted to her? Regardless of the requirements of his job, Orion was a kind, sensitive soul. A description he would deny. Distracted by her impatient child, Lyra left the doorway to return to the living room, thinking about how abruptly her brother had left the room.

Lyra sat Skye down on her blanket in the middle of the room, collecting toys all around the child, hoping to keep the little girl occupied. "If you'll keep an eye on Skye, I'll check Alessandra's luggage for a phone charger and find some clothes to change her into. Doc should be here soon." Orion smiled at the opportunity that had presented itself. He cherished the time he was able to spend with his niece and enthusiastically accepted his sister's offer. He knew he would never have children of his own, so the time he spent with Skye allowed him a chance to exhaust his paternal instincts. Orion lowered himself to the floor and picked up a book, *Baby Bear Sees Blue*, instantly gaining Skye's attention. Orion settled in with his niece and began to read.

It didn't take Lyra long to find some pajamas in Alessandra's smallest suitcase. She was about to begin her search for a phone charger when she heard the knock at the door. Doc Sterling had arrived to check on his patient; however, he had been detained by the enthusiasm of her daughter. Doc was good with the children of Hideaway Canyon, but the special relationship he had with Skye was apparent. Doc Sterling was the grandfather Skye would never know. It brought tears to Lyra's eyes, witnessing their special relationship. Doc looked up as Lyra entered the living room to greet him, using the opportunity as a signal to check on his patient.

"How is she this afternoon?" Doc asked.

"Alessandra seems to be doing the same," Lyra replied.

"Alessandra?"

"Yes, our patient has a name. Alessandra Petrovich. Jess and Orion were able to get down the mountain on Iker's snowmobile to secure her car and gather her belongings. They found her purse, which had a driver's license in her wallet," Lyra explained.

"That's good news. It never seems right, not using my patient's name. Now, let's take a look at the young lady." Lyra assisted Doc Sterling as he changed Alessandra's bandages, checking the laceration on her forehead first. The sutures were doing their job, and the opening was healing. Changing the bandages on her wrist and ribs came next. Overall, Doc indicated he was satisfied with his patient's progression. But as a precautionary measure, he gave the woman another shot of antibiotics and changed her IV. "Let's keep her on the IV one more night," he suggested. "Her vital signs are good, and I think one more night with additional fluids and the antibiotic shot will help her gain some strength and hopefully bring her back to consciousness," he continued.

Orion walked into the bedroom. Nodding toward the living room, he told Lyra that little Skye had fallen asleep on the couch.

"I guess I wore her out." Lyra sent Orion downstairs to grab something to eat and check on Jess. She sent a message with her brother for Jess, asking him to let her husband know she would be at The Rip by dinner hour, expecting a crowd at the bar again tonight.

Meanwhile, Doc finished his exam and assisted Lyra as she bathed and clothed Alessandra in preparation for the evening. Both were hopeful that the woman would regain consciousness soon. Lyra watched the doctor tenderly care for the woman, turning her slightly on the side to prevent any bedsores from developing. He took a seat in the same chair Orion had been sitting in, next to the woman. He gently picked up her hand, the one that wasn't bandaged, and held it, whispering, "Miss Alessandra Petrovich, it's a pleasure to meet you. I want you to know that you are in a safe place. There are people here who are watching over you and caring for you. We are strangers to you, but please don't be afraid. No harm will come to you during our watch. Sleep tight and know that it's all right to wake up." Doc sat, holding her hand for a few more minutes. Lyra turned and walked into the next room so the doctor wouldn't see the tears streaming down her face.

Doc Sterling positioned himself beside Lyra, wrapping an arm around her shoulder. Lyra laid her head on his shoulder, finding comfort in the simple embrace he offered her. "She needs to rest. The IV and antibiotic shot are more precautionary than anything, right now. Her fever has gone down, and her wounds are mending. Like usual, there's nothing more I can do. Let's see how she's doing by morning," Doc shared. Lyra thanked Doc Sterling as he opened the door to leave.

She glanced at the couch to see Skye was still sound asleep. Lyra decided to take the opportunity to finish looking for the power cord so they could charge Alessandra's phone. The sooner they were able to identify her contacts, the sooner they would be able to notify her family that she was safe.

After reorganizing the smallest piece of luggage and not finding the charger, Lyra moved onto one of the larger pieces of luggage. It could be anywhere. *Thank goodness this piece was on rollers,* Lyra thought; it was so heavy she could hardly move it. Unzipping the opening and laying out both sides of the suitcase, she saw two additional zippers to open. Opening the zipper on the left, she was stunned. She left the suitcase sitting right where it was at and slowly backed out of the bedroom. She went to the couch and sat down, picking up Skye as she was waking up. She cuddled with her little girl, appreciating the moment and thinking about the money she saw. She had never seen so much cash in her life.

Orion walked through the door carrying, what looked to be a to-go container from the bar. The break had been good for him; he was smiling. It didn't take long for his smile to disappear, seeing Lyra's face and knowing something was wrong. Skye was cuddled up in her lap. It must be the woman, Alessandra. Was she awake? Had she died? All these thoughts navigated through his mind. Before either had time to speak, panic began to take over Orion, and his heart began to race. Lyra could only watch as she saw her brother drop the container he was carrying on the small table, next to the door, and take three long strides into his bedroom. His heart was surging through his chest. Closing in on the bed, he saw the woman looking more peaceful than he had seen her look. She was beautiful. There was a soft pink glow to her cheeks, which hadn't been there earlier. He could tell the doctor must have replaced her IV, and it looked as if she had fresh bandages on her forehead, wrist, and ribs. He gently picked up Alessandra's hand, feeling for a pulse and finding it very strong. Reaching to check for a fever, he couldn't resist a soft caress down her pink cheeks. Her fever was subsiding. She was alive. Relief eased through his body. Alessandra Petrovich appeared to be doing quite well. Looking tenderly at the woman lying in his bed, Orion's pulse quickened. As before, heat began to rise in his body. He couldn't stop touching her. Without realizing several minutes had passed, Orion jolted back to reality, considering what he had read wrong in Lyra's face. He turned to leave the room and talk to his sister. As he turned, he saw the open suitcase on the floor. He saw a suitcase filled with cash. Orion stood speechless looking at the cash, wondering, *Where had that money come from?* He turned to find Lyra standing in the doorway holding Skye, who had just begun to wake up. Lyra stopped him before he could say anything, "I'll send Jess up when I get downstairs." She turned and walked out the door with her daughter. Orion listened to Lyra's footsteps slowly walk down the stairs and the door opening as she entered The Rip.

It was almost an hour before Jess made it up the stairs and into Orion's apartment. The Rip was packed, as expected, and he just couldn't leave his crew without his help. Although there wasn't much wind, Orion had seen the snow continue to fall outside. By the time Jess arrived, Orion had moved the luggage out into the living room, so he wouldn't disturb Alessandra as he counted the money and placed it in organized piles. He searched through all the pockets of the suitcase to see if he would find any information that could give him a clue about the money or if he could find anything else suspicious. He was sitting on the couch when Jess opened the door. Immediately, Jess saw stacked money, two guns with magazines, and a phone arranged neatly in rows. *I think I'm going to need a beer*, he thought, going into the kitchen and grabbing two beers, one for himself and a second for Orion.

As Jess walked back into the room, Orion started, "There's almost two hundred and fifty thousand dollars in this suitcase." "I found the charger for her phone and plugged it in about twenty minutes ago. I also found two guns and a burner phone. A SIG 229 was in the suitcase hidden in a compartment underneath the money."

Jess looked at Orion in disbelief, "You said two."

"I hadn't had the opportunity to tell you, but yesterday, when we cleaned out the woman's jeep, I found a gun in her glove box, Glock 22 with a standard mag-15 round capability," Orion said matter-of-factly.

Remaining calm, Jess said in disbelief, "You are telling me that for the past twenty-four hours there's been an unconscious woman lying in your bed who has over two hundred and fifty thousand dollars in cash on her and a gun used by seventy-five percent of America's police force and a SIG 229 issued to every United States Secret Service operative."

Orion replied, "Yes," just as they heard the door click shut.

The men looked up, unaware anyone had opened the door and saw Iker standing rigid. "Lyra sent me up. She thought you might need me."

Lyra was right. Knowing Iker's ability to gather information, the man was one of the most sought after by special operations organizations in the United States and many countries throughout the world. Both men were happy to include him in their discovery. Iker was connected, not that they weren't, but if anyone could find out who this woman was, it would be him. Like other members of The Firm, Iker had been a guest in Orion's apartment many times. Knowing where the kitchen was, he searched through the refrigerator and helped himself to a beer. Grabbing two extra bottles and tossing the caps in the trash, Iker strode back into the room and handed both men a cold one. He sat down in the large leather chair, the one that fit his size the best. He stretched his legs, facing Orion and Jess, who sat on opposite ends of the couch. Iker, six feet six inches tall with mahogany skin, was an imposing sight to most. He was an irreplaceable member of The Firm, having served in the Navy and with the Navy SEAL team for twenty years, resigning to take a position as a commander in special forces and then became one of the founding members of The Firm.

"What did you say the little lady's name was?" Iker asked, and he reached into his pocket and brought out a small notepad and pen.

"The Illinois driver's license I found in her wallet identified her as Alessandra Petrovich. Address is 7100 South Shoreline Drive, Apartment 3A, Chicago, Illinois 60649. Date of birth, October 4, 1982. Light brown eyes, brown hair. Five feet eight inches and one hundred and thirty-two pounds. She's an organ donor. Her license indicates she wears glasses. She wasn't wearing any when I found her, maybe contacts. Otherwise, they could still be in her jeep," Orion responded with details. "I also grabbed some papers out of her glove compartment. I didn't look at all the documents, but I know one piece of paper was a vehicle registration." He stood up walked into the bedroom, returning with the registration. "There are miscellaneous receipts we can use, if we need them for a deep dive into her background," Orion added.

"We've got enough to get the ball rolling. I will call Micah and fill him in on what we are doing. See if he can check his resources while Iker wipes the cobwebs from his computers," Jess said humorously. "Let's keep this information under wraps. We don't need the residents of Hideaway Canyon getting involved. We also don't know that Alessandra Petrovich has done anything wrong." Standing up, Jess said, "We don't need to worry about Lyra. She knows the job."

Jess continued to talk, "Iker, if you want to get started, go on ahead. I don't need you in the bar. Lyra and Josie are downstairs and can help me close up. All of us need to get home. The snow's getting deeper."

Orion reached over and picked up Alessandra's cell phone and charger and handed it to Iker, "See if you can get anything off of this."

Agreeing that they would meet in The Rip's office tomorrow morning around ten o'clock, the three men parted ways knowing each would spend the evening checking their sources. There was more to Alessandra Petrovich's story, and the three friends who were exceptional intelligence collectors intended to find out.

After everyone left, Orion began picking up the bundles of money he had sorted, deciding to return them to the suitcase and to his bedroom. He took the burner phone, two guns, and magazines, checking to make sure neither was chambered, and placed them on his dresser in the bedroom, feeling more comfortable that all was out of eyesight, at least from the living room. He looked at the woman. *Alessandra Petrovich...just who are you?*

Orion stood and watched Alessandra, unable to walk away. He saw the slow rise and fall of her chest. Although she now had a light pink hue to her cheeks, she was still very pale. The cuts and bruises on her face and arms were slowly dissipating, and Orion could see the swelling from her forehead laceration was gone. Like the other times, Orion felt her cheeks and forehead for a fever. Although she didn't seem that warm, he picked up a washcloth, dipped it in the basin of cool water and began washing her face. He felt an intense desire to touch her, and washing her face provided him with an innocuous way to do so. She was beautiful. Her skin was like porcelain, like the dolls his niece would play with. She had small ears, perfectly shaped. He had put the cloth down and gently fondled her earlobe between his finger and thumb. So delicate to his touch. They were pierced; he could tell by the small punctures he saw in each. She had freckles across her cute little turned-up nose, and one freckle on her right cheek was shaped like a star. Her cheekbones were prominent, and her jawline strong. He could tell by the shape of her body under-neath the covers, she had a slender build. Not emaciated, the kind he liked. The toned muscles in her arms revealed she was strong. He gently picked up her hand, the one that wasn't bandaged and studied it. She wore no jewelry on either of her hands. There wasn't a ring nor a tan line indicating a ring had been previously worn and removed recently. She must not be married. Or maybe she was one of those people who chose not to wear a ring. Her short nails were covered in pink polish. Her fingers were long and fingertips soft. He caressed them with his own, only to stop abruptly thinking his rough hands might hurt hers. No, she was unconscious and would never know. He asked himself again, *Alessandra Petrovich…who are you?*

Hearing the wind shake the window brought him to his senses. He gently placed her hand back under the covers and walked out of the room. He felt a chill in the air, knowing he needed to carry wood, his never-ending chore, from the deck into his apartment for the expected cold evening. Slipping on his jacket and gloves, he tended to the chore. After stacking more wood and stoking the fire, Orion knew he would have enough wood for tonight. He flipped on the television, turning the volume down low. Alessandra was unconscious, and the level of noise would make no difference; however, it just seemed like the right thing to do having a patient in his house. Relaxed, Orion pulled out his laptop from the desk, knowing he was on a mission to find out more about Alessandra Petrovich.

Hideaway Canyon, April 22, 2013

Residents of Hideaway Canyon woke up to a spectacular post-card-perfect sight. Another one and a half feet of snow had accumulated throughout the night, leaving in its wake a backdrop of snow-capped mountains, pine trees whispering in the light wind as branches bent slightly because of the heavy snowfall that tried to weigh them down. A blanket of white snow covered the miles and miles of terrain that could be seen from rooftops throughout the valley, sparkling as if a handful of glitter had been tossed into the mix of snowflakes as they fell to the ground. Slowly, the community began to rouse. Residents freed themselves from the warmth of their home to collect outside in parkas, snow boots, and mittens, talking about the storm and plans for the day. The chore began, everyone digging themselves out of their homes, shoveling paths through snow so they could check on neighbors.

As Orion walked out onto his deck to collect more wood for his stove, off in a distance he could hear the roar of a snowmobile engine starting up, sputtering to a stop, then starting again in a purr. The sound seemed so normal; it made him think he was home. The canyon residents were used to waking up to large snowfalls, so taking care of the burdens brought on after every snowstorm wasn't much of a chore. He could see the streets of the small community come alive. He could hear people calling out to their neighbors with cheery greetings, dogs barking, and the laughter of children delighted from playing in the snow. Stopping for a moment, Orion paused to listen, having grown to appreciate the sounds of this community. He knew this would be the place he would want to call home, knowing it would never be possible for him.

It had been a quiet evening for Orion in his apartment. He woke at dawn, like usual, finding himself lying on his couch with his laptop in his hands. Orion instantly knew he had been overwhelmed by a need for sleep and hadn't accomplished the search he planned to do on Alessandra. Collecting wood needed off his porch, he turned and walked inside to feed the fire. He started a pot of coffee before walking into his bedroom to check on the woman lying in his bed.

Before long, Orion heard footsteps coming up his stairway, knowing Doc Sterling would be doing his rounds about town, checking on any patients he had. It would be another day that residents of Hideaway Canyon would be stranded on the mountain. Orion had listened to the news station before falling asleep last night, and he knew that the forecast looked clear, and residents would begin the slow chore of digging themselves out and beginning to work their way down the mountain and into the city. Opening the door, Orion held out his hand to shake Doc's and thank him for coming. After a brief discourse about the weather and how things were looking in town, Doc walked across the room to Orion's bedroom to check on his patient. Orion followed close behind. The doctor proceeded to check Alessandra's vital signs, nodding his head as he did so. Both men remained silent as Doc performed his job.

"Hello," Lyra called as she slipped into Orion's apartment and set her squirming daughter on the floor. "Unca O, Unca O," the child called as she ran as quickly as her short little legs could carry her, searching the familiar apartment for her Uncle Orion. Within moments, Lyra heard screams of delight as Orion stepped around the corner of the door leading to his bedroom, startling the little girl. He grabbed Skye unexpectedly, slinging her up in his arms and rubbing a day's growth of beard over her cheeks as she giggled and squirmed to get away from him. Skye loved her uncle and the games she played with him.

Taking off her coat and mittens, "Please don't get the child riled up. I've spent the past hour trying to calm her down. She's already excited about the snow," Lyra scolded. "I promised her that we could play in the snow after we helped watch Alessandra for you, so you could join her daddy and Iker at The Rip. Getting her to agree to that was even a chore!"

Orion let his niece slide down his leg to land gently on the floor. The child took off running toward the couch, her blond curls bouncing with delight that she was freed. "Doc's in the bedroom." Orion nodded. "I'll watch your little hellion, if you want to help him" as he walked over to join Skye on the couch. The child became entranced in her own little world after Orion offered her a box of some of her favorite toys.

It wasn't long before Orion returned to the bedroom to offer his assistance to Doc and Lyra; however, most importantly, he wanted to hear the woman's prognosis. Doc had removed the IV and bandage from Alessandra's forehead, indicating her wound was healing very well, and he didn't want it to be covered any longer. The air would help the healing process, and the stitches would dissolve on their own. He rewrapped her wrist and ribs in fresh gauze, pointing out there wasn't anything else he could do. It would take time and rest to heal these wounds. Taking Alessandra's blood pressure, pulse, and temperature, he gave the brother and sister a big smile. "I think our patient is well on her way to mending."

"But, Doc, she's still unconscious," Lyra worried.

"That's not uncommon in an accident, and this little lady had a doozy of a head injury," Doc replied. "I'd like to be able to tell you she will gain consciousness by noon, but medical science just doesn't know the answer to that. What I do know is that the body's a wonder among machines, and whatever is happening inside her right now, is a good thing. Her body's doing what it needs to do to heal. Give her time. I'm confident she'll be awake and talking to us soon," he consoled Lyra. "Nothing for us to do now but sit and wait. Lyra, I'll help you give our patient a sponge bath, change the sheets and get her in some clean clothes, if you would like," Doc offered.

Knowing the doctor was a busy man and he could help Lyra, Orion offered, "No, Doc, you finish your rounds. I have another hour before my meeting, so I can help Lyra with our patient."

Doc accepted the offer. Putting away his stethoscope and gathering the IV equipment, Doc headed into the living room. He found Skye busy playing with a doll. She looked up at Doc Sterling, holding her doll to him and said, "My dolly has a booboo."

Doc sat down on the couch next to the child, checked in his medical bag, and pulled out a Band-Aid. Holding it up to the little girl, he offered, "Want to put a Band-Aid on her booboo?" Skye nodded, and Doc worked his magic on his new patient. When he was done, he patted the little girl with the blond curls, stood up, said his goodbyes, and walked out the door.

Lyra, with Orion's assistance, worked methodically nursing the beautiful woman lying in her brother's bed. They changed the sheets on the bed, and Lyra gently bathed and clothed Alessandra, her brother helping move the woman when instructed. As they worked, neither did much talking. Lyra wondered whether Orion noticed how beautiful the woman was. Since her fever had subsided, color returned to her cheeks. The sallowness of her skin began to change, giving her a warm glow. Lyra questioned the woman's story, her thoughts, wondering to the money and gun she found. Hopefully the men would have more information soon. Someone had to be wrought with fear, wondering where the beautiful woman was. She could only imagine what her feelings would be, had her own daughter been missing.

Searching her brother's eyes, trying to read his thoughts. "I know you have a meeting with Jess and Iker. I've got this covered. If you throw a load of clothes in the washing machine on your way out, I'll make sure they get changed to the dryer. I brought some nail polish with me, promising Skye to polish her nails in her favorite peachy-pink color. I think I'll do Alessandra's nails too, while she sleeps," Lyra said.

With warmth in his eyes, Orion wrapped his arms around his sister and pulled her close. "Thanks for helping me," Lyra offered. "You're a good man, Orion." She continued, "You know, not all people are bad in this world. I know we all have a few concerns about what we found in Alessandra's luggage. There could be a reasonable explanation. Don't let your job let you think the worst."

"Or we could be lucky the woman's been unconscious and incapable of shooting us," spilled out of Orion's mouth. Giving his sister one last big squeeze, he thanked her for watching the woman, said he'd be back soon, and slipped out the door before Skye realized he was gone. As he moved down the stairsteps, he knew something was very wrong. That sixth sense that had always helped him "get the job done" was telling him beware. He had too much to lose in Hideaway Canyon, to let anyone, including a beautiful woman, harm the people he loved.

Knowing she would be at her brother's apartment for a few hours, Lyra went into the kitchen to see what Orion had in his refrigerator. She would make lunch while she waited. It didn't take long before Skye sought out her mother, holding her favorite peachy-pink nail polish in her hand. Smiling at her daughter, she asked, "Are you ready for mommy to polish your nails?" Skye eagerly nodded her head yes. "How about we paint your nails and then paint Alessandra's to match? That way, when she wakes up from her nap, she will look so beautiful, like you, and be surprised!" Lyra offered.

"Yes!" her daughter squealed without hesitation as she ran into the bedroom. Lyra spent the next hour painting fingers and toes, talking and giggling with her daughter.

The morning had gone smoothly for Orion. Doc Sterling made his rounds early, checking in on Alessandra, and Lyra and Skye showed up shortly after Doc's arrival, freeing up Orion's time as care-taker to meet with Jess and Iker at The Rip. Having offered the men a beer; and all three men opting for a cup of coffee instead, the men began their meeting.

Jess began. "I ran the woman's driver's license. Nothing pulls up—no tickets, no arrests, no outstanding warrants, at least for the name Alessandra Petrovich. Her driver's license looks legit. The address exists and I've sent men to Chicago to verify the photo with the driver's license and to check records in Illinois to see what they can dig up." Orion and Iker listened intently. "Records show an Alessandra Petrovich was granted a student visa and entered the United States in early 1998, through Canada. I've got people work-ing on a deeper dig, to find out how Alessandra Petrovich arrived in Canada and if she's a resident. If everything matches, the woman has lived in the US for fifteen years…uneventfully."

Having more information to relay to his friends, Jess continued, "It looks like Alessandra Petrovich was accompanied by a woman with the name of Alina Ulanova Petrovich, presumably her mother, could be an aunt, cousin, relative of some sort. Here's where it gets interesting. Alina Ulanova Petrovich has no record—of anything. Just like Alessandra, no tickets, no arrests, no outstanding warrants, also no driver's license. No record of a job, social security number, or paying taxes. Unless Alina was independently wealthy, and if she's Alessandra's mother, it would have been difficult for them to survive, not impossible. Good chance we could be looking at an undocu-mented immigrant. Records do show an Alessandra Petrovich applied for a social security number when she was twenty-two years old, and she's been paying taxes ever since. But neither women are United States citizens," Jess let the other two men absorb the information he gave them.

Clearing his throat, Iker started, "I might have your connection." Glancing at both men, he began, "Like you, I didn't find any significant records in the United States. Nothing that interesting, anyway. However, there was an Alina Ulanova Petrovich in Western Europe, very promising young ballerina with the Mariinsky Ballet in St. Petersburg, Russia. Traveled as a premier ballerina for several ballet companies prior to joining Mariinsky."

Jess and Orion stared at their friend. Glancing up, Iker said, "What?" seeing the two men and their questioning expression. He continued, "The information was in my research." Frustrated by their looks, he continued, "Just listen, it gets interesting. Ms. Petrovich, the ballerina, seems to have disappeared. Records show her marrying a man by the name of Anton Petrovich, then leaving ballet for good. She never reappeared in any other dance company, which is almost unheard of in the world of ballet, particularly for someone who has made it to the top as a prima ballerina."

Jess and Orion continued to listen silently, not knowing what to say, dumbfounded by Iker's familiarity with the world of ballet. "The man our little ballerina married, Anton Petrovich, was a young officer in the Yugoslav People's Army. Later becoming a top commander for Mikozavich." He paused.

"Butcher of the Balkans." Orion could feel the heat rising from within him. The three men made eye contact, acknowledging their recognition of the name and knowing the atrocities associated with the man's reputation.

"According to my sources, Petrovich's wife disappeared fifteen years ago with a daughter. Alessandra could be the Butcher's daughter," Iker finished. "As soon as I have more information, I'll let you know. Could take a few more days. The question I'd like us to answer is, if she's Petrovich's daughter, what's she doing here?"

"If I get the serial numbers off the guns, can you run them through the system? If the check comes back positive, we'll turn the guns in for fingerprinting," Orion asked Iker. "Also, I'd like to pull some random numbers from the bills we found. Can you run them too?"

"Sure, tell me what you need. Let's find out if the guns and money can be identified with any crimes, national and international level," Iker agreed. Orion indicated he would gather the information for Iker right after their meeting, so he could get started on his search.

"I'd like to wait and see what additional information we gather, which is going to take a few days, but I'm not sure this is anything we should be worried about. If the guns are permitted and the money legit, I don't see there's been any crime committed. At the most, it looks like we have two females showing up in the United States fifteen years ago, possibly undocumented immigrants, neither having done anything wrong. If that's it, I'd say there's nothing to move on. Immigration isn't in our purview, and I see no reason to interfere in the lives of either woman. If the women are who we think they might be, they are safer here," Jess concluded.

"I wonder where the other woman is. Why is Alessandra alone? Doesn't make sense she would leave her mother? Maybe she's not alive," Iker questioned. Neither of the men commented, knowing Iker's questions needed to be answered.

"What did Doc say about Alessandra?" Jess asked Orion.

"She still isn't conscious, but the prognosis looks good. Her fevers gone, he took her off the IV and removed the bandage from her forehead. She just needs more time for her wrist and ribs to heal. She could regain consciousness any day," Orion answered.

"Guess we are lucky she's unconscious. It buys us a little more time to search her background," Iker added.

Josie walked into the office, wanting some help out front. The bar was beginning to get busy; lunch hour was upon them. Jess and Iker hurried out to man the bar and kitchen, while Orion hastened up the back steps to his apartment to collect information for Iker's search.

When he opened his apartment door, Orion could hear faint giggles coming from his bedroom. Glancing in the kitchen, he saw that Lyra had set the table and was making something for lunch. He strode into the bedroom to find Lyra painting Alessandra's toenails. Caught off guard, he asked, "Is she awake?"

"No, since I was painting Skye's nails," she said, looking over at her daughter. "We thought Alessandra would be surprised when she woke up to find her own nails done."

"Unca O, look at my nails," Skye called. Turning, Orion witnessed Skye sitting on her bum with both her hands and feet in the air displaying her pretty peachy-pink finger and toenails and a few other body parts. He smiled, feeling his heart about to burst, hoping no other man would ever see what he just saw. He loved the little girl. No man would ever be good enough for his niece. He leaned over and kissed Skye.

"I have a few things to collect for Iker, then I'm going to help Jess in the bar. Are you girls okay?" he checked. Indicating they would be fine, Lyra told him she made some lunch for him and Jess and would have it waiting for them when they got a break. She watched her brother walk out the door, turning her attention back to her daughter and the unconscious woman.

The little village of Hideaway Canyon had been bustling throughout the day. After three days of snow and having been unable to get into the city, residents were excited to be out and about, visiting friends and neighbors, talking about the snowstorm, and restocking their supplies. Although the road down the mountain was still treacherous, a path in the snow had been plowed, and a few residents were successful making a trip into the city. After helping during the lunch hour rush at The Rip, Orion and Jess used their trucks to pull Alessandra's vehicle out of the ditch and have it towed to Rob Taylor's Automotive to find out what repairs were needed.

By the end of the day, Orion was exhausted. He had returned to his apartment to relieve his sister and niece from serving as nursemaid to Alessandra, knowing Jess was taking the evening off so he could spend time with his family. Iker and Josie would close The Rip tonight. After a quick check on his patient, Orion went into the bathroom to take a nice warm shower. He knew the shower would help him relax and hopefully help provide a good night's sleep. He came out of the bathroom after showering, in a pair of old gray sweatpants, towel drying his hair. He grabbed a beer from the refrigerator while microwaving a leftover dish Lyra had left for him. He took his meal into his bedroom, setting up a TV table next to the chair by his bed. He decided he would have his meal with Alessandra tonight. Taking a long draw on his beer and a bite of his meal, Orion gazed curiously at Alessandra.

Remembering what Doc Sterling had told them about an unconscious person being able to hear, he began to talk, "You're not much for talking, are you?" Orion looked around the room and then back at Alessandra, feeling rather silly. *She is beautiful,* he thought. *What's the matter with you? Stop thinking about the woman that way,* he scolded himself silently. It had been a long time since he'd been in a relationship, or for that matter, with a woman for any reason. The job always seemed to get in the way, and love was a complication he never needed. His attention turning back to Doc Sterling's words, Orion began to talk to the woman out loud, "I'm going to eat my dinner with you, if you don't mind. You know, Doc says he needs you to wake up soon, or he'll need to start you on a feeding tube." He paused for a moment to take a bite. "My sister's a pretty darn good cook, and I'm sure you'd agree what I am eating is better than liquid through a tube." Feeling more comfortable, Orion continued to talk. "We pulled your jeep out of the ditch today and took it to a local mechanic. Rob Taylor. He's a good man and will do right by you. We've been trying to figure out who you are. We want to help you."

As Orion ate, he continued watching Alessandra wondering if she could hear him. "Someone's got to be looking for a pretty lady like you." He smiled, realizing he had surprised himself for stating that out loud. "You've been here three days. I found you along the road, in the ditch, with your jeep headed down a deep ravine. It was snowing pretty bad. You're lucky to be alive." He finished his meal. Not knowing what else to say, "Thanks for having dinner with me." Feeling like he had followed the doctor's instruction, Orion stood up and walked out of the room.

After putting his dirty dishes in the dishwasher and cleaning up the counter, Orion took another beer out of his refrigerator and headed into the living room. He picked up his laptop as he sat down on the couch. Tonight, he would accomplish something with his research. After logging into The Firm's database, Orion typed in the words "Anton Petrovich." Immediately a list of files displayed on the screen. One caught his attention, marked "CLASSIFIED." The word didn't detour his effort, knowing he held a top security clearance, which would allow him access to the information. It wasn't long before Orion realized he had spent the past two hours reading through files on his computer. *Could Anton Petrovich be this woman's father?* he thought.

Glancing at the clock, he signed off his computer and placed the laptop on the coffee table. He walked back into his bedroom, turning on a small night light for Alessandra and sat down in the chair next to her lying in bed. He had turned the night light on for her every night since her arrival, knowing she could gain consciousness in the middle of the night. He knew the light was only a small attempt to provide comfort for the woman, if she woke in the middle of the night. He suspected she would not only be disoriented but would be terrified waking up in a stranger's apartment. He leaned over and brushed the back of his hand against her soft, warm cheeks noticing color continued to return to her face. He tenderly outlined her jawline with the tips of his fingers, finishing with a stroke down her small nose.

He was unable to control the effect stroking the woman had on his body. Why did he want to touch her so badly? he thought to himself. He'd seen many beautiful women before, even dated some. But none seemed to captivate him the way she did. He picked up her hand, the one that wasn't bandaged, and placed it safely between the two of his. He dipped his head toward her, feeling the warmth of her shallow breath on his skin, and a powerful surge struck his loins. There was a connection he felt for her that he didn't understand and didn't have the strength to want to break. He had to touch her. A force, beyond his control, lured him into her. Orion gently touched his lips to Alessandra's forehead offering a light kiss. He touched her lips, starting at her forehead, down to her brow, tracing her cheekbones. He slowly lifted his head, only long enough to gaze at her pretty face. Not wanting to wonder what it would be like to kiss

Alessandra, he lowered his lips to hers, offering the woman a delicately warm kiss. The woman showed no awareness of the kiss; however, Orion felt like he'd been struck by a bolt of lightning.

After taking a moment to recover from the kiss, Orion whispered, "Alessandra Petrovich, you are safe in my home. I won't let anyone hurt you." He felt her move her fingers. A wave of excitement rushed through his body as he looked down into his hands. He watched closely beginning to talk to her again. "Alessandra, you can hear me, can't you? You just moved your fingers. Do it again. Show me you can hear me." He waited and watched patiently for a sign. Minutes passed. He tried once more. "Just one more time, Alessandra. Let me know you can hear me. Just move your fingers a little. I know you can do it." Still nothing. Wondering whether he had let his own attraction to the woman unravel him, he placed her hand softly under the sheet, tucking the blankets around her. "Good night, Alessandra Petrovich." Discouraged, he left the room.

Orion's apartment, April 23, 2013

Awakened by unrecognizable sounds that he thought were coming from outside, Orion slowly opened his eyes. He felt like he had just fallen asleep. The wind must have picked up. As Orion lie on the couch stretching, he glanced toward the window, seeing that it was still dark outside. He had wanted to get an early start on the day, planning to meet with Jess and Iker again, to discuss the information they received from their searches; however, it must still be the middle of the night. Sitting up, he found his watch. It was four thirty in the morning. Reclining back onto the couch to get more sleep, he heard the noise again. And it didn't come from the window. It came from his bedroom.

Without any reason for alarm and trying to wake up, Orion sluggishly made his way into his bedroom. Standing in the doorway, he looked toward Alessandra lying on the bed—nothing moving there. As he slowly turned away to scan the rest of the room, his eyes darted back to the bed, realizing Alessandra wasn't in the bed. He heard a click and felt an explosion in his arm. Instantaneously, he knew he had been shot. His reflexes dropped him to the floor as he searched on his knees for shelter around the corner of the doorway.

Orion yelled out, "Alessandra, put the gun down." He could hear weeping coming from the room.

"No, leave me alone! How do you know my name! I will kill you!" the woman whimpered.

"Damn it, I'm not going to harm you. You don't even know me. Why would you want to kill me?" Orion tried to reason, thinking this couldn't be happening to him.

Another shot came from the bedroom. "I don't know who you are! Where am I? What do you want?" Alessandra yelled through tears.

Orion could hear terror through the tears, coming from the voice in the bedroom, knowing the woman must be terrified. He didn't like being shot at…he never had. And it only made him angry. "Alessandra, my name is Orion. This is my house," he commanded.

"Did my father send you? I won't go back!" she screamed.

"Who? No, your father didn't send me. I don't even know your father. Please, put the gun down," Orion pleaded. "I'm not going to hurt you. I've been helping you," he tried to reason with the insane woman holding a gun. Knowing he would soon lose patience with the situation and his training would kick in, Orion made another attempt to calm the woman down. "Please, I'm begging you, hear me out first, then you can shoot me."

"Don't come any closer," the woman warned.

"Alessandra, please let me reach around the corner and turn the light switch on," Orion pleaded.

She sent out another warning shot, "No, I said, stay where you are!"

"Alessandra, if you can see me, I'll be easier to shoot," Orion suggested, knowing he was crazy for making himself an easy target. He'd always trusted his intuition in the field, and his gut was telling him the woman was terrified. He couldn't imagine the beautiful woman lying in his bed for the past three days was capable of killing someone; he could hardly believe she owned a gun, or in her case, two guns. Obviously, she wasn't afraid to fire a gun. She managed to hit her target, gratefully not a perfect chest shot. If she could just see that he was an actual person, not her father or his henchmen, and if he could get her to listen to him, he hoped he'd be able to talk his way out of getting shot again.

He heard the woman's tears lessen, but she warned, "All right, but don't come closer. I will shoot you,"

He needed to keep her talking. Her voice would let him know where she was in the room. It was dark in the bedroom, except for the nightlight, which didn't give off much light. Orion concentrated on slowing his heartbeat, knowing he needed to talk to her in a calm voice, "Alessandra, I am slowly standing up, in the doorway of the bedroom. The light switch is on the wall to the left of the door…I'm reaching for it…I found the switch." The woman remained quiet.

"Now, I'm going to switch it on. The light will be bright. It will be blinding, but I promise you, I won't move from this spot. Please, Alessandra, don't shoot me." There was no response. As his heart raced, Orion switched on the light, not knowing whether or not he would be shot.

The man and woman stood staring at one another. Neither saying a word. He wasn't what she had expected. The man stood where he said he would, wearing a pair of gray sweatpants and no shirt. At a glance, he looked like a man having spent a day surfing on the beach, but the lines in his face revealed more. His hair, messy from sleep, was sandy blond, curling above his shoulders. He stood, not smiling, but then who would be, after having been shot at? His eyes were dark and penetrating, as if searching her for information she wasn't prepared to give. She kept the gun pointed at him, as her teary eyes wandered to his shoulder. She winced, seeing blood dripping down his upper left arm, knowing she caused it. As her eyes lowered, she saw the muscular torso of an athlete. Her legs began to ripple as though they would give out. She willed herself to remain standing, not understanding why his presence made her weak in the knees. Orion watched, without speaking, as the woman seemed to discover the bandages that were holding her together. He knew he'd had a moment to rush her and wrestle the gun away, but the sadness he saw in her eyes when she discovered her bandages alarmed him. When he was on the job, he looked to take advantage of every moment like this; however, right now, he couldn't make himself tackle her.

Orion, knowing he needed to deescalate the situation and get the gun away from Alessandra, began to talk, "Alessandra, I am not going to hurt you. If I had wanted to hurt you, I would have done so before now. You had an accident three days ago, and I found you along the road."

Alessandra's head pounded as she tried to recall how she arrived at the man's apartment. She touched her hand to her forehead. Could this be true? Nothing was making sense.

"Why don't you come into the living room with me, and we can sit down, and I can explain how you ended up here?" Orion asked, hoping for some sign that Alessandra would put the gun down. "You've been hurt, and I know you must be feeling weak."

Keeping his hands up, he slowly started to back his way out of the bedroom, never allowing her out of his sight. As if the two were attached by an invisible rope, she mimicked his movement and moved out of the bedroom and into the living room with him. The gun remained pointed at him. Orion continued to talk, "Why don't you sit on the couch, it's the most comfortable." He quickly gathered the pillow and blankets he had been using for his bed and tossed them to the end of the piece of furniture.

"I'm going to stoke the fire, it's a little chilly in here," he said as he pointed to the extra wood by the stove. Alessandra didn't offer any argument, so he moved to tend to the chore, making every action slow and deliberate, while keeping an eye on Alessandra and the gun pointed at him. The warmth felt from the stove was almost immediate, offering comfort to the situation. Although the gun remained pointed at him, Orion could see the woman had taken her finger off the trigger. *A good sign*, Orion thought. Feeling confident that he would be able to talk the gun out of Alessandra's hands, he told her that he wouldn't get any closer but motioned that he was going to sit in the chair facing her. Orion could see pain in Alessandra's eyes as she slowly and painfully lowered herself to the couch. Without knowing for sure, he suspected her head was throbbing and watched as each and every breath she took was taken in agony.

Without warning, Jess and Iker burst through Orion's apartment door, both men with guns intent on removing any threat. Startled by the entrance of his friends and desperate to save the woman's life, knowing both men possessed the skills to kill Alessandra in one shot, Orion jumped in front of her. At the same moment, as if watching a fantasy movie of *Xena: Warrior Princess*, Alessandra jumped to her feet, positioning herself behind Orion holding a gun butted up against the back of his head. All four stood motionless.

Orion, Jess, and Iker were awestruck. *Sweet Jesus. Who is this woman?* Not one of the men anticipated Alessandra's ability to move so swiftly and with such precision, almost as if she had been trained. Alessandra's movement had placed Orion as her shield.

"Nobody shoot! Nobody shoot!" Orion commanded. His two friends stood glaring at Alessandra, guns pointed with their infrared sites activated on a spot between her eyes.

Calming his voice, Orion began to talk. "Alessandra, these are my friends, Jess and Iker." He paused. "Jess, Iker…Alessandra has regained consciousness." All three remained motionless, assessing the potential threat, not saying a word, thinking about their next step.

"I don't know why they are here," he said quietly, searching his two friends' faces.

A couple of seconds passed, and Jess responded, "I let Charlie use the cot in the back room of The Rip last night to sleep off his alcohol consumption. He woke me up a few minutes ago, saying he heard gunshots coming from your apartment. I called Iker, and he met me here."

"Ah, my good friends, thank you for checking on me. As you can see, I am fine. Ms. Petrovich and I were just about to sit down and talk," Orion informed them with a look the men would understand, trying desperately not to get shot.

Iker, giving a side glance to Jess and Orion, and making eye contact with Alessandra, said, "You don't look fine to me. You've been shot."

Alessandra winced as she saw Orion look down at his arm, having forgotten about the gunshot wound that she inflicted. "It's a flesh wound. I haven't had time to clean it up," Orion said, responding to his friend.

"Alessandra was startled early this morning when she woke up in a strange apartment. She was afraid, seeing me walk into the bedroom. She accidentally shot me," Orion added. Knowing she had intentionally and purposefully shot Orion, Alessandra refrained herself from speaking. She was beginning to think there might be something wrong with the man and wondered why Orion was seemingly defending her to his friends. The thought crossed her mind to shoot him again; however, the look in his two friend's eyes prevented her from doing so. She had no doubt Jess and Iker would, in fact, shoot her between the eyes.

"I can see why she would shoot you," Jess retorted without smiling.

With only a knowing glance to his friends, Orion suggested, "Why don't the two of you put your guns down? Would that be all right with you, Alessandra?" Although the woman remained silent, Orion recognized a sign of relief in her face.

"I'm not going to put my gun down until she puts hers down," Iker stubbornly retorted.

"Oh, come on, boys. I'm the one with a gun pointed at my head, so give me a little leeway here. I'd really like to show a little more hospitality toward my guest…she's the one that's been wounded and unconscious for days," Orion declared, hoping both gentlemen would understand the message he was sending.

Without any further discussion, Jess and Iker removed the magazines from their guns and set them on the table, keeping a close watch on their friend and Alessandra. "Now, Alessandra, if it's all right with you, I'm going to sit down in the chair, like I planned earlier, so we can have a talk." He kept his hands in the air and turning slowly so he wouldn't scare the woman into accidentally shooting him again, Orion took a step sideways to lower himself into the chair. He suspected Alessandra wasn't feeling well; the color had gone from her cheeks.

He relaxed his arms slowly, dropping them onto the arms of the chair, keeping his eye on Alessandra as he spoke, "Gentlemen, if you would excuse the lady and me, we'd like to have our talk."

"I'm not leaving here when your arm's bleeding, and there's a gun pointed at your head," Iker indignantly stated.

"If the only way I can get rid of you is to let you play nursemaid, I have antiseptic and bandages in the bathroom closet. Alessandra, is it all right if Jess grabs the supplies from my bathroom?" Orion asked, trying to keep the woman feeling as though she was in charge of the situation. A tactic the three men had been trained in and used on many missions.

"Of course," the woman replied, having been in a daze, completely confused by the situation, feeling the weight of the gun she had pointed at Orion. It didn't take long before Jess had gone into the bathroom and returned, handing the supplies to Iker. Iker cleaned and dressed the wound. Looking satisfied, he set the remaining supplies down and glared at Orion.

"Alessandra, my friends would probably feel more comfortable leaving if you didn't have that gun pointed so close to my face." Keeping her eyes on the two men, she took a couple of steps away from Orion toward the couch.

Sensing that Alessandra was beginning to trust Orion, exactly what the men had hoped for, Jess turned to Iker and said, "I think Orion has everything under control. How about the two of us head downstairs and get the coffee on." He glanced at Alessandra and Orion for approval. Immediately seeing the relief on the woman's face, he added, "Ms. Petrovich, you had the whole town worried. We're glad you came to visit us in Hideaway Canyon and hope the remainder of your stay is better than your first few days have been. We'll be downstairs if you need anything."

"Orion, why don't you bring the lady to The Rip for dinner tonight. That way she can meet everyone." He winked at Alessandra, who stood with an incredulous look upon her face. Jess and Iker picked up their guns and walked out the door.

Orion studied Alessandra from the chair he was sitting in, as his friends walked out the door. The color was gone from her face, and her hand trembled, trying to hold the gun, no longer pointed at Orion, falling toward the ground as her arm dropped to her side. Orion bolted from his seat in time to catch Alessandra as she collapsed into his arms. A rush of desire erupted from his core, more intense than he had ever felt before with any woman. With a slight curl at the corners of his lips, Orion thought, *Our standoff must be over.*

Orion carried Alessandra back to his bed, gently placing her upon it. He tucked the blankets around her and tenderly wiped her face with a warm cloth. He had never felt such an attraction to a woman. Yes, he had relationships before, even one that was long-standing, but most were to fulfill a momentary visceral need for both parties involved. He knew he was not destined for a more meaningful relationship. He would never have a permanent one that allowed him a wife and family to love, the kind you made a home with. A relationship like the one Lyra and Jess had. Worried about Alessandra, Orion picked up his phone and called Doc Sterling. He wanted Doc to check on her. After the quick phone call, Doc assuring Orion he would be there soon, Orion sat in the chair next to Alessandra. Who was this woman? He was fascinated by her. Not only did he find her beautiful, but the strength she had just displayed as she stood against Orion and his friends perplexed him. He had witnessed only a weak and delicate side of Alessandra for the past three days, yet he remained in awe of the strength and agility she had shown, as well as her surprising use of the gun in his apartment a few moments ago. He felt so uncertain about this woman yet so much desire.

By six in the morning, Doc Sterling had already arrived to check on his patient. Orion explained to the doctor the scene that had occurred in his apartment early that morning. Doc roared with laughter as he started to examine Alessandra. Glancing at Orion's arm, he saw that it was bandaged. He recognized the work to be Iker's, knowing the man had skills as good as any doctor. Orion had been taken care of. He wished he had been in Orion's apartment to witness the scene that occurred in the early morning. He couldn't wipe the grin off his face as he cared for the brave woman.

Orion took the opportunity to gather the guns that he had laid on the dresser and locked them in the hidden safe he had installed in his apartment. Like his friends, he was always prepared, this time recognizing his own stupidity by being caught off guard. He was the one who set the guns he had found in Alessandra's suitcase and car on his dresser. Wanting to make sure there wasn't a repeat of the morning's scene, he secured them.

There was a soft knock on Orion's apartment door, Lyra appearing at her husband's request. "How is she?" Lyra asked concerned.

"Doc's checking on her right now. She fainted right after Jess and Iker left." Knowing her husband would have filled her in on what happened, he said, "Maybe it would be good if you were here when she wakes up."

"Our thoughts were the same. Jess and Iker already filled me in. It was their idea to send me up here. Waking up to a woman might help her feel a little more comfortable." Orion nodded in agreement. "I remember my first run-in with Jess. There was nothing comfortable about that," Lyra recalled with a smile toward her brother. "I can't imagine how frightened she would be to see you in the dark. Add Jess and Iker to the mix. She must have been terrified."

Doc walked out of the bedroom. "Good morning, Lyra."

"Morning, Doc. How's our patient?" Lyra inquired.

"She's fine. The eventful morning your brother described would have made anyone faint." Lyra and Orion had hopeful looks. "I just spoke with her. With a whiff of smelling salts, she's come around. The girl just had a little fainting spell. Go easy on her...she's confused and weak. She just lost the last four days of her life."

Knowing patients were often comforted by the presence of their doctors, Doc suggested, "Why don't the two of you come into the room with me so I can introduce you properly?" The siblings glanced at each other in agreement and followed Doc back into the bedroom.

Alessandra sat, silently propped up by pillows the doctor must have helped her with, her eyes focused on her hands in her lap. "Miss Alessandra, I have a couple of people I'd like you to meet," Doc started as he walked into the room. "This is Lyra, she's been assisting me as your nursemaid." The woman raised her eyes to meet Lyra's and offered a shy smile as Lyra walked through the door.

Lyra approached Alessandra's bedside, smiling. "We're so glad you are feeling better. You had us all worried. You must be so frightened. I cannot imagine how you must feel. But please know we have all been here to help you, and you are safe with us."

"Thank you, Lyra." Alessandra returned a smile, embarrassed. "I am grateful for everything you and the doctor have done for me."

Afraid to go into the room any further, Orion stood in the doorway. Doc Sterling drew Alessandra's attention from Lyra to Orion, "And this gentleman is Orion, Lyra's brother and the owner of the apartment you've been staying in. Hideaway Canyon was in the middle of a snowstorm when he found you unconscious along the mountain road. He brought you here, so we could take care of you."

Alessandra cautiously watched the man from the bed. Her eyes roamed the man's face, scanning the length of his neck to his upper left arm. When she saw the bandage on his arm, her eyes immediately returned to his. It was impossible for her to look away. Alessandra was the first to break the silence. "I shot you?" Orion gave a single, slow nod without taking his eyes off her. "I am so sorry to have hurt you. I've never shot anyone before, and I am ashamed of myself. I was afraid. Please forgive me," she asked.

Not fully believing the woman but acknowledging her apology for the sake of Lyra and Doc, Orion said, "Apology accepted. I hope you know none of us mean any harm to you. We were only trying to help. When you feel better, and with Doc's approval, we'll sit down and explain everything we know."

Doc interjected, "But for right now, young lady, I think you need some more rest. You've got more healing to do, and a good nap will go a long way to getting you healthy." Doc asked his patient, "Will you be all right if I go on my rounds and leave you in Lyra's hands?"

"Yes, thank you, Doctor Sterling."

"After you wake from your nap, I'll make some soup for you for lunch. And if you're up to it, I'll help you shower and wash your hair. I know how good that might feel," Lyra added, seeing Alessandra's smile of appreciation.

"I'm around too, if I can be of any help to you," Orion's voice sounded from the doorway, knowing he was not someone she wanted help from, but he thought it was polite to offer.

Alessandra watched as Doc Sterling encouraged the brother and sister to leave the bedroom, closing the door behind him. Feeling somewhat relieved and finding Lyra and Doc Sterling nice, she glanced at the top of the dresser. Her guns were gone. Panic ran through her body from head to toe. The man took them; she knew it. Where were they? Could she trust these people? Could she trust the man they called Orion? Alessandra knew there was nothing she could do now. Her head still pounded, the doctor telling her it was to be expected because of her injury. She felt weak. Her wrist and ribs ached from her earlier activity. She slowly adjusted the blankets around her. Accepting her circumstances, she let the medicine Doc Sterling had given her take effect, and she fell asleep.

The three convened in Orion's kitchen after leaving Alessandra in the bedroom to get some sleep. "I'd like to order an MRI and a couple of x-rays for Ms. Petrovich. I'm not worried about anything in particular, she seems to be healing. It's more precautionary. The mountain roads are open now, and we can get her down the mountain to the hospital. Orion, I was hoping you could help me out, using your truck?" Doc asked.

"Of course, anything you need," he responded.

"I'll call the hospital and see if I can set something up for tomorrow and let you know later today. I'd like to check in on her before this evening, I think it might be wise for me to be the one to tell her about the MRI and x-rays." With a nod of agreement from all three, Doc left the apartment.

"Orion, I need to pick up Skye before she gets into too much trouble at The Rip. Jess and Iker are watching her. If it works for you,

I'll come back, and Skye and I can keep an eye on Alessandra. Having a woman around might be more comfortable for her for a while, or at least until she gets used to all of us. And, Skye, if nothing else, could amuse her. Plus, I'd hate for you to get shot again." Her brother's face reminded her of a wounded animal, yet he agreed with his sister's logic. It had already been planned that he would meet with Jess and Iker today, so Lyra's suggestion was helpful and would allow for the men's meeting to still take place.

Now that Alessandra was conscious, Orion felt an urgency to know who she was. He wanted more information about the woman, Alessandra Petrovich. Approaching the topic again, as delicately as she could, "You might want to think about moving her to our home. It's not far away, and she might be more comfortable with another woman around," Lyra suggested.

Orion surprised his sister by responding without seeming to give her suggestion a thought. "No, she's staying right here!" Orion wasn't quite sure why he used that tone with his sister.

Knowing her brother well enough by the sound of his voice, Lyra didn't argue but gave Orion a quick hug and said she wouldn't be away long. As she closed the door and descended the stairway, she grinned from ear to ear. She knew her brother well. She had a sense the stars were aligning. Orion liked Alessandra Petrovich.

After his sister left, Orion thought about opening the bedroom door and checking on Alessandra. However, after a second thought, he felt it was better for him not to appear to intrude on her privacy. Remembering the scene from early this morning and his sister's words, he thought it best if he let her sleep. *If she is awake, won't she come out, anyway?* he thought. After a moment, he realized, *No, she's probably looking for her guns.*

Orion realized he needed to remove any weapons he could find in his apartment or anything that could be used as a weapon. He had been shocked by Alessandra's agility and speed with a gun in her hand. He suspected he was lucky the room was dark, suddenly feeling lucky he wasn't dead. *I wonder what other talents the woman possesses*, was running through his thoughts. He knew all the guns were locked safely in his hidden gun safe; however, he also had some knives in various strategic places around his apartment. Gathering his Leatherman, a Deejo, and Swiss Army knife in various places, he went into the kitchen to continue his search. Pulling open the silverware drawer, he removed all the knives he could find. Glancing at the forks, he recalled a time when he used a fork to kill a man. It was one of those kill or be killed situations. It saved his life. Without further thought, he grabbed all the salad and table forks and added them to his pile. He took his stockpile of weapons to his gun safe, closing the door and double-checking to make sure it was secure. He didn't come to Hideaway Canyon to be shot or stabbed. Feeling immune from harm, he went to the kitchen to make a pot of coffee and have a sandwich.

About the time Orion finished cleaning up from his lunch, Lyra returned with Skye. There was no one better suited to distract him than little Skye. He grabbed the little girl as she entered his apartment, carrying her into the living room and tossing her gently on the bean bag chair in the corner of the room. He dropped himself into its softness, tickling his niece as she tried to wrestle herself from his grip. Their usual game. When she finally got away and familiar with her uncle's apartment, she ran to the toy box, sitting next to the door to the deck. Opening the lid to her treasures, she pulled out her stuffed koala bear and her favorite book. Skye took it to her uncle and dropped in his lap. Lyra smiled, already knowing the loving relationship her daughter had with Orion and walked into the kitchen. While Orion kept Skye busy, she would prepare lunch for Alessandra. She would be awake soon.

Lyra prepared a small lunch with soup and cheese and crackers. She set the table, hoping Alessandra would feel like joining her and Skye. From the kitchen, Lyra could hear Orion reading to Skye about African animals. Her brother roared like a lion and chirped like a bird when the book required it. Realizing she had everything set for lunch, Lyra headed for the living room. She stopped suddenly. She could see Alessandra leaning against the doorway of Orion's bedroom, quietly watching and listening as Orion read to Skye. Lyra could see tears rolling down Alessandra's cheeks. Moving to the doorway unnoticed, Lyra slipped her arm around Alessandra's waist, giving her a compassionate hug of understanding. The women stood silently and watched together. As Orion closed the book, he discovered Skye had fallen asleep on the bean bag chair. Picking up a small blanket laying on the floor next to the chair, he carefully covered his niece and kissed her little forehead.

As he stood, he heard Lyra's voice. "That's a scene I never tire of." Locating the direction her voice came from, Orion saw the two women standing in the doorway to his bedroom with watery eyes. As he did not immediately understand their despair and wanted to fix it, his long heavy strides advanced him quickly toward the women, stopping short in front of them. Alessandra stiffened. Knowing her brother would be worried about the woman's comfort and recognizing the look of concern on Orion's face as he easily crossed the room, Lyra stepped forward and wrapped her arms around Orion. "They are happy tears, Orion, no need to worry." He held his sister in his arms, seeming to understand her need for the comfort and warmth of his arms. As he did so, he peered over Lyra's head meeting Alessandra's eyes. Seeing the tear stains on her cheeks, he wanted to offer her the same. It didn't take long before Orion recovered from the moment, knowing the offer would only frighten her, he politely asked Alessandra if she had been able to sleep.

"Yes, thank you. I feel much better," she replied. "And your arm?" she continued, ashamed. "I really am sorry."

With sincerity he replied, "Nothing to worry about."

Releasing Lyra, "I'm going to let you ladies enjoy your lunch before our little tornado wakes up. I'll be downstairs with Jess and Iker, if you need me. I'll be back before Doc Sterling returns to check on you," he said, hoping Alessandra accepted his concern. Feeling the need to escape from any uncomfortableness, he left without grabbing a jacket, "see you two after bit," he opened the door and was gone.

Lyra looked forward to Orion's departure, wanting the opportunity to talk to Alessandra alone. She was hoping to learn more about the woman and put her own mind to ease. She knew Jess and Iker had some concerns, concerns the men worried, their friend Orion

90

didn't recognize. According to Jess, Orion had taken some risks with Alessandra earlier this morning that made them uncomfortable. However, trusting the man, they had followed his lead, leaving the apartment while Orion had a gun pointed at him. Jess and Iker's exhibition of trust in their friend didn't curtail their concern. The two men were worried Alessandra posed a danger to Orion and to Hideaway Canyon. Lyra loved her husband, and she loved Orion and Iker. She was, however, very aware that the line of work the three men pursued took them into the darkest arenas of the world, and all three looked at life through dark glasses filled with evil and despair.

Lightly taking hold of Alessandra's hand and squeezing it, Lyra asked if she felt like sitting at the table and having some lunch with her. Without any hesitation, Alessandra responded, "I would love to. I'm feeling much better, and it's nice not being in bed."

"Let me check on Skye," Lyra said, releasing the woman's hand and crossing the room where Skye slept. Alessandra watched as the mother checked on Skye, smiling at her sleeping daughter. As she witnessed the gesture of love, Alessandra's heart lurched with an emotion she concealed.

The ladies went into the kitchen. "Why don't you have a seat at the table so we can talk while I serve? I just made some soup, and here's a plate of cheese, crackers, and fruit we can nosh on."

"Thank you, this looks wonderful, and for some reason I am starving." Alessandra began to nibble on some crackers and cheese as Lyra filled their bowls with soup. Alessandra noticed the fresh polish on her nails.

"Skye and I kept you company yesterday, and we thought you might like it if we did your nails. They match Skye's," Lyra said when she noticed Alessandra seeing her nails.

Alessandra smiled. "Thank you. I do like it. Seems cheery!"

"I was going to cut up some apples, but for some reason, I couldn't find Orion's knives. My brother's never been known to be the handiest around the kitchen. But he manages well enough to prevent starvation," she laughed. Lyra continued, "I don't doubt you are hungry. I'm not sure what you ate the day of your accident, but since your arrival, the most nourishment you have received has been saline and dextrose through an IV." Both women chuckled. With a sympathetic look, Lyra said, "Doc Sterling warned us last night that he would have to start you on a feeding tube, if you didn't wake up soon."

Alessandra continued nibbling, this time selecting fruit. Everything tasted so delicious to her. "Umm, Lyra, this taste so amazing. I can't thank you enough." Lyra could see the hesitation in Alessandra's eyes.

"What is it?" Lyra asked.

"I don't…I don't want to sound ungrateful…but I…I don't know why you are being so nice to me," she said.

"We have no reason other than to want to help you. You were hurt. You had a terrible accident," Lyra responded.

Lyra handed her a bowl of soup, thinking maybe she should have made something more substantial. The woman was hungry. Of course, that made sense because she hadn't eaten in three full days. "I kept lunch simple because I wasn't sure how much your stomach could take," she said in apology.

"It's perfect," Alessandra answered. Realizing the appreciation Alessandra had for the food, Lyra kept silent for a few minutes and let the woman enjoy the meal.

Catching Alessandra glancing around the room, Lyra began to talk. "This is an apartment above my husband's, Jess's, bar. The bar's called The Rip. Orion brought you here after finding you along the side of the road. We were in the middle of a two-day snowstorm, and Orion had gone down the mountain for supplies. Driving back, he found your car off the side of the road. You were unconscious. The roads were closed, and we couldn't get you to the hospital. He brought you here and called Doc Sterling." She paused, giving Alessandra time to process the information.

"I don't remember any of that." Tears trickled down Alessandra's cheek. Lyra handed her a napkin and waited for the woman to wipe away her tears. "I'm sorry…I don't mean to be so silly."

Touching Alessandra's shoulder, Lyra said, "It's all right. We're all here to help. I can't imagine what you must be feeling. But please know we will fill in whatever pieces we can in order to help you.

When you feel up to it, we can take you to Rob Taylor's. He's the local mechanic. Nice guy. Jess and Orion towed your car to his shop after the snow stopped, and it was safe to have it removed."

The women finished their soup, enjoying some small talk. Lyra chatted about the weather and the community of Hideaway Canyon, suspecting a change of subject would be good for a while. Alessandra could feel the love Lyra had for her family as she spoke, revealing funny little stories about each of them.

She appreciated the woman's attempt at distracting her. "Thank you so much, Lyra. I guess I should be happy I remember one thing."

"And that is?" Lyra asked questioningly.

"Early this morning, after I shot your brother." She recalled the moment. "Orion told me my name was Alessandra Petrovich. I knew he was right. Something inside me told me so." With a smile, she stood up and started to help pick up the dishes. "It felt good knowing my name. Now, if I could only remember more, I don't remember my car or the accident. Do I live around here?" she said with a sigh. Lyra shrugged, not able to answer her question. Before long, the dishes were washed and put away, and the counters and the table were cleaned.

Not long after the final dish was put away, giggles came from the living room. Lyra knew her daughter was awake. "That would be my daughter, Skye." Believing Alessandra might need a few moments to herself, Lyra allowed her intuition to give way to a suggestion, "Orion will be downstairs with Jess and Iker for hours. So why don't you take a shower. Jess and Orion stacked the luggage and boxes they found in your jeep in the corner of the bedroom. I'm here if you need any help finding your things, let me know. And when you are done, I will introduce you to Skye."

"I like that idea," Alessandra responded with a smile. She had enjoyed her lunch. She felt relaxed and happy. Something told her she hadn't felt that way in a while. She looked at Lyra's hand, wanting to reach out and touch it, a gesture of thanks and appreciation. She liked the woman. Feeling too shy to carry through with her thought, she did nothing.

As if reading Alessandra's mind, Lyra reached out to her. "You are safe here." Releasing Alessandra's hand, she turned toward her daughter, still giggling in the corner.

Looking forward to washing her hair in a nice warm shower and putting on some clean clothes, Alessandra walked into the bedroom and closed the door. She knew she had met a nice woman and silently wished they could be friends. After closing the bedroom door, Alessandra looked around an unfamiliar room. She knew she had been in the room for four days yet couldn't seem too remember much else. Lunch had been perfect. She enjoyed Lyra's company, and the woman put her at ease. She knew she would ask more questions after she showered.

The Rip, April 23, 2013

Orion found Jess and Iker in the kitchen. "So you're still alive?" Iker commented facetiously. "That wasn't the smartest decision I've seen you make, asking us to leave with a gun pointed at you."

"I had the situation handled until you two goons burst in the room," Orion said, defending himself.

"The woman had already shot you. Doesn't sound like it was handled all that well!" Iker argued.

"All right, boys, let's stop bickering," Jess interjected. "Let's go into the office, this isn't the place to be talking." He called out into the bar for Josie.

"Yes, boss." Josie walked into the kitchen, sparkling as she came into the room with bright pink hair.

"The three of us are heading into the office. Can you cover things?" Jess asked.

"Sure," the woman replied.

"Just give a shout if you need us." The three men left the kitchen and headed into the office.

Orion led the conversation. "Here's what happened." Jess and Iker listened in silence. "Alessandra must have gained consciousness in the middle of the night. I woke up at about 4:30 a.m., hearing some noises I couldn't identify, so I started searching. The sounds led me to the bedroom." The two men looked at each other hesitant about Orion's next words. "I must have startled Alessandra because before I knew it, I was shot. It was dark, and I'm sure she was terrified." The men's faces were stunned by how little Orion knew about women. "I'm not trying to make excuses for her, put yourself in her place. We all knew how frightened the woman might be when gaining consciousness."

"Okay, so you want to believe it was an accident. I get it. But you forget, the gun was still pointed at your head, and you were asking us to leave!" Iker argued.

"She doesn't know any of us. The last thing she knew she was driving up a mountain road. I can handle myself anyway," Orion continued, "and like I said, before the two of you charged in, I had her almost convinced to put the gun down so we could talk." It made sense. "You startled her, and her defenses were back up."

"Okay, okay, okay, you two," Jess calmed his friends. "You can assure me that my wife is safe upstairs with Alessandra?" Jess asked his brother-in-law.

"Absolutely. You do remember she's my sister." Orion mouthed back insulted Jess would even suggest he wouldn't make sure his own sister was safe. "The minute the two of you left my apartment, Alessandra fainted." He continued filling them in. "I carried her back to bed. While she was out, I hid all the guns in my gun safe. And knives too. Double-checked the lock." Not wanting to be tormented by his friends, Orion didn't admit he hid the kitchen knives and forks too. "Doc came over and checked on her again. When I left a few minutes ago, Alessandra was awake, and Lyra was going to make lunch for them. Lyra thought her talking to a woman would be more calming and comforting to her."

"She's probably right," Jess agreed.

Orion confirmed the safety of the two women, "No guns are accessible to either woman in the apartment. I think we are safe to assume, there's no chance anyone will be shot today."

"So let's move on to what we do know about Alessandra Petrovich," Jess started, reading from a report he received. "She checks out in Chicago. The address on her driver's license is legit.

My man talked with the building supervisor, Bob Thomas. He verified Alessandra had lived in his building for about five years or so. She always paid rent on time, always with cash. Nice girl. She was quiet and kept to herself. She drove a jeep. Tags match the tenant application to the jeep she was driving when Orion found her and is now sitting in Rob's shop. The sup says he never saw anyone coming or going. No boyfriends that he knew of. The day before she moved out, a man did stop and ask questions about her. The man was professionally dressed. The note says his comment was 'didn't think it was a boyfriend...too old for her.' According to Mr. Thomas, the man that was asking about her had money. Mentioned the guy was wearing a fancy suit but also drove up in a black Mercedes SUV. Didn't recall anything about the license plate. Only saw the man once. Would probably recognize him in a lineup. Thomas indicated he saw Alessandra leave for work every Friday morning and did not return until Monday evening. Same pattern for the past five years. Alessandra mentioned to him once that she visited her mother on weekends, so he didn't give it much thought. She never gave any other details. He never met or saw a woman who looked to be her mother. She kept her apartment neat and orderly. Not one tenant complaint about her. When she left, she didn't leave a forwarding address and told him to keep the deposit for him and his wife. It was her gift to them for their kindness. Her tenant application showed she was employed by a company named Global Research and Analysis. She listed Alina Ulanova Petrovich, her mother, as her point of contact, phone number listed is not active."

"I can fill in some blanks," Iker interjected. "Our contacts at The Firm indicate Alessandra Petrovich started working at Global Research and Analysis at the time you said she lived in the apartment, five years. Her boss, Dimitri Osmond, said she walked in off the street. Apparently, she showed up every day for a week. He felt sorry for the girl, so he hired her in their housekeeping department, paying cash. She insisted on cash. Within six months, he realized she was worth much more, becoming one of the research assistants, and then, for the past three years, he promoted her to Global Research Analyst. He helped her apply for a social security card, and gave her a regular paycheck, taxes deducted like everyone else. He did say that every payday, he would take her to lunch and his bank, where he would assist her in cashing her check. He encouraged her to open a checking account, but she refused to do so. He didn't ask any more questions. She was a good employee and he didn't want to lose her." Pausing for a moment, Iker looked at his friends, giving them an opportunity to ask questions.

"Did she have any friends at work? Did any other employee know anything about her?" Orion asked.

"No, she seemed to be respected for her work ethic and the job by everyone in her department. No one knew very much about her. She always brought lunch from home and ate at her desk. The only socialization she did at work was the trip to lunch and the bank with her boss every payday," Iker said, answering his friend's question. "A couple of employees thought she and the boss were having an affair."

"Just a couple more follow up points. I did run the serial numbers on a few of the bills in her suitcase. Nothing illegal there. As for the phone, we were only able to find one number, and that number went to a phone in Seatonville, Illinois, a small town on the western border of Illinois, close to Iowa. In the past week, there's been a consistent call, one each day, for less than a minute. There were also a couple of texts to the same number. All short. Difficult to trace. The calls stopped four days ago…when Alessandra arrived here." Iker told the men his guess was the number belonged to Alessandra's mother, Alina Ulanova Petrovich, although he hadn't sent one of the Firm's agents out to check on his suspicion. "I'm having one of the men follow up in Seatonville, Illinois. A Kosovo birth certificate verifies that an Alina Ulanova Petrovich gave birth to a daughter, Alessandra, on October 4, 1982. Father of the child was listed as Anton Petrovich."

There was a knock at the office door. "Come in," Jess said.

Josie opened the door holding a coffee pot, "Hey, thought maybe you might need a refill." She entered the room as all three men pushed their cups forward on the table.

"You need any help out there," her boss asked.

"No, not yet. It's picking up a little. Mostly pouring drafts, a little too early for dinner orders. I've got it handled for now," she said as she filled their cups and walked out the door.

"Well, I guess I have the last piece, that fits everything together," Orion shared his research. "I've been checking all the files we had at The Firm on Anton Petrovich. A file marked 'confidential' provided some alarming information. The man's a real piece of work. His nickname, the Butcher of the Balkans, fits him well. He and his men are willing to use any tactics necessary in the name of Kosovo's president, Mikozavich. Both men, described as monsters. Many people fled their homes, hundreds of thousands becoming refugees. He was one of Mikozavich's commanding officers in charge of ethnic cleansing. If people didn't leave their homes, he forced them out by burning their homes and raping their women and sometimes children. He massacred entire villages in the name of ethnic cleansing. Confidentially, the International Criminal Court is taking action to charge him with war crimes and other charges, although right now they don't have enough evidence to convict. He's a powerful man with the backing of his government."

Orion continued, "No one seems to know where Petrovich's wife and daughter went. The family was living in a small village in Kosovo called Gjakova. Some believe Petrovich had them murdered along with the hundreds of thousands of others. Burned in mass graves in Kosovo's countryside. Other's believed they went into hiding. Some stories say the man loves his family; others say he wants them dead. Seems to be many stories, not enough proof. Yet. The International Criminal Court is looking for Alina Ulanova Petrovich and Alessandra Petrovich, hoping the two women are alive and might have information they could share." His eyes darkened as he finished, "If they aren't dead, and Commander Petrovich would know one way or another, it would be in his best interest to locate them first."

"I think we have a good idea who's staying in Orion's apartment. Now, what do you boys want to do about it?" Jess asked.

"We don't need trouble with the Kosovo government or the International Criminal Court. I say we get her jeep fixed and send her on her way. Tensions have escalated in that part of the world, and we don't need to be a part of it," Iker gave his opinion.

"We can't send her on her way. She's not fit to defend herself if her father's coming after her. She hasn't even recovered from her accident, if it was an accident," Orion argued.

"We don't need to bring the Kosovo War to Hideaway Canyon. It's up to us to figure out if we need to protect her, or if we need protection from her. She's pretty skilled with that gun." Jess deliberately paused. "The gun problem is resolved. Orion has taken care of that. Unless she's deceiving us, I don't believe we can send her on her way. She still hasn't healed from her accident. Let's give her a few more days and see if her memory comes back."

"If she's even lost her memory," Iker stated with grim necessity.

"We can all keep a close watch on her. Orion, I trust you can take lead and see what you can find out from Alessandra," Jess instructed. "Let's see how forthcoming she is with us as her memory returns." With some hesitation from Iker, the men decided to continue gathering as much information as they could. The meeting ended, and Jess and Iker returned to their duties in the bar. The dinner hour was approaching, and like always, The Rip would get hectic.

Orion could hear laughter coming through the door of his apartment as he walked up the stairs. He hesitated for a moment before opening the door, not wanting to interrupt the fun. He found his furniture had been pushed to the side of the living room, and the girls were playing the game Twister. Alessandra's beauty stunned Orion speechless. It had been difficult for him to ignore the attraction he felt for her as she lay in his bed, but the sight of her now, laughing, smiling, playing. He couldn't force himself to look away. Skye was the first to break the spell, "Unca O, come play." Smiling, he approached the three, unable to take his eyes off Alessandra.

"Yes, please, Orion. I think I need a break," Alessandra pleaded. Knowing the energy spewing from his niece was hard to keep up with, he grabbed the little girl and hauled her up to his shoulders.

"I can't believe these two conned you into a game of Twister," Orion worried. "Isn't this a little rough on you?"

Rather than letting Alessandra answer her brother, Lyra responded, "She had never heard of the game! We thought it was time she was introduced to some fun. And we went easy on her."

There was a knock at the door, "Come in, door's open."

"I came to check on my patient," Doc responded as he entered the apartment. Seeing the game on the floor, he smiled. "Guess I missed all the fun!" He laughed. "My wife's always telling me I have bad timing."

"We've taken good care of her today, haven't we, Skye?" The little girl nodded, curls bouncing.

Alessandra shared her day with the doctor, "Lyra made me a wonderful lunch. I couldn't believe how hungry I was. Being able to take a shower and wash my hair felt so good." She turned away from Doc Sterling, captivating Orion with her golden-brown eyes. "And I thank you for your kindness in hauling the contents of my jeep to your apartment. I appreciated opening my suitcase to find some of my own clothes." Unable to take his eyes off her or to find words, he nodded. His thoughts deviated from the beautiful woman to the money in her luggage. Would she be forthcoming about the cash stowed in them?

"Well, Ms. Petrovich, how about you let me give you a once-over. It will put this old doctor's mind at rest tonight, knowing you are well on your way to recovery." Doc Sterling joined Alessandra on the couch, going about his business as the town's doctor. "So how are the headaches?"

"They're better. After my nap, they were gone, but now I have a slight headache. I might have enjoyed myself a little too much," she admitted. "I can't seem to remember anything. I recognized my name when Orion said it and when I searched through my suitcases for clothes, I recognized that the items were mine. I don't remember the accident or anything before."

"It's our fault, Doc," Lyra said, taking responsibility for her and Skye's involvement in convincing Alessandra to play Twister.

"I think the game did all of you a world of good," Doc exclaimed. Looking back to Alessandra, he said, "I'm pleased with your progress. As for the lapse in memory, give yourself time. You are already showing small signs of remembering. With the head trauma you suffered, I've seen patients take months to regain their full memory. Sometimes, parts never come back. I would like you to go to the hospital and have them do an MRI of your head injury and take a couple of x-rays, one of your wrists and the other of your ribs. The storm wouldn't permit a trip to the hospital when you arrived." Seeing a frown of concern cross the woman's face, Doc continued. "It's only precautionary. Even though I've had years of practice without modern technology, and I'm pretty good at my diagnosis, I'd rather not take the chance I missed a splinter size break. Even an old doctor like me can appreciate a new trick," he said with a wink. "An MRI will show even the smallest of brain bleeds, that could turn into something worse down the road. It's better to know now," he said with a wink.

Lyra noticed the wrinkle of concern that appeared on Orion's brow. She knew her brother had witnessed, firsthand, results of undiagnosed head trauma. He knew soldiers that suffered from consequences of combat, some surviving, some not. "We'll take good care of her," she announced.

"Orion, I made an appointment for ten o'clock at the Imaging Center for Ms. Petrovich. Can I trust you to get her up and down the mountain and to her appointment safely? That truck of yours seems to power its way through almost anything."

"Absolutely, it would be my pleasure. I'll see that Alessandra arrives where you need her to be," Orion acknowledged.

Doc Sterling said his goodbyes, saying he would check in late afternoon tomorrow with test results. Lyra encouraged Skye to pick up her toys so they could join her daddy at The Rip. "Alessandra, you are welcome to join Jess, Skye, and me at The Rip for dinner," Lyra asked. Looking at her brother, "And as you know, you are always welcome."

"Thank you for the offer. You have been so kind, and I've had a wonderful day. I'm rather tired, though, and think I'd like to get a good night's rest before our trip to the hospital tomorrow," Alessandra's eyes shifted shyly to look at Orion, feeling self-conscious she had referred to the two of them.

"We completely understand. Maybe a raincheck then?" Lyra said silently aware of the reference and realizing her brother hadn't.

"Yes, another time sounds fun," she responded with a smile.

Already knowing what her brother's response would be as to the invitation she had given him to share dinner with her family, Lyra peered at Orion while she picked up toys with her daughter. She knew her brother was interested in Alessandra. What she wasn't sure of, was how much that interest was professionally motivated and how much was personal attraction. Lyra knew tonight would give him time alone with her.

"I'll join Lyra and Jess another time," he said, searching Alessandra's face, "assuming you are comfortable with my being alone in the same apartment with you tonight?" She gave him a slight nod, not knowing how comfortable she would really be. She knew it was his home, and it would be impolite to say anything else. As she stood looking at the man, Alessandra felt a twinge of excitement; she was attracted to him. Her heartbeat quickened at the opportunity she was given to be alone with him, yet a fear rested in the pit of her stomach. She sensed there was more to Orion and his friends. There was so much she didn't know, and she suspected they could be dangerous.

"I'll make some dinner for the two of us tonight. We can relax and turn in early. If all goes well at the hospital and Alessandra is up to it, maybe we can convince our guest to join us at The Rip tomorrow evening. It would give her an opportunity to meet the town," he said, smiling at the two women. "Tonight, we can have a quiet evening," Orion said, wanting time alone with the woman.

At their last meeting, Jess and Iker made it clear they wanted him to find out more about Alessandra; they were sure she was Anton Petrovich's daughter. What they didn't know was why she was in Hideaway Canyon, and where was the woman's mother? Had Alessandra Petrovich brought danger to their peaceful little community? Was Alessandra as dangerous as her father, or was she marked to be one of his victims. The only person that could put the pieces of the puzzle together for them was Alessandra if she was willing to do so and if she could remember.

It wasn't long before the commotion created by goodbyes to Lyra and Skye left a deafening silence in Orion's apartment. Knowing this beautiful woman would be sleeping in his bed, Orion struggled to control his urges. He focused on getting his mind back to making dinner. He wiped his brow as he turned to Alessandra, "I'm not an expert in the kitchen, but I do know how to make a decent salad and pot of spaghetti, if that will work for you?"

"That sounds perfect. What can I do to help?" Alessandra responded, smiling.

"You can be my sous chef," he chuckled. "I'm not even sure what that is, but it sounded official." Both chuckled as Orion motioned for Alessandra to join him in the kitchen. The two strangers made small talk as they prepared a meal together. The kitchen was small, and it didn't take either long to feel the temperature rise in their limited space. Orion began the spaghetti. As he stooped to collect a pot from a bottom cabinet, Orion's eyes focused on the pair of long legs covered in denim leaning against the cabinet. His eyes slowly perused the legs he knew belonged to Alessandra, caressing each inch with his eyes. When he finally arrived at her face, he was met by a pair of golden-brown eyes. Not being able to hide the desire in his eyes, he stood abruptly, almost knocking Alessandra over. He grabbed her around the waist to prevent her from falling, feeling the heat rise from his core. *Did she feel it too?* he wondered. Slowly, ever so slowly, he dropped his arm to his side. He turned to the refrigerator and opened the door, appreciating the coolness that passed over him. He gathered a few items, then pointed to the vegetable bin. "How do you feel about making a salad?" he asked Alessandra. Needing a distraction from the sensation she felt from having Orion's arms around her, she eagerly agreed and set to work on a salad. Orion pointed from a cupboard to a drawer as Alessandra asked where she could find a bowl and a knife.

As he stirred the sauce on the stove, Alessandra said, "I don't know if I'm in the right spot, all I see are spoons." His face turning red, he looked at Alessandra not knowing what to say. Perplexed by Orion's behavior, she began explaining why she needed the utensil, "I need a knife to cut the vegetables."

"The…the knives…well, I…," he said, his chin dropping to his chest, as if receiving a scolding as a little boy, "after you shot me, I gathered the guns and all the knives and forks in the house and locked them in my gun safe."

"Forks?" Alessandra said in disbelief as she stared at the man.

"Well, I was afraid you could use them as a weapon," he said sheepishly.

With her eyes trained on Orion, her lips slowly moved into a curve. "Would you get them out for us to use for dinner if I promise you, I won't use a fork or knife to harm you? You can even lock them back up after we do the dishes, if you would like." Alessandra was having a nice time and it felt good to tease Orion.

"Sure." He walked out of the kitchen embarrassed, but on a mission to provide the utensils Alessandra needed. By the time he returned with all the forks and knives he had removed from the kitchen, she had found plates and salad bowls in the cupboard and arranged them neatly on the table. Both went back to prepping for their dinner, not mentioning the utensils again. When the salad and spaghetti were plated and placed on the table, Orion held a chair for Alessandra to sit in.

He picked up the bottle of red wine he had placed on the table earlier and began to open it. Holding the bottle up for Alessandra to see, he said, "Would you care for a glass?"

"Yes, thank you," she said. As they ate, Orion quietly watched as Alessandra seemed to savor each bite. With each fork full, she closed her eyes and relished in the flavors she tasted. She had no idea how attracted to her he was. As she chewed, the sensual movements of her lips made him wonder what it would be like to have them against his own skin. He imagined her savoring his flesh with those lips. Would her eyes close for him, too? He grabbed his glass of wine and gulped the contents hoping to put out the flame that had been ignited by his thoughts.

"Dinner is delicious, Orion. I'm very grateful for all you are doing for me. I know you must have a lot of questions; I wish that I had some answers," Alessandra started a conversation.

"Maybe after dinner, I can show you some papers we found in your jeep. Looking at them and your driver's license might help your memory," Orion volunteered.

"I have a jeep?"

"Yes, do you remember it?" Orion asked.

"No, I don't," she said, looking sad. "Lyra told me you and her husband had my car towed to a local mechanic."

"Yes, and maybe tomorrow, before your hospital appointment, I can take you by the shop to see it. It might bring back some memories, but remember what Doc said. Don't push yourself too much," Orion responded. "Would you like me to top off your wine?"

"Yes, thank you. When I was in Paris, we had wine at almost every meal," she revealed as she ate. Seeking Orion's eyes from across the table, she realized she had another memory. "I've had wine in Paris," she giggled, seeming pleased with herself. Orion wondered if the memory or second glass of wine caused the smile. She seemed more relaxed tonight than he'd seen her since she gained consciousness. Both having finished their meal, Alessandra was first to stand and begin clearing the table. Orion joined her. The two worked efficiently, one washing, one drying. As he worked, he plotted a way to get her talking after dinner. Before they knew it, the kitchen was cleaned up.

"What would you like me to do with these?" Alessandra asked. Orion turned to see what the lady was referring to.

Laughing, he picked up the knives and forks on the counter that Alessandra had collected and opened the drawer with spoons, placing them in their designated spots. "I didn't mean to insult you with the forks and knives. I am sorry." He apologized to his guest.

"Lyra's always telling me that work has jaded my perspective on things." Keeping his thoughts to himself, still worried about her ability to handle a gun, grabbing a second bottle of wine and two clean glasses, he said, "Let's relax in the living room." Orion knew this would be a good time to talk to the woman. Alessandra followed him into the living room and, to his surprise, started the conversation.

"Why do I have a gun?" she asked.

"Well, we found two. One in the glove box of your jeep and one with the money in the suitcase. And to answer your question, we don't know." He added to the answer, "Iker did check the serial numbers, and there isn't anything connecting either to a crime. The Glock 22 is standard issue in many police departments around the United States, and SIG 228 is commonly issued by the Drug Enforcement Administration. We couldn't find any record that either gun had been permitted. Unless you have friends in one of those places, we're not sure how you ended up with them," he said, hoping to make her feel better.

"I don't remember buying a gun."

"Do you remember ever shooting one, other than at me last night? Have you been trained to use a gun?"

"No."

"Alessandra, I'm going to be honest with you. Based on the way you moved and the way you shot in the dark the night you wounded me, I believe you've received some type of weapons training." Orion stared at the woman searching her face for answers wondering if she was lying to him.

Stunned by his words, Alessandra defended herself, "Orion, I really have no memory of training with a gun or buying one. I surprised myself shooting you. I know I never explained myself to you that night, but I was sure you meant to harm me. Before I knew it, I had grabbed the gun, knowing I needed to defend myself. I had no idea I knew how to hold a gun, let alone shoot one. Please believe me, I am telling you the truth." She watched Orion, frustrated that he didn't seem to believe her. Waiting for a response, he said nothing. Alessandra couldn't understand why it should be so important to her that the man sitting beside her believed her. But it was. "I'm telling the truth. I wish you would believe me. I don't know any reason why I would even carry a gun, and I have no desire to shoot anyone."

Orion knew, all too well, Alessandra had shot him; however, the evening had gone well. He didn't want Alessandra to be upset. He wanted to see what memories he could provoke. With an attempt to relax the woman, Orion said, "Alessandra, I believe you, and maybe one day soon, your memory will come back, and you will remember why you have the guns."

Orion set the bottle of wine and glasses on the coffee table, leaving the living room to collect the papers and driver's license he had found in her car. He said, "You pour. I'll be right back." Within moments he had returned with the information in his hands. As he looked into her eyes, wondering whether the information would jog her memory, he could see her hesitation. "Everything will be all right. These are what we found in your glove compartment. Maybe this will help," he said to her as she extended her arm to take the papers. His hand brushed hers as she took the papers from him. Her hands felt warm and soft; he didn't want to let go. Orion joined her on the couch, making sure to sit down on the opposite end of the couch. Not too close yet not too far. Alessandra took a sip of her wine and began to peruse the papers he had given her. Orion sat silently, watching the woman's every expression.

"Alessandra Petrovich, 7100 South Shoreline Drive, Apartment 3A, Chicago Illinois 60649." She paused. "I'm from Chicago. I wonder why I said Paris?"

Not wanting to interject his own thoughts and opinions, Orion simply said, "Maybe you visited Paris some time. Remember, Doc said not to worry about your memory coming back in bits and pieces. It's to be expected."

"I'll be thirty-one years old this year. October 4 is my birthday," she smiled, thinking her birthday was a happy time. *Why did she think birthdays were a happy time for her?* she thought without asking out loud. "Light-brown eyes, brown hair, five feet eight inches, and one hundred and thirty-two pounds. I'm an organ donor," she added seemingly pleased. She flipped the license over. "I wear glasses?" she asked, looking for an answer from Orion.

"I don't know. We didn't find any glasses in the jeep, but we didn't look that closely. There was still a lot of snow, and the jeep wasn't very secure, so we gathered as much as we could and as quickly as we could. They could have fallen under the seat," Orion said in an effort to explain.

"Well, I must not need them that much," she said, her eyes wide with laughter. "I can see you!" Leaning back and forth toward Orion, pretending to focus on him at the end of the couch, she said, "Come closer. Let me see if I can see you better." She continued to laugh. Orion couldn't believe his luck. She wanted him to get closer. Then he remembered the wine, knowing it wasn't his nature to take advantage of a woman having had a little too much to drink. He smiled at Alessandra. He did like this woman.

Did she just say come closer, or was I imagining that? He hesitantly moved closer, wanting to take advantage of the invitation, but not quite knowing whether he heard correctly or that she meant it. He inched closer to the beautiful woman. She didn't seem to mind, or had the effects of the wine numbed her senses? Either way, he kept going. Orion had inched himself past the middle of the couch, and he knew he was in her territory. "Now, let me see," her words stopped him abruptly from his mission. Alessandra leaned in closely, a warm smile on her face. Her cheeks were rosy, her lips wet from wine, seeming to offer him an invitation to move closer. "You have the darkest eyes I've ever seen," she told Orion pausing from her movement toward him. "I can see you," she giggled again. He sat mesmerized by the beautiful woman and how playful she became. It was an unexpected surprise.

In one swift movement, his lips softly brushed hers. Not taking his eyes off hers, he pulled away to look at the beautiful woman who sat next to him, not saying a word. Golden eyes stared back at him. "I'm going to kiss you again, Alessandra," Orion whispered as he inched closer and closer to the woman, recognizing the musky smell of his own shower soap on the woman. Alessandra had no idea how alluring his scent smelled to him on her. When his lips reached hers, he closed his eyes, letting all his senses take over. The touch, the smell, the sound, the feeling of her lips began to overwhelm him. Her lips parted slightly, taking him in with a slight breathy moan. She responded, accepting his warm kiss. Wanting to explore further, but knowing he shouldn't, he slowly pulled away, reaching his hand out to touch her hand, knowing he didn't have the will power to break a connection with her completely. He didn't just want to touch her; he needed to.

"Maybe we can look for my glasses in the jeep tomorrow?" Alessandra suggested, surprised by her own response to the man's touch and wanting to focus attention away from their kiss. She had wondered what it would be like to have Orion kiss her; however, she never imagined it to feel that good. She knew she couldn't let it happen again. A feeling deep inside told her she needed to find out where her home was, and Hideaway Canyon wasn't it. Another kiss might prevent her from leaving, and she'd only known Orion and his friends a few days. They had been very kind to her, but she suspected she didn't know everything she should know about them. Alessandra sat back and began looking at the papers. As she read, she hoped something would trigger a memory. Orion silently watched her, unable to take his eyes off her. He wanted the woman to say something about their kiss, but she didn't. After seeing her yawn, and knowing tomorrow would be another long day, he suggested they call it a night. He told Alessandra they would need to leave about an hour before her appointment; he wasn't sure what the roads and traffic would be like.

While Alessandra took the wine bottle and glasses into the kitchen, Orion went out onto the deck to collect wood for the stove. Returning to the living room, gathering a pillow and blankets, beginning to make his bed on the couch, Orion asked Alessandra if there was anything she needed before they went to sleep. "No, but, Orion, thank you again. The evening was wonderful," she said, picking up the papers she had been reading. "Good night." She walked through the bedroom door, suspecting it would be difficult for her to fall asleep.

"Good night." Orion stripped his shirt off and flipped the light switch. *What was I thinking kissing her? I can't let that happen again,* he thought as he laid on the couch, body warm, remembering the kiss he had just shared with Alessandra.

Hospital run, April 24, 2013

Orion was up early in the morning. Like always, he stoked the fire; it was another cold morning in the little mountain town. He wanted to get up before Alessandra to shower and dress and to make breakfast before their trip down the mountain. He had assured Doc Sterling that he would get her safely to and from her appointments at the hospital. Maybe today, during their trip, Alessandra would remember more. As he scrambled the eggs, he heard noises coming from his bedroom. He knew Alessandra was awake and would be out for breakfast soon. Orion's thoughts wandered back to the kiss they shared the night before.

"Good morning." Startling Orion from his thoughts, Alessandra entered the kitchen. "Something smells good."

"Good morning. Pour yourself a cup of coffee. I hope you like bacon, scrambled eggs, and English muffins," Orion said as he placed a plate filled on the table. He pulled out a chair, indicating Alessandra should sit. "There's butter and jam on the table."

As he joined her, Alessandra said, "I'm starving. And yes, I love it all. Thank you again for your kindness. You know, you don't have to wait on me, I really can fend for myself."

"I'm sure you can," Orion chuckled, recalling the evening she shot him. "Like Doc says, you're still recovering. So we'll take it one step at a time until your memory comes back. I was thinking we could swing by Rob Taylor's shop before heading to your appointments. You can look for your glasses, and we can see the shape your jeep is in."

"I'd like that!" Alessandra finished her breakfast and went back into the bedroom to finish getting dressed while Orion stacked the dishwasher and cleaned up in the kitchen. "Ready," she said, walking back into the kitchen with her coat in her arms. "Any chance we could stop at the grocer's after my appointment. I have a few things I would like to pick up," she asked.

He grabbed his coat from the hook on the wall and motioned Alessandra toward the door. "Of course, there's a few items I need too. I'll check with Jess to see if there's anything he and Lyra need too." Smiling back at him, she opened the door and headed down the stairs, realizing this was the first time she had left the apartment. She wasn't sure where she was going, and suddenly, she felt afraid. She hesitated after taking a couple of steps, looking back at Orion. Seeing the fear in her eyes and understanding Alessandra's hesitation, Orion joined her on the step where she was standing, taking her hand in his to lead the way.

Opening the door leading into The Rip, Orion saw Jess wiping down tables. Lyra was behind the bar stacking clean glasses, while Skye ran around the tables laughing and playing, a usual site at The Rip each morning prepping for the day's business. Orion knew Iker would already be tucked away in the kitchen working on the daily special, although he couldn't hear or see him. The aromas passing through the bar gave the man's location away. When Jess took ownership of the bar, it needed a lot of work, but hard work wasn't something Jess ever backed away from. Before long, The Rip became a local hang out, a place that welcomed residents and tourists, alike. Jess and Lyra, along with their curly blond-haired daughter, Skye, had built themselves a place to call home.

Looking up, Jess caught a glimpse of Orion holding Alessandra's hand. He had suspected his brother-in-law was attracted to the woman. Even though his wife was the most beautiful woman in the world to him, he gave credit to Alessandra's beauty. He could understand Orion's attraction to her, hoping that attraction didn't lead his friend into danger. Orion dropped Alessandra's hand as he met his friend's eyes, "We're on our way to the hospital via Rob's shop. I told Alessandra I would take her to her jeep to find her glasses and see if something might jog her memory before we headed down the mountain."

"That's a great idea," Lyra said, joining them from the bar. Smiling at Alessandra, she asked, "How have you been feeling? Did you get a good night's sleep?"

"Yes." Alessandra paused, looking toward her ribs and wrist, "I'm feeling better every day. Orion is treating me like a guest. He made a salad and spaghetti for dinner last night, and it was delicious.

I looked at my driver's license and the papers found in my jeep, hoping they would trigger my memory." Alessandra looked around the bar, "Everything seems new."

"Give yourself time. You've only been conscious for two days. And you haven't healed." Lyra looked at her husband, then brother, and back to Alessandra. "You are safe here and have a place to stay as long as you need it."

"My wife's always right," Jess joked as he slipped his arm around Lyra. "If you feel up to it this evening, why don't you join us tonight? Maybe we can convince Lyra to even sing?" Jess gave his wife a sweet kiss on the cheek. "But for now, I need to get back to work. You two be safe and enjoy your trip," Jess said with a wink toward Alessandra and Orion. He returned to wiping tables.

Protective of Alessandra, Orion said, "Let's see how Alessandra is feeling after our trip down the mountain and to the hospital. If she's up to it, we'll join you," Orion said, responding to the request to join them at The Rip. "Do you guys need anything from town?"

"No, we're all set," Lyra answered as she heard her daughter approaching. "Unca O, Unca O," the little girl yelled, racing toward Orion. Sweeping Skye up into his arms, he tickled the little girl pink until she was begging for mercy. "I wuv you, Unca O," she said, squeezing him around the neck before struggling to be let go.

Orion set his niece on the ground, "I love you too, you little hellion!" Laughing as he gently placed his hand on Alessandra's back, ushering her out the front door.

The brisk mountain air took Alessandra's breath away. She pulled her gloves out of her pocket with a shiver. Concerned, Orion asked, "Are you warm enough?" Looking at the woman he knew wasn't used to the weather, he wanted to wrap his arms around her, however, refrained from doing so.

"Yes, thank you," she said softly. Looking up into his eyes, she said quietly, as if telling a secret, "I love the mountains." Waiting for a reaction from Orion that never came, she repeated herself louder, "I love the mountains. I know the feeling of cool mountain mornings. I've been in mountains before I wanted to see the mountains again."

She stood looking around at the surrounding area, Orion watching her, both knowing her memory was returning.

Orion gave Alessandra a few minutes to absorb her surroundings before interrupting her thoughts. "You had another memory return." He smiled at her, offering his reassurance.

"Not anything specific, but just like I knew my name was Alessandra Petrovich when you said my name, I know that I've always loved the mountains," she said.

"Maybe getting out of the apartment today will help to jog your memory more," Orion stated. "If you are warm enough, it's only a short walk to Rob's shop to check on your jeep?" he asked.

"I'd like the walk. I've always loved the feeling of the cool mountain air on my face," she knowingly said.

Offering his arm, he said, "I'd feel better if you took my arm. It's a little slippery out here, and you already have enough injuries."

Realizing he was right, she smiled, bowing her head in jest, "Thank you kind, sir." On the short walk to Rob's, Orion pointed out a doe with two fawn grazing off in the woods and a couple of rare cardinals sitting in a tree. *I know why I've loved the mountains,* Alessandra thought.

It wasn't long before they arrived at a large dark building with a sign, "Rob Taylor's Automotive," across the top in bright colors. Orion opened the door for Alessandra, both needing a moment for their eyes to adjust. Alessandra was startled by what she thought was a large dark shadow approaching them. Seemingly frightened, Orion watched as Alessandra moved a couple of steps back and behind him. Surprised by her actions, but saying nothing, Orion stepped forward, offering his hand. "Morning, Rob."

The young man, not quite as tall as Orion, greeted the couple, "Morning." Dressed in dirty dark blue coveralls, the man grabbed a rag out of his pocket, wiping his hands before offering one too Orion.

Hearing sounds of metal coming from the other side of the shop, Orion observed, "I see you've got the crew working today."

"Yes, you'd think business would slow down with all the snow, no one being able to go anywhere. But I'm busier than I've ever been during the winter. I'm not complaining though. I'm doing what I love and loving what I do," the man said jokingly.

Stepping to the side, Orion allowed Alessandra to come into full view of the man. "Rob, this is Alessandra Petrovich. Owner of the jeep Jess and I pulled out of the snow a couple of days ago."

Wiping his hands for a second time, knowing he would never get all the dirt off, "Nice to meet you, Ms. Petrovich. Sorry, my hands are dirty and sorry to hear about your accident," Rob said.

"Nice to meet you," Alessandra extended her hand hesitantly.

"I wanted Alessandra to drop by and take a look inside her jeep to see if she could find her glasses. Also, I thought we'd check to see what the repair prognosis looks like," Orion continued talking with Rob about the repairs needed on the jeep. As he talked, he watched Alessandra move cautiously around Rob, working her way toward her jeep. It was the only jeep in the garage; however, Orion wondered to himself whether there was something familiar about the vehicle to Alessandra. Orion and Rob stepped in line, following behind Alessandra, as she moved to her car.

When she arrived at the jeep, she peered inside, then turned to the men and asked, "Is this my jeep?" Both men nodded their heads yes as they watched her. Orion knew why he was watching Alessandra—she was beautiful, and he could hardly take his eyes off her, but he turned to see Rob staring at her too.

"Let me help you look inside," Rob said. "There's still a lot of broken glass and some metal pieces hanging off your jeep, and I don't want you to get cut." Rob jerked on a door so Alessandra could look inside easier. Orion watched as she climbed cautiously into the back seat, checking underneath the seats for what he knew were her glasses. He continued to watch, not able to tell everything she was collecting. It wasn't long before he noticed a big smile appear across her face as he noticed she held out her hand so he could see the pair of glasses. He smiled at her. He turned his attention to Rob. Orion and Rob finished their discussion of the repairs needed on the jeep and the plan on finding the parts. Rob leaned up against the jeep, causing the vehicle to move a little. Checking on Alessandra, both men saw the woman sitting apprehensively in the back seat. Orion moved quickly to Alessandra, knowing from her facial expression she was struck by fear.

"Alessandra, let me help you out," he offered.

Shaking, she reached for Orion's arms, as he helped her out of the vehicle, "Than…thank you." Alessandra remembered being in the back seat of her jeep and afraid of a dark shadow. She didn't know why she was in the back seat, and she didn't see any face on the dark shadow, but she knew she should be afraid. And she was.

"What's wrong?" Orion asked as he looked from Alessandra to Rob for answers. Rob, bewildered, only shrugged.

Embarrassed, Alessandra answered quietly, "Nothing. Maybe we should get going." She moved toward the door, thanking Rob for working on her jeep. Orion trailed quickly behind her, wondering why Alessandra had been overcome with emotion. He caught up with her, pulling her arm through his, not wanting her to fall on the slippery road. As he wrapped their arms together, he felt Alessandra lean into him. She seemed completely unaware of the feelings she stirred in him. Wanting to stop and wrap his arms around Alessandra and pull her body in close to his, he willed himself to keep walking. They walked side by side to his truck without saying a word. When they arrived at his truck, he opened the passenger side door and helped her inside. He turned up the heater to warm the cab and pulled Alessandra across the seat, close to him. He put the truck in gear and headed down the mountain. He wanted to ask her what happened in the back of her jeep but decided against it. He suspected she remembered something, and his guess was it wasn't a pleasant memory.

As Orion drove down the mountain, he wondered if Alessandra would recognize the area where she had veered off the road. She hadn't revealed any memories had returned from her accident, but somehow he knew, sitting in the jeep had affected her. What was she hiding? He wouldn't press for information, at least not now. He would wait for a better time. Maybe he could get Lyra to talk to her tonight. Feeling Alessandra's head gently rock against his shoulders, Orion knew the woman had fallen asleep. He took every caution driving down the mountain and to the hospital, so his driving wouldn't disturb her rest.

Before he knew it, the two had arrived at the hospital where Alessandra's tests were scheduled. "We're here," he said, gently shaking Alessandra awake, watching closely as the woman opened her eyes. She smiled, recognizing the man's face, feeling like she was safe. Orion delivered Alessandra to the office Doc Sterling had arranged for him, making sure she was signed in and filled out the necessary paperwork. When the nurse called Alessandra into the office, she told Orion her tests would take about two hours. Orion assured Alessandra he would be waiting.

Knowing that Orion had a couple of hours, he decided to do some shopping. First, he found the hardware store so he could pick up a couple of hinges for some cabinets in his apartment. He had told Jess and Lyra he would fix them for their generosity in allowing him to stay in the apartment above the bar. While he was in the hardware store, he selected two new light fixtures for the bathroom and a ceiling fan for his bedroom. He might as well make himself useful during his stay at Hideaway Canyon. He had not only covered at The Rip sometimes but made himself useful by serving as a handyman to any residents of the town that needed help.

After putting his purchases in his truck, he walked over to the nearby gift shop, thinking he'd find a little present for Skye. Orion selected a couple of books and a small bracelet for the little girl. As he browsed the jewelry counter, he saw a necklace with a silver star. In the middle of the star was a citrine stone. Immediately he thought of Alessandra, the funny little star-shaped freckle on her cheek, citrine stone matched her eyes. Looking at his watch, he knew it was time he headed back to the hospital. He signaled to the store clerk that he wanted to buy the necklace. After paying for his purchases, he walked out the door, slipping the necklace in his pocket.

Alessandra was sitting in the lobby, waiting for him when he walked through the door. "Hope I haven't kept you waiting," he said.

"No, I just sat down about five minutes ago," Alessandra stood as she responded.

Dismayed by his immediate attraction to the woman, Orion sought a reason to be near her. "How did the tests go?" Orion asked as he picked up the coat lying on a chair and helped Alessandra into it. She seemed so strong yet vulnerable. Orion suspected Alessandra's memory was returning and was concerned she wasn't as forthcoming about it as he would like. What was the woman hiding? He was determined to find out more about his house guest.

"Everything seemed to go well. The nurse said they would let Doc Sterling know my results. Thank you," she smiled as Orion held the door.

Knowing it was lunchtime, Orion suggested they grab some lunch before finishing their shopping and heading back up the mountain. Alessandra still wanted to run to the grocer. He knew a great little cafe within walking distance and could see Alessandra appeared to be more relaxed than she had been earlier this morning at Rob Taylor's Automotive. Although the surrounding mountains were filled with snow, the sun warmed the sky, making it a beautiful day for a walk. Orion hoped the walk would do Alessandra some good.

The two walked several blocks window shopping and talking. He pointed out area landmarks and told the story of how the valley was discovered, filling Alessandra in on stories about the locals. It wasn't long before Orion and Alessandra arrived at the Green Bean & Bistro for lunch. The sign by the door said, "Seat Yourself," so Orion led Alessandra to a booth by the window, where he sat with his back to the wall. He knew Alessandra would appreciate the view of the mountains, knowing the sun through the window would help keep her warm.

"Well, if it isn't Orion Grey," a waitress called as she approached them with glasses of water. As she set the glasses down, Orion stood and gave the woman a hug. "What brings you to town?" the waitress asked.

"You, of course." He smiled.

"Now, don't waste your words on me. You save them for those pretty young girls we know your charm will work on." The waitress laughed, looking at Orion's companion and handing out menus.

"Jazz, I'd like you to meet Alessandra Petrovich." Orion smiled as he introduced the waitress to Alessandra. "Alessandra, Jazz…the woman who refuses my heart."

"Nice to meet you." Alessandra laughed at the friendly exchange between Orion and the waitress.

"Nice to meet you. Don't you let this man fool you, there isn't a woman alive who would refuse his heart. Not even me. He just never offers it. He's one of those wanderer's, always out saving the world, never home long enough to take root," the waitress revealed. "Now what can I get the two of you?" Jazz asked. "The special is our BLT with cottage fries."

"The special for me," he winked at Jazz and looked toward Alessandra, setting his menu down.

"Sounds good to me. With a glass of tea," Alessandra ordered.

Holding up an empty coffee cup, "Coffee," Orion said before the waitress gathered the menus and walked away.

Not more than a minute passed, and Jazz returned to their table with a glass of tea and a pot of coffee to fill Orion's cup. Hearing a little bell ring, Orion looked over to the front door as two well-dressed men arrived, finding chairs at the counter of the cafe. He studied the men, thinking they looked out of place. They must be in town on business; the conference center hosted meetings, and the men weren't dressed for the slopes. "You two came in at the right time. The storm dropped several feet of fresh powder bringing in skiers from out of state. We have nonstop customers from morning to night. Your food will be up shortly." She walked away to take more orders.

"It sounds like you and our waitress get along well," Alessandra began the conversation.

Hoping he would have an opportunity to find out more about Alessandra, he smiled. "Yes, Jazz and my family go way back. Jazz and my mother were best friends." Orion began to share information about himself, hoping Alessandra would feel more comfortable and do the same. "I grew up around these mountains and valley. I guess you could call it our stomping grounds." He smiled at the woman across the table, wanting her to know more about him. "My parents were Oaklin and Abel Grey. They had three children. Me, of course. Lyra, who you've already met and Crux, my older brother." Seeing Alessandra listening intently, he continued. "My grandfather started a ranch in the valley over one hundred years ago. My mother was an only child. She loved growing up on the ranch, and eventually, she and my father took over the management of it as my grandfather got older. It's a long story. Maybe I'll tell you the rest of the story one day."

Jazz walked up with their lunch. "Here you go. Ketchup's already on the table for your fries. Can I get you anything else?"

Checking with Alessandra, Orion responded, "Looks like we have everything we need for now."

"I'll be back to check on you later," the waitress said, walking to the next table.

Alessandra and Orion started eating. "This is wonderful. I know why you suggested we come here," Alessandra said, wiping her mouth with a napkin. "Tell me more." She took another bite.

"I'll have to save the story for when we're not eating. It's rather long. Maybe when we have more time," Orion replied, worried that his mother's free spirit might unsettle Alessandra. Seeing the disappointment on Alessandra's face, he added, "I will tell you that my mother, Oaklin, was a free spirit and loved the freedom she had growing up on a ranch. She daydreamed endlessly of the stars in the sky. Hence, her naming her children Crux, Orion, and Lyra. We were all named after constellations. My mother would ride the trail with her father on her horse, Galaxy. At night on the open range, you can see constellations for miles. She would sleep on a bedroll under the stars, just like all the trail hands. She would sit on our beds and tell us stories about Greek gods and how constellations came to be. She really was a great storyteller." He smiled, taking another bite of his sandwich.

With a forlorn look, Alessandra spoke, "My father used to take me riding in the mountains. I know how your mother felt."

She immediately aroused Orion's interest. Did Alessandra understand the meaning of what she just said?

Not wanting to alarm the woman, Orion gently encouraged her memory, "Remember yesterday when you talked about drinking wine in Paris?" he watched Alessandra nod yes. "You used the word *we*." He continued to carefully watch the woman. "You must have been in Paris with your father?"

The little bell on the front door of the cafe rang again, catching Orion's attention. He looked up to see the two well-dressed men open the cafe door to leave. The taller one turned and looked over his shoulder at Orion, then Alessandra, too, who had her back toward the door. Within a moment, the man turned back and walked out the door. "No, never," Alessandra said with alarm. Orion's eyes trailed back to Alessandra, attentive to her words. His thoughts wandered. Did Alessandra mean to say that out loud? How should he respond to what she just said? He remained quiet watching the woman. "My mother." She stared across the table. "It was my mother." Helplessly looking at Orion for answers, she asked, "Where is my mother?"

Realizing this was a good time to signal Jazz for their check, he gulped the last of his coffee and asked Alessandra if she needed anything else. With a look that told him he needed to get her out of the restaurant, Orion stood up, tossed a couple of twenty-dollar bills on the table, and reached for Alessandra. He helped her put her coat on and ushered her toward the door. As they left the café, he heard Jazz call after them, "Bring Alessandra back for dinner one night." He acknowledged the waitress with a wave, hustling Alessandra out the door and down the street to his truck.

Before long, Orion and Alessandra were headed up the mountain toward home, it didn't seem like the right time to suggest going to the grocer. Orion knew bits and pieces of Alessandra's memory were returning, and he wanted to get her home, to a safe place, where he could give her his full attention.

"Your memory is coming back, isn't it?" Orion glanced over at the woman sitting next to him in his truck.

"Yes." She shivered, staring at the road ahead.

Orion reached over, gently pulling Alessandra close to him, offering her the warmth of his body. With the hand he wasn't using to steer with, he took her hand and cradled it in his. "Alessandra," he said. With a pool of tears forming in her eyes, the woman looked up and into Orion's eyes. "You are safe. I won't let anything harm you." Hearing those words and unable to hold back her tears, Alessandra began to sob. Orion slowed the truck to a stop in the middle of the small mountain road, knowing there wouldn't be much traffic. After putting the truck in park, he wrapped both arms around Alessandra, holding her until her tears were dry. Orion knew, as he sat holding Alessandra, it was time to come clean with the woman, filling her in on the details he, Jess, and Iker found. His feelings for Alessandra were too powerful; he knew he needed to be honest with her. Sitting in his truck holding her, stirred a passion from within him, a passion he was so unfamiliar with. Something he didn't recognize. He couldn't deny his physical attraction to Alessandra; however, his attraction was much deeper than outside appearances. She was beautiful to him in so many ways; no one else seemed to matter. Maybe it was the star-shaped freckle on her cheek; maybe it was the golden-brown eyes; maybe it was even the bad-assed way she handled a gun that kept him mesmerized. Whatever it was, Orion knew that the stranger who slept in his bed for the past four nights was his. Everything about the woman told him the stars were aligned, and he'd never believed the story his mother told. He pulled Alessandra in closer to the warmth of his body and kissed the top of her head. "Oaklin Grey was right all along." He smiled.

Hearing Alessandra's tear subside and keeping one arm wrapped around her, Orion put the truck in drive and started to slowly ascend the mountain again. "Is this where I had my accident?" she asked quietly as she raised her head to look at the window.

"Just a short way ahead," Orion responded. "Would you like me to show you?"

"Yes, if you don't mind."

Orion drove ahead another mile and stopped the truck. He pointed off to the right. "See that little group of aspens?"

"What are aspen?" Alessandra asked.

Smiling Orion answered the woman, "A type of tree. Guess I assumed everyone knew what aspens were. A tree common in Colorado and a few other states, known for their leaves turning to a beautiful golden color in the fall."

Looking off on the side of the road, she stated, "Oh, yes, I see the ones that are broken."

"Those broken ones are the ones that saved you from plunging into the ravine below," Orion told her. "Jess and I secured your jeep with ropes, just so we could get your things out of the vehicle. We didn't trust that our weight wouldn't push it over."

"I think I was being followed," Alessandra revealed her thoughts to Orion. "Was there another car?" she asked.

"No, just your jeep. Why do you think you were being followed?" Orion asked.

"I've been seeing this dark shadow of a man in my dreams. I feel like someone has been following me," she explained.

Orion shook his head, knowing he hadn't seen anyone around. "By the time I saw you, you were already in the ditch. I didn't see any tracks from another vehicle, but it was windy and snowing pretty heavily," Orion told Alessandra, wondering if the information would help her remember. He hadn't seen any significant evidence from the accident, but then, he hadn't looked for some either. It had been five days ago, and with the weather as it was in Hideaway Canyon, evidence that might have existed had long blown away or was covered in the layers of snowfall. Orion suggested they leave.

"Let's get back home." Alessandra smiled at Orion's words. "We can sit down and try to put some of the pieces of your memory back together, if you'd like."

Taking a deep breath, fearful of what she might find out, she nodded. Alone in her thoughts as she and Orion traveled the last leg of the trip, Alessandra feared what Orion would say. He had shared such wonderful memories of his family, particularly his mother, and his childhood. Deep inside Alessandra, something was telling her she had a very different one. Clearly, Orion had been raised with the love of both parents growing up. She was fearful of Orion's reaction to the information she was remembering. And if Alessandra's memory served her right, she could be putting Orion and his family and friends in danger.

Orion pulled his truck up to the front door of The Rip. He walked around the truck to help Alessandra safely out onto the slippery sidewalk. He offered her an arm, leading her through the front door. Orion could see the lunch crowd had been exhausted, and the bar was rather quiet. "How was the trip?" Jess called out from behind the bar as Orion and Alessandra entered.

"It went well," Alessandra answered.

"Well, pull up a chair. Are you up for a glass of wine?" Jess asked the woman, immediately seeing her nod of acceptance. "Lyra's in the kitchen. I'll let her know you are here." Jess opened the door to the kitchen, letting Lyra know her brother and Alessandra had returned. He collected a bottle of wine and two glasses for the ladies and headed for the table. "Orion, how about you? A beer?"

"Absolutely. Give me a minute to unload the truck, and I'll join you," Orion said as he motioned to Alessandra, he'd be right back.

Lyra came out of the kitchen and joined Alessandra at the table. She sat down just in time for her husband to hand her a glass of wine. "Did you have a good day?" she asked Alessandra.

"Yes, my appointments went well. Then Orion took me to a wonderful little cafe, the Green Bean & Bistro, the food was delicious." She smiled. "I also met Jazz."

Lyra watched the woman talk, "Let's drink to a good day!" She raised her glass against Alessandra's. The woman toasted and sipped. Alessandra talked to Lyra about her MRI and x-rays and shared some of the tales told her about the locals. Both women laughed as they sipped, as Orion emptied his truck. A smile crossed Lyra's face when she heard Orion had shared information about their mother and the family ranch, knowing he rarely divulged personal information. Lyra, like her mother, had an appreciation for Greek mythology and stories of how the constellations came into being. She knew the stars were beginning to align for her brother, and whether or not he liked it or believed it, Lyra knew Orion would accept it.

Soon the ladies were joined by Orion and Jess at the table. Orion and Jess caught the end of the women's conversation, laughing at funny little stories from Lyra and Orion's youth. "I have some memories," Alessandra announced, surprising everyone.

"Hey, didn't I get invited to the party," Iker interrupted as he walked out of the kitchen.

Looking from Alessandra to Jess, then Lyra, Orion said with a smile, "Do we really want him here? Of course, you're invited! Just grab a round for everyone before coming over," Orion teased, knowing Iker would join the table with refills. They waited for Iker before they continued, making small talk to pass the time. Recognizing the tension in the woman's body, Orion reached over and placed Alessandra's hand between his, hoping to squelch her nerves and give her courage to share her memories at the table. Lyra looked at Jess approvingly, as Iker approached with a tray filled with drinks for the table. Iker served everyone at the table, scanning Jess and Lyra's faces when he, too, noticed Orion holding Alessandra's hand. Clearly the relationship his friend had with the woman had changed since he last spoke with his friend. Orion wasn't one to show affection toward anyone, let alone someone he had only known a few days. Iker never remembered seeing Orion with any woman, except on the few occasions the job required his association with one. Orion's gesture toward the woman brought a smile to the faces of his three allies. Iker sat down, giving Alessandra a big smile, "Good news today, little lady?" She smiled back at the man who intimidated her, not knowing whether or not he even liked her.

Alessandra felt Orion squeeze her hand, and she began, "Some of my memory is coming back." Her eyes met Lyra's with a smile. "Not all of it makes sense, but I'm remembering bits and pieces that I know are real."

"Why don't you share what you remember, and we'll see if we can help put some of it together for you," Jess encouraged her.

"I don't know how much Orion has told you about last night," Alessandra started but was interrupted by Iker.

"Orion hasn't told us anything about last night." He paused. "Is there something we should know?" Iker grinned at his friend. Orion ignored Iker's smirk and gestured for Alessandra to continue.

"When Orion and I were having dinner last night, I mentioned having wine in Paris. I didn't even remember my comment until Orion brought it up at lunch today. He's right, I did say it." She paused. "I said *we* had wine in Paris. I know the *we* was me and my mother—and another woman, but I don't know who she is. And I don't know where my mother is. I don't know if she's alive or dead. I don't even know how long ago that was, but I know I've been to Paris." She continued, "And then this morning at the automotive shop, when I crawled into the backseat of my jeep looking for my glasses, I had another memory. I can remember being in the back seat of my jeep. The jeep started rocking, and I felt like I was being watched. I keep having flashes of a man in black clothes. No face, just a silhouette. I felt like I was being followed. I can't remember anything else." Alessandra looked around the table at her new friends or at least a group of people that wanted to help her. All four watched and listened intently to Alessandra as she spoke, encouraging her to continue. "Then today, when we were having lunch, Orion talked about his mother riding horses in the mountain with her father." She paused for what seemed like a long time. Taking a deep breath, she continued, "I know I used to ride horses in the mountain with my father. Not these mountains but some other mountains. I think he's a very bad man. He might be dead." Orion could feel Alessandra's hand tremor as she revealed what she knew.

Shocked by Alessandra's last words, Lyra asked with eyes show-ing concern, "Are you all right?" There was a pause from everyone at the table as Alessandra nodded. "Your memories are starting to come back, like Doc Sterling said. Don't push yourself too much. One day it will all make sense." While Alessandra's attention was on Lyra and what she was saying to her, the men cast looks between each other. Orion wasn't sure the timing was right to reveal the search the three men had done. The looks Orion was receiving from his friends told him Jess and Iker would wait for a lead from him as to whether or not the timing was right to approach the subject of the search and the information they had gathered. Regardless of who Alessandra's father was, her new friends were concerned for her recovery.

"Yes, I'm fine. I just wish more made sense. I am not sure how to connect the pieces. Also, where is my family? My mother, my father, do I have brothers and sisters? Why was I driving up this mountain road?"

Orion decided it was time to share some of the information they found, although he wasn't sure he wanted to share it all. He hoped the information would trigger more memories for Alessandra. "Alessandra, you know that after I found you and brought you here, Jess and I went back to your jeep to gather your things and tow your car to the shop." He paused. With an attentive look toward Orion, she listened. "As you know, we found your driver's license. We also found a cell phone."

The information didn't seem to upset Alessandra, so Jess picked up where Orion left off. "We started looking for your family by using the address we found on your driver's license. We used some of our professional contacts, trying to locate anyone who might know you," he added.

"We knew someone had to have been worried about you. You must have just disappeared to them. I can't imagine how I would feel with the disappearance of my daughter," Lyra explained, worried Alessandra would take offense to what might seem like their interference.

"Thank you." Alessandra looked gratefully at each person sitting around the table, "I really do appreciate it."

Jess continued to provide Alessandra with the information his search team was able to collect. He told her that she had lived at the address for five years and that she worked at a company called Global Research & Analysis. He gave her the names of her building supervisor, Bob Thomas, and her boss, Dimitri Osmond. Not wanting to reveal all the details of the reports, he told Alessandra the reports were in his office, and he would be happy to give them to her to read tonight, if she would like.

"We're not trying to rush your memory, Alessandra. Doc Sterling said it would take time," Orion reminded her. "Our search initially started only to help find your family, knowing someone had to want to know what happened to you." He gave Alessandra a moment to think about what he said, then added, "Maybe the reports will help you put some of the pieces together."

"Remembering bits and pieces is completely normal," Lyra added.

Iker sat quietly, listening to the conversation, sipping his beer. "Jess also told you Orion found a phone." He looked into Alessandra's eyes, watching closely for any sign she remembered. "I was able to pull only one number off the phone. I tried multiple times to call the number. However, no one ever picked up. From what I can tell, it was a burner phone. I have that number written down. You might want to take a look at it to see if it jogs your memory. The phone log shows you either placed a call or text, once a day, to that number only for about four days prior to your accident." He waited, like everyone else sitting at the table, for a response from the woman.

Alessandra sat, tears collecting in her eyes, looking down at the hands in her lap. She hadn't noticed, but at some point, during the conversation, Orion had stopped holding her hands. "I don't remember. Why do I remember Paris and not Chicago? Whose number was I calling?" Alessandra asked, quietly crying. Glancing from one person at the table to the next, she asked, horrified, "Why do I have a gun?" Wanting to know the answers to the same questions, Orion reached over and wrapped his arm around her, pulling her close, feeling the warmth of her body next to his, not knowing what to say. His gesture was made to comfort Alessandra; however, his body's reaction to the woman was nothing short of lust.

"I think Alessandra's had enough new information given to her to process," Jess said in an effort to end the conversation, knowing they had upset her.

"Yes, I do too," Lyra offered with a smile. "Alessandra, why don't you join me in the ladies' room. We'll wash our faces and make ourselves more presentable," wanting to save Alessandra from embarrassment. Customers would see the mascara streaks running down the woman's cheeks and know she had been crying.

"I've got a pot of chili simmering in the kitchen. How about I serve up five bowls with some cornbread and honey butter?" Iker suggested. "The dinner crowd will begin soon, so we'd better eat while we have a chance.

"And I'll top off everyone's drinks," Jess added.

Orion stood and began clearing the table of glasses and beer bottles, as everyone parted to prepare for their meal. He knew the conversation had been a difficult one for Alessandra and wondered what effect the remaining information would have on her.

Jess and Iker were waiting for Orion in the kitchen. "Let's give the lady some time before we brief her on the remaining information we gathered," Jess suggested. Orion concurred.

"The lady's either an excellent actress, or she really doesn't remember. I didn't get any sense that she was lying, but we need to be cautious. If Anton Petrovich is Alessandra's father, he's a dangerous man and one we don't want involved with," Iker said as he walked into the office to collect Alessandra's file, handing it to Orion. "See if anything in these reports makes sense to her."

"I will tonight after dinner, after she's relaxed and had a chance to calm down. I'll see if she can make anything of the information." Orion noticed his friends seemed hesitant. The two men stood side by side, looking from Orion to each other. "Okay, what gives," Orion said, losing patience. He knew his friends too long not to recognize the subtleties of their actions.

"Listen, don't go off half-cocked," Jess started. "We're only concerned about your well-being." Seeing frustration rise within his friend, he hurried to finish what he was about to say, "We're worried Alessandra's situation is becoming too personal for you."

Orion responded in anger, "Since when do I let my personal feeling interfere with my professional duties!"

"Look, brother." Iker stepped forward, placing a strong hand on Orion's shoulder. "No one's saying you don't do your job. Alessandra fell into our laps, she's not one of our jobs." Seeing his friend's temper subside, he continued, "You've put it out there, in plain sight, you have more than professional feelings for the woman."

"We're good with that." Jess and Iker simultaneously nodded at Orion. "But the facts remain, whether any of us like it or not, Alessandra's father isn't someone we want to mess with. Good chance he wants to find his daughter, and if he does, all of us could be in danger."

Stepping back, Orion knew his friends were right. "I'm aware." He paused. "I don't know why. I can't explain it. She's beautiful, but that's not just it. She has no one, and I need to protect her. Just trust me, I need to see this thing through. I won't let any harm come to her or any of you." Understanding Orion's words and trusting their friend, Iker gave Orion a heavy-handed slap on the back, and Jess offered a quick fist bump. The three friends walked out of the kitchen, joining Lyra and Alessandra for a quick dinner before customers began to arrive at The Rip.

Josie showed up at the bar with her twins and Skye, whom she'd been babysitting, just as the friends were finishing dinner. A few people had trickled into The Rip, most for a quick draft. Iker parted the group, heading to the kitchen, while Lyra said her goodbyes. When she was finally able to corral her child, who thought The Rip was her personal gymnasium, she kissed her husband and headed home.

After checking with Jess to make sure he didn't need an extra hand, Orion ushered Alessandra up the back stairway to the apartment above the bar. The sun was just beginning to set, so he knew it wasn't late but also knew Alessandra had a long day. Even though he could see the dark circles under her eyes, suspecting she was exhausted, he couldn't help enjoying the thought of being alone with the woman. The file in his hand could wait until morning. Tonight, he wanted her alone in his home.

When they arrived upstairs, Alessandra slipped into the bathroom to shower and change into something more comfortable. She'd had a long day and relished in the thought of a warm fire and cozy pajamas. Orion tasked himself, gathering wood off the balcony, stacking enough by the stove for the night. He gathered a couple of glasses and opened a bottle of Sutcliffe Cabernet while waiting for Alessandra to return. Just as Orion was about to turn the television on to pass time, Alessandra walked into the living room. Her hair had been released from its earlier ponytail and hung softly over her shoulders. Light from the small lamp Orion lit when they walked through the door illuminated her skin, giving it light peach glow. Wow, she was beautiful. He almost laughed, recognizing his flannel pajamas on her. She had rolled the waist so she wouldn't trip on the legs, and the pajama top hung loosely over her body, hiding any indication she was a woman. He knew better. He could see the tips of her fingers sneaking out the long sleeves that were rolled up. He wondered if she was aware the pajamas belonged to him. He remembered the first night Lyra had given Alessandra the pajamas to wear. The stranger didn't have any clothes. Lyra told him his pajamas would be easier for her to get on and off because of her bandages. It all made sense. He never gave it any thought as to the effect his seeing his pajamas on a woman would have. As he stood staring at Alessandra, thinking about the first night he saw her in his bed, he never imagined his feelings would grow so strong. Now, as he watched Alessandra enter the room, he only hoped he would be able to ignore his desire.

With a smile, Orion motioned for Alessandra to sit on the couch. He reached for a blanket and tucked the edges around her. "How about a glass of wine?"

"Yes, thank you. The shower helped wake me up," she said, thinking how kind and gentle the man was as he filled her glass with wine, how attractive the man was, dismissing the thought, reminding herself it must be feelings of gratitude. She'd only known him a few days, and she had to ignore whatever personal feelings she felt about the man.

"I'm going to take a quick shower. Would you like the remote to the television, or I could put on some music? Your choice?" Orion asked.

She gazed at the file on the coffee table and then back to Orion. "How about some music. Something soft and relaxing." Not feeling like opening the file, she propped her head up against a pillow, ready to listen to music that would relax her. Orion headed to the stereo, tuning the station to one with country music, the only one that existed in the area. He slipped out of the room without Alessandra seeing him.

Alessandra let her mind wander. So much had happened today. She had been to Paris, most likely with her mother, seeing her jeep and remembering a shadow following her, riding with her father in the mountains, the trip up and down the mountain at Hideaway Canyon, and hearing the results of the investigation led by Jess. How could she make sense of it? She kept playing the conversation she had with her friends at The Rip over and over in her head. The more she thought about it, the more frustrated she became. She had to find some answers. We're the Grey's right to think someone would be looking for her? And wouldn't that most likely be her mother and father? She obviously had been keeping in touch with someone, multiple calls and texts to the same number had to mean something. Could she trust these people she thought of as friends? Could she trust Orion? Hearing water splashing in the shower, she peered at the file sitting on the table. She wasn't going to get any answers by just sitting here. Alessandra picked it up the file and began to read.

"I don't seem to have a lot of friends, do I?" Alessandra sighed as Orion joined her on the couch. He could see she had the file open and must have already read part of the report. It wasn't a question; he breathed easy, not wanting to respond. She was right. He, Jess, and Iker noticed the same thing when they read the report. The team wasn't able to find anyone that knew anything about her. A beautiful woman like Alessandra would receive lots of attention, especially from men. He believed she had lost her memory, but now, as it came back, he sensed she was keeping other secrets. Was Anton Petrovich her father? And if he was, did she know it? Was she protecting the Butcher of the Balkans?

Alessandra reached for the wine bottle, filling a glass for Orion and handed it to him. She topped her own off before continuing to talk. "Where did I go on weekends? The report says my building supervisor. Let's see..." She shuffled through the report looking for the name, "Bob Thomas, thought I was visiting my mother. But if my memory is correct, I couldn't have been visiting her. Paris is too far away. So where did I go, gone forty-eight hours, every weekend?"

"Alessandra, remember, Doc Sterling said it was natural for your memory to return piece by piece. Today's been an unusual day, you've really been overwhelmed with information," Orion tried to offer reassurance, recognizing her frustration. "He said it could take months, but it is a good sign that some of your memory is returning." He wanted to tell her about the additional information Jess and Iker had discovered but worried thinking of Doc's warning, too much too soon could do more harm than good.

Wanting to cry, but forcing herself not too, she said, "Orion, you don't understand. I have to know." Tears began to surface in Alessandra's eyes as she covered them in embarrassment with her hands. Orion enveloped the woman in his arms, offering the soothing warmth of his body. After a few moments, he gently pushed Alessandra away from him and reached for the file.

"Alessandra, you know the answers better than any of us do," he said, knowing he wasn't a man known for his patience. "I'll do whatever I can to help you remember, all of us will. You have to be honest with us and share what you do remember." Orion paused for a moment as he searched Alessandra's eyes, wondering if she had been telling him all she remembered. "Do you remember the first night you gained consciousness, and you shot me?" he asked.

"Of course, please don't remind me. I am truly sorry."

"I'm not bringing it up for another apology," he grumbled, "you asked, 'Did my father send you?' And then you said, 'I won't go back.' Why would you say those things?" He began leafing through the report documents as if looking for something as she responded.

"I didn't remember saying that." She paused deep in thought. "You are right. I did say that. That doesn't sound like I would be happy to see my father." Alessandra looked surprised. "I keep seeing a dark shadow of a man. I have this sense of being followed. I've wondered if it was my father."

Orion stopped flipping pages and began to read, "It says in the report that you're building supervisor, Bob Thomas, was visited by a man he described 'had money.' The man was well-dressed and drove a nice car...he was older. The man wanted to see you. You weren't home. Could that be your father?" Orion flipped the page as he looked at Alessandra, wanting some answers.

"I don't know."

"Then it says, your rental application lists an Alina Ulanova Petrovich, as a contact," Orion pressed Alessandra, knowing he might be pushing her too hard. "And in your handwriting, in parenthesis, you wrote the word mother." Holding the pages up for Alessandra to see, "it's right here." His impatience was growing. "You listed a phone number for her, but it's no longer in service. Like the number from your cell phone, Iker already checked the number out. The numbers didn't match, and no one answered either one, but both were Illinois numbers. We believe your mother was with you five years ago in Illinois and not Paris."

Alessandra sat stunned, realizing Orion and his friends had more information on her than she knew or that they had shared with her. She hadn't heard him be so direct since the night she shot him. "I don't remember, I really don't remember! I don't know why I think my mother is in Paris!" Alessandra defended herself. "But if that's what the report says, it must be right. I'm sorry I don't remember!" she cried. Alessandra's head was pounding, her heart racing, feeling like she would vomit. Why couldn't she remember? She abruptly stood up. "You don't believe me," she said, refusing to let Orion see the tears gathering in her eyes, heading for the bedroom. Without looking back, she called out, "I'm tired and going to bed. Good night."

Orion walked out onto his deck to stare at the stars. He had just done the very thing he hadn't wanted to do. And that was, upset Alessandra. Feeling like a fool, Orion walked back into his apartment and picked up the phone to call Lyra. Jess answered, "Hello."

"You're home?" Orion asked, surprised Jess answered the phone.

"Yes, it was a quiet night, so we closed up at nine o'clock." Jess told Orion everything had been cleaned up and prepped for tomorrow. "Charlie was the only one left. I told him to turn the lights off and use the cot in the back. He wasn't in any condition to drive home. I hope you or Alessandra aren't planning on shooting each other tonight. Charlie's heart couldn't take another night of it," Jess joked. Orion remained silent on the other end of the phone. "You didn't call to talk to me, did you?"

"No, but I don't mind listening," Orion answered.

"Are you doing all right, buddy?" Jess asked before calling out to his wife to come to the phone.

"Sure." He paused. "I think I did something pretty dumb," knowing he would pay for the admission he made to his brother-in-law. Orion heard Jess chuckle as he handed the phone off to his wife.

"Hello." Lyra came on the phone.

"Hi. I made a bad call," Orion said as he began to explain what happened with Alessandra earlier in the evening. As Orion spoke, Lyra walked out onto the porch to look at the sky and listen attentively to her brother. She remained quiet, thinking how she had become both her brothers' sounding board since their mother's death. Oaklin Grey used to give the best advice, Lyra remembered, yet she couldn't recall her mother ever telling her what to do.

When Orion finished his story, Lyra talked, "Can you imagine how you would feel, waking up in a strange place, with strange people, not knowing who you are?" Knowing her brother would be listening, she continued, "To Alessandra, she has no friends, no family, no one to trust. I can't imagine what an awful feeling that would be. I do know how desperate and frightened I'd feel?"

"I suppose so." Orion knew his sister was right.

"I think I'd want to know yet, be terrified of what I might find out. What if her story isn't one that comes from storybooks? Does it matter?" Lyra asked her brother.

"No," he answered, "it doesn't matter. I don't care where she's come from."

"Then what's the hurry to find out. If she remembers today, or tomorrow, or not for another month. Don't push her. She doesn't need the pressure. And you, Orion, have feelings for Alessandra that are not just professional. They are personal."

"Well, yes, yes, I do. I definitely didn't want to hurt her."

Lyra smiled as she looked up into the stars. She loved her life. "Then tell her that," she recommended to her brother. Neither sibling said anything to the other for a few seconds, both looking at the stars.

"How did I get so lucky?" Orion asked his sister.

Recognizing the private joke, "It's in the stars," Lyra replied with a smile. "Good night."

Feeling more settled after speaking with his sister and knowing what he needed to do, Orion checked his watch for the time. He wondered if Alessandra was still awake, it wasn't that late. He knew he wouldn't be able to sleep, if he didn't at least try to talk to her. He upset her, and he didn't mean to. Orion knocked gently on his bedroom door. There wasn't any answer. He knocked for the second time, a little louder. Still no answer. He slowly turned the door handle. Flashbacks from the night Alessandra shot him raced through his head. Calling out Alessandra's name. The guns were locked up, he thought to himself. The light was on, and as he opened the door wider, he could see Alessandra wasn't in his bed. Fear dissolved from his body as he opened the door wide to see the woman sitting on the floor surrounded by open boxes and her suitcases. She had been searching through her personal items. Thousands of dollars were scattered about the floor in stacks, as if having been counted. A few photos lay among the piles. When she raised her head to meet his eyes, Orion could see she'd been crying. "I'm a thief. I think I stole this money." She looked so frail, her eyes dark and sunken, her skin pale, like the day he found her.

Having read the report and knowing there was an explanation for the money, he reached for her and gathered her up in his arms, "No, you're not," Orion murmured as he carried her to the bed.

"How do you know?" Alessandra sobbed, knowing she was a thief. Not able to let go of her as he placed her on the bed. He joined her without asking, holding her close to him as they lay in his bed. The warmth of her body next to him made his pulse quicken and his heart pound. He knew Alessandra remained unaware of his desire for her as a woman. He was grateful Alessandra had closed her eyes and buried her head under his chin, not wanting her to see the evidence of his desire. He knew now was not the time to act on his fascination.

"Alessandra, I need to tell you something. Nothing I am going to tell you is being said to hurt you. None of my actions, none of those done by Jess or Iker, have been done to hurt you. Some of what I am going to tell you might not feel good to hear. It could hurt you," Orion said cautiously. Aware Alessandra's sobs began to diminish, "Will you listen?" he asked gently. He felt her nod her head.

"Jess, Iker, and I own a business called The Firm. The work we do provides us with resources to find out information. When I found you, we used those resources to try to find out where you came from and notify anyone who might be looking for you. Your driver's license was our initial source. However, that did provide us other leads which we were able to follow up with to find out more about you," introducing Alessandra to how their research started. "Do you have any questions?" he asked.

"Do you know more about me than what you've told me?" Alessandra asked Orion.

"Yes, we think."

"What does that mean?" she asked.

"The probability is high that we know who you are and have collected substantial information about your background, but really, it's only you that can totally verify it at this point. We would need to do further investigation to know we are one hundred percent sure of our findings." Orion answered her.

Alessandra quietly encouraged Orion, "Will you tell me?"

Orion began to tell Alessandra everything they knew. He started from the beginning with everything contained in the report. He knew she hadn't had time to read the entirety, so filled her in where she left off. He told her that she entered the United States from Canada on a student visa. There were a lot of holes in the information they knew from before that time. She had read most of the information they had collected from her building supervisor in Chicago, so he began talking to her about her job. Orion told her everything they had learned from Dimitri Osmond, her boss at Global Research & Analysis. She was a good employee, well liked but stuck to herself. Her boss took her to lunch every payday, and he helped her cash her paycheck, which was where they thought the cash Alessandra had in the suitcase came from. Orion told her Iker ran the serial numbers on the bills, and none were reported missing or stolen. Evidence showed she earned the money legitimately. Her boss tried to talk her into opening a bank account, but she refused.

He continued by telling her they found a birth certificate with her mother's name, Alina Ulanova Petrovich, and her father's name, Anton Petrovich. He handed her a copy of the birth certificate. She was born in Kosovo, and as she already knew, her birthday was October 4, 1982. He told her how they believed her mother was a classically trained ballerina, performing around Europe, serving as a prima ballerina for the Mariinsky Ballet Company in St. Petersburg, Russia. From what we can tell, your mother gave up ballet after marrying a man by the name of Anton Petrovich, an officer in the Yugoslav military. Apparently, your mother joined your father in Kosovo, and little, if anything, was heard from her again. There is no record of her, that we could find, in the ballet world after her marriage to your father.

"This is the part that is difficult to share with you." Orion pulled away from Alessandra so he could look in her eyes. "I'm not saying this to hurt you, nor is our investigation one hundred percent conclusive." Orion relayed to Alessandra that they believed her father was the same Anton Petrovich associated with a man by the name of Mikozavich, President of Kosovo. Mikozavich was suspected of deliberately creating conflict among the ethnic groups in his country, in addition to ordering the slaughter of hundreds of thousands of people, and forcing the exile of even more, who became refugees in other countries. Alessandra's eyes filled with tears, but she refrained from making a sound. She continued to listen, "Anton Petrovich is one of Mikozavich's top commanders, and he was in charge of raiding villages and killing and forcing people out of their homes. It was his job to carry out all orders given by Mikozavich," Orion waited for a reaction from Alessandra.

How could a man like that be her father? Alessandra asked herself. The photo she found, where was it? She had forgotten about it. Leaping out of Orion's grasp and away from the bed, she dropped to the floor in search of the photo she had glanced at earlier. She knew it was here. Wanting to help, Orion lowered himself from the bed to the floor, "What are you looking for Alessandra?" he asked.

"I saw an old photo earlier, right before I found the money." She shifted stacks of bills to the side and frantically looking under them. "I know it has to be here. The photo was of a man, woman, and child. I must have dropped it when I saw the money."

With a little more shuffling, she found it. She held up the photo as Orion moved in closer so he could see. Alessandra and Orion sat with their eyes fixed intently on the photo, black and white, close to twenty years old, with a tear in the corner. As they examined the photo closer, they saw a man standing in what looked to be a military uniform, in front of a large, ornately decorated building. Orion could see something written on the building; however, it was written in another language, one he guessed to be Russian. People could be seen walking behind the family whose picture was being taken. Orion's eyes followed the man's arm around the woman and up into what he knew were Alessandra's eyes. Jealousy raged in the pit of his stomach. He didn't like seeing another man's arms around Alessandra. As he looked closer at the photo, he could see that the beautiful young woman who was laughing at the dancing child in front of her wasn't Alessandra at all but had to be Alessandra's mother. The child, probably nine or ten years old, must be Alessandra. As if coming to a decision, Orion announced with conviction, "The woman looks just like you. This has to be your family…you, twenty years ago with your mother and father. Why else would you have it?"

Orion stood, offering his hand to help Alessandra off the floor. She hadn't let go of the photo. He joined her as he ushered her to the edge of the bed where they both sat. Still, claiming Alessandra's hand, he said, "It's getting late." He looked into the woman's eyes. "I'm an impatient man, Alessandra. And I know I've pushed you hard today. I'm sorry. I never meant to hurt you with any of this information. I only want to help you find out who you are?"

With dark eyes, begging for sleep, she said, "I thought I wanted to know too, but now, I'm afraid what else I might find out."

Saying good night to one another, Orion left the room, closing the bedroom door on his way out. He wished she had asked him to stay, but he accepted Alessandra needed a night alone. Not caring that his living room was in disarray, he grabbed a blanket off the floor, hit the light switch, and sank into his couch.

Hideaway Canyon, April 25, 2013

Orion was awakened by a knock at the door. He hurried to answer it, not wanting the noise to disturb his guest. After unlatching the deadbolt and peering around the door as it swung open, he stumbled back onto his couch. "You look like shit," Iker provoked as he and Jess walked through the door.

"You better have something damn important to say," Orion warned. "I'm only working on five hours of sleep."

"Two men showed up at the bar last night, looking for Alessandra and her mother. Is that important enough for you?" Iker sneered as he watched his friend jerk awake.

Sitting up straight, Orion looked from one friend to the other, "Any idea who it was?"

"Not a clue," Jess answered. "It didn't take long for The Rip to fill up after you and Alessandra headed upstairs after dinner last night. We had the usual crowd. A mix of locals and tourists, mostly here because of the new powder." He continued, "I saw the two men come in. They didn't do anything wrong, just didn't belong. Spent a couple of hours scanning the crowd from a booth in the back of the bar. Didn't seem interested in any of the local girls or ski bunnies. Josie waited on them. Neither seemed very talkative. Ordered expensive vodka and tipped well."

"What makes you think they were looking for Alessandra and her mother?" Orion asked.

Iker jumped into the conversation, "That's where I come in."

"Don't you always," Orion retorted with an appreciative smile toward the man.

"I had a smoke with them."

Orion gave a questioning look to Iker. "You don't smoke."

"I did, last night. Went outside for a break to enjoy the cold mountain air, gets hot in the kitchen. Barely had time to locate the

Milky Way before I was joined by the two men. We had a chat," Iker spoke, watching Orion and Jess look at each other and chuckle. They knew Iker didn't chat, but both knew the man was cunning and would take advantage of any opportunity offered. "Before long, we were having a cigarette together, and one of the men pulled out a photo of a woman with a girl. Asked if I'd ever seen them. I looked at the photo a couple of times. The woman could have been Alessandra's sister. Told them I hadn't seen either of them, but I sure would like too."

Orion's face changed from an expression of approval to one preparing to punch someone. He didn't like the thought of anyone talking about Alessandra, and it pissed him off. As Orion's face saw red, Jess focused the man's attention back to their reason for the visit. "I've already checked the cameras, and we've got a couple of good photos of the men. I'd like you to come down to the office and view the footage. We might want to show Alessandra and see if either man looks familiar to her."

"She's still sleeping. Yesterday was rough on her." Orion's expression showed his concern. "But when she wakes up, we'll get her to take a look." He went on to tell his friends about his evening with the woman and how he had pressed Alessandra with additional information. He also told Jess and Iker about Alessandra finding the money and a photo of what they think to be her mother and father. "She seemed as surprised as we did. Claimed she didn't know where it came from." He stopped. "And I believe her. She asked me if she's stolen it. I told her what you found out when running the serial numbers, not connected to any crime, that we can find."

"We'll be in the bar," Jess said, and he and Iker turned to leave. "Come down when she wakes up to look at the video. We need to find out who these guys are and if they are friendly or not."

"Right now, doesn't look it. I am running facial recognition on our two visitors, so far nothing matches in our database. Could be Petrovich's men, could be government officials searching for Alessandra and her mother hoping they could provide evidence to prosecute the man? We just don't know," Iker reiterated what he knew his two friends suspected. Jess and Iker walked out the door.

Shortly after his friends left, the phone rang. Doc Sterling was on the other end, indicating he had Alessandra's test results and would be stopping by in an hour to talk with the woman. Orion readied himself by showering and making a pot of coffee. By the time Alessandra wakened, he had breakfast sitting on the kitchen table.

Orion knew Alessandra was nearby even before seeing or hearing her. His olfactory glands recognized the honey, lemon, and mint aroma he found so alluring. As he turned from the stove to greet the woman, he found himself unable to articulate the commonest of greetings. He marveled at her beauty. She stood barefoot in the doorway, in a pair of faded jeans, jeans he knew she'd worn before, and an oversized sweater. Nothing a clothier would find stylish, definitely not haute couture. Her hair, long and straight, resting on her shoulders, was still wet from her shower, and her face glistened without makeup, maybe a touch of lip gloss. Why did women wear lipstick? he wondered. He'd never liked kissing a woman with lipstick on, but for some unknown reason, he didn't care what she had on her lips; he wanted to kiss them. To Orion, she was the most provocative woman he'd ever met, as heat rose from his toes and up through his body.

"Good morning." Alessandra smiled as she walked into the kitchen, already showered and dressed, distracting Orion from his thoughts.

"Morning. Coffee's hot. Help yourself. Hope you're hungry, I made us omelets."

"That sounds perfect. I am famished...Alessandra paused. "You know, I'm getting spoiled. You've made breakfast for me every morning since I became conscious. I'm not sure how I can ever repay you," she said.

Knowing exactly how he would like to be repaid, but keeping the idea to himself, "no need...it's my pleasure. Just don't shoot me, and we'll call it even," he teased.

As Orion and Alessandra enjoyed the breakfast he had prepared, Orion told Alessandra about Doc Sterling's call and Jess and Iker's visit. Alessandra dropped the fork she was holding, startling not only herself but Orion too. Alessandra's mind flashbacked the man in the dark clothes she thought was following her. She had never seen his face but knew someone was there. When she went to bed at night, the memories were always there, hiding somewhere in her mind. She couldn't remember a time when she didn't have them. The memories themselves were so frequent. They didn't frighten her anymore. However, the actual person showing up, terrified her. Orion could see the fear rising in Alessandra's eyes, knowing it wasn't because of Doc's house call. He reached for her hand and held it for a few moments. With a slight squeeze, he let go, picking up her fork and handing it to her. "You don't need to worry, you are safe here. I'm not going to let anyone hurt you," Orion said, never taking his eyes off the woman as he finished his breakfast.

Alessandra jumped at the knock on the apartment door. Suspecting it was only Doc Sterling's arrival, "Stay right here," Orion said as he rose from the table. Alessandra sat motionless, fearing the arrival of the dark shadow that had been buried deep in her memories. Relieved, she heard Orion call from the living room. "Doc Sterling's here to see you Alessandra." Knowing Alessandra was in good hands with Doc Sterling, Orion went back into the kitchen to clean up their breakfast mess.

Doc's visit didn't take long. He didn't have any additional concerns to offer after viewing the x-rays and Alessandra's tests results. He told her she was well on her way to mending. Doc said it was no longer necessary to keep her ribs wrapped; however, he cautioned she would need to be careful, and her ribs would eventually heal on their own. He rewrapped her wrist to keep it immobile for another couple of weeks. The wrap would be a reminder to her to refrain from placing any significant pressure on her wrist until it was fully healed. With the exception of the wrist, Doc granted her a clean bill of health and was on his way to see other patients.

Alessandra stayed seated on the couch in Orion's living room deep in thought. Doc Sterling's visit had provoked something in her memory, a place far away, a place she didn't recognize. She remembered the pain she felt lying on a cot in a small dark room with a woman sitting on the edge of the small bed holding her hand. From the walls, two men came walking into the room, up to the bed and stood over her. She remembered one of the men bending over to give her a gentle kiss on the forehead, saying the words "kroshka." The other man said, "She'll be all right," as walls seemed to close around her. Lost in her memory, Alessandra was not aware Orion had been watching her. Why couldn't she see their faces? Who were the men and woman in the room with her? Was it her mother and father? When he saw her wipe a tear as it trickled down her cheek, Orion made sure Alessandra knew he was there.

Before he could stop himself from doing so, Orion scooped Alessandra into his arms, placing her in his lap as he sat down. He had been standing in the doorway watching Alessandra, seeing her obvious discomfort, suspecting her memory was returning. What could have happened to Alessandra that she was too afraid to tell him? Or was she remembering and choosing to hide her past from Orion? As Alessandra's head lay snuggled under Orion's chin, he recognized a coolness on his chest caused by tears running down her cheeks and dampening his shirt. Orion didn't speak, not knowing what to say. Knowing he didn't have the strength to only hold her in his arms, he reached for her chin, gently lifting it so his lips would meet hers. Without asking, he kissed her, first only wanting to kiss the tears away, and then losing control to satiate his appetite. Alessandra responded without hesitation, exploring the depths of what Orion offered. Realizing what she was doing, Alessandra pulled away from Orion's arms, searching his dark eyes. "I'm sorry. I didn't mean to. Well, yes, I did mean to…to kiss you, but I can't…I shouldn't." She looked down at the floor. She was afraid to look at Orion, fearing those dark eyes would see right through her. She had wanted Orion to kiss her since the first day she set eyes on him. She feared he would find out she lied. "Jess and Iker are expecting us downstairs, remember?"

Loosening his grip on the woman and knowing she was right, he said, "You have nothing to be sorry about. Neither do I." She knew he'd act the same way if he had the chance again. "You are right. Jess and Iker are expecting us."

"Give me five minutes and we'll head downstairs." Alessandra jumped up, relieved by the excuse to put some distance between the two. Alessandra knew she should stay away from him, like a person needs oxygen to stay alive. Alessandra was beginning to feel like Orion was her oxygen.

Alessandra followed Orion down the stairs and into The Rip. After exchanging greetings with Josie, Jess, and Lyra, the four headed into the office where they found Iker at a desk. Alessandra stood in awe. The office looked like a whole other world, something she never would have guessed hidden behind the door. The office was large and looked official. Next to the American flag, she glimpsed at plagues on the walls, not able to read what they said. She perused the room, recognizing the state-of-the-art technology, several laptops were open on the desks and what she recognized as a supercomputer occupied an entire wall. The room was furnished with comfortably stuffed leather sofas, and a conference table surrounded by enough chairs to fit a dozen people. Multiple flat screens were mounted on the walls for viewing, and when she turned to look back toward the door they entered, the wall appeared to be a sheet of glass. She could see everything on the other side of the wall, looking out into the bar. She had never seen anything like it. Who were these people and why would they need an office like this?

Seeing the shock in Alessandra's face, Iker suggested to his friends, "Maybe we should switch the wall?"

"Alessandra, will the glass wall be too distracting?" Orion asked. Realizing that Alessandra wasn't able to respond, Orion offered, "The wall is for our staff's protection. We can see out, but no one can see in. If we're working in here, we can watch our customers and staff. Keeping everyone safe. But if it bothers you, we can hit the blackout switch, and we'll be prevented from seeing out," he explained.

"No, it's fine. I've just never seen anything like it before." Without asking, she sat with her back to the wall, with a view of The Rip in front of her. Orion glanced at Jess and Iker, noticing Alessandra's choice to sit with her back to the wall too, and wondering if the choice was done intentionally, something all members of The Firm would habitually do. Lyra, hoping to make Alessandra more relaxed, seated herself in the chair next to the woman. She remembered being intimidated by the office the first time she saw it. Lyra had become used to the reality of the three men's job but understood it did take her some time to adjust to it. Iker began searching for the video footage of the two men from the night before, while Jess and Orion found the comfortable sofa they always chose to lounge in. The first two screen feeds were continuous ones, of the men entering and leaving The Rip. The other four screens showed still shots of the men; two zoomed in, focusing on the men's faces. Everyone sat silently watching the feeds, watching Alessandra, and waiting for her to talk. Could one of these men be following her? Were these the two men she remembered when she was lying on the cot? Why couldn't she remember? Alessandra thought about the shadow she kept seeing in her dreams at night. More of her memory was returning, but none of it made sense. She remembered being in her jeep and seeing a shadow walk by. She knew now, she had been sleeping in the back seat. She thought about being with her mother in Paris, and she thought about horseback riding with her father. She searched for the three faces she remembered this morning and wondered who they could be. Her mind flashed back to the old photograph she found in her belongings and then back at the two men in front of her.

Alessandra felt a gentle touch on her hand, returning her focus to the present day and back into the room. Alessandra's look met Lyra's, in a gesture of gratitude. Her eyes continued to travel from Jess to Iker and, finally, rested on Orion. Who were these people? These people she wanted to trust yet, knew nothing about. Fear began to consume her. Not only did she not know anything about herself, but she didn't know who these people were either. She looked around at the room, confused by what she saw. None of this made any sense. No one spoke. Everyone waited, hoping something had jogged Alessandra's memory.

Orion was the first to speak. As though seeing right through Alessandra, he knew she was keeping a secret. He could tell she knew more than what she was saying. Like a couple of nights ago, his patience had waned, and he needed to confront her. This time, he wasn't waiting until tonight. He called her out, in front of everyone in the room, not concerned with his doing so and how it would affect Alessandra. "You remember something. I can tell."

Stunned by Orion's words, fearing she might reveal too much, she said, "No. No, I'm just trying to make sense of my memories."

"Do you know these men?" Orion demanded.

"No." Alessandra paused, becoming more alarmed.

"I don't believe you. You are hiding something from us." Orion's voice began to rise as he demanded answers. Jess gave Iker a look of concern, surprised by Orion's accusation toward Alessandra. Both worried for the man's behavior, thinking one of them might need to jump in soon. Jess had assigned Orion lead on the case, knowing he found the woman. He had nothing but respect for Orion's intuition and loved him like a brother, but he also knew Orion's lack of patience and interrogation skillset could be terrifying, particularly for the young woman. More times than not, though, Orion got the answers he was looking for. He and Iker also knew their friend's objectivity could be thwarted by his personal feelings. Both waited patiently, cautiously, watching Orion and Alessandra.

"You're wrong. I don't know who these men are," Alessandra yelled at Orion, defending herself. Orion was right that she was hiding some of her memories, but why should she tell him everything? She didn't know anything about him and suspected he wasn't telling her everything either.

"You're not telling us everything," Orion lowered his voice flatly, knowing he had stepped out of the line of professional questioning.

She stood up, pointing around the room, "You're not telling me everything either!" Alessandra walked out of the room.

Lyra halted the interrogation, knowing Alessandra's nerves were on edge. Fearing her brother's anger would only cause more harm than good. With one look of warning to the three men seated in the room, she said, "Are you satisfied? Did you have to upset Alessandra? I'll go talk to her—and all three of you leave her alone." She angrily glanced at her brother. "Especially you don't go near her!" Lyra headed for the door. Before stepping through the door and into the bar, she turned back and looked at the three men sitting in the office. "And Alessandra's right. You haven't told her everything either!"

Lyra found Alessandra in Orion's bedroom in tears. "Seems like all I do is cry," she said.

"I'm sorry. I love those three idiots, more than there are stars in the sky, but sometimes they just don't know when to stop," Lyra said. Alessandra handed Lyra the photo she was holding. Looking at the photo, Lyra asked, "Do you remember who this is?"

"No, I don't," she replied quietly. "But I wish I did. I even showed it to Orion last night. I don't know why he doesn't believe me."

Thinking a change of scenery and a little retail shopping could be just what Alessandra needed, Lyra suggested, "Let's go down the mountain, have lunch and do a little shopping. What do you think?"

Smiling at Lyra, Alessandra replied, "Sounds fun! Are you sure?"

"Absolutely. Would it be all right if I took this photo to Jess and Iker so they could run facial recognition? Maybe they can get lucky, and the man in the photo is just a younger version of one of the two that showed up at the bar last night," Lyra asked.

"Sure, but can you give it to them. I don't feel like having a face-to-face with any of them right now."

"I understand. And no harm will come to the photo. You will get it back. It's a long shot, but worth the try," Lyra told her. "And, Alessandra, for what it's worth. I believe you."

"Thank you."

"You get ready and meet me downstairs in thirty minutes. I'll drop this off and run home to change and make sure Skye's covered." She giggled. "I miss having a female to shop with. This is going to be so fun!" Lyra was out the door and down the steps.

She walked into the office with the photo, handing it to her husband. She leaned over and kissed the man while keeping an eye glued to the other two. "Maybe you can use this to check facial recognition on the young man in the photo to the two that showed up at The Rip last night...make sure Alessandra gets it back."

"Thanks, great idea," Jess stated, proud of his wife, knowing Lyra wanted to keep the peace between Orion and Alessandra.

"Alessandra and I are going to lunch and shopping. I'm going to ask Josie to bring Skye with her to the bar tonight when she arrives for her shift. I'm sure the three of you can handle work and our little angel." The three men knew better than to speak as she walked out the door for the second time.

"Your wife," Orion said disgruntled.

"Your sister!" Jess shot back at him. Iker laughed.

After Lyra walked out of the office, Orion turned to his two friends. He told them about having lunch at the Green Bean & Bistro with Alessandra the day before and how the same two men from the photos had been in the restaurant. He'd gotten a good look at them but was sure they hadn't seen Alessandra, nor she them.

Alessandra went into Orion's bedroom to get ready. Glancing at the piles of cash she had counted and left on the floor last night, she knew she had time to return it to the suitcase she found it in. As she did so, she slipped a few bills into her purse. Orion had verified the money hadn't been obtained illegally. *I won't feel guilty spending money I earned.* The thought stunned her. Just like she knew, her name was Alessandra when Orion told her, and just like she knew she had been in Paris with her mother, Alessandra knew she had earned the money; she would never have stolen it.

Within twenty-five minutes, Alessandra headed down the steps from Orion's apartment into The Rip wanting to be on time to meet Lyra. Not seeing Lyra, Alessandra selected a stool at the end of the bar, closest to the front door. Jess was working behind the bar. After placing a tray of wine glasses into their slot above the bar, he walked over to Alessandra. "Sorry about what happened in the office," he apologized. "Can I get you anything?"

"No thanks. I'm as frustrated as the rest of you. A little retail shopping therapy will work wonders," Alessandra joked, trying to make light of the situation. "Did you get the photo?"

"Yes, Iker's running facial recognition as we speak. It should be able to tell us if the young officer in the photo matches either man that showed up last night. And you'll get your photo back, unharmed."

"Thanks. Jess, I'm really not trying to hide anything. I am getting bits and pieces of my memory back. I admit it, but nothing makes sense to me."

"It will, when the time is right." Jess looked at Alessandra. "Orion's a good guy. He's not the most patient, but he means no harm. He just wants answers. Unfortunately, he's a little more zealous than he needs to be. He's very good at his job."

"His job?" Alessandra questioned. "Just what would that be?"

Avoiding the question, Jess replied, "That's for him to tell you."

"Ready to go?" Lyra asked Alessandra as she breezed through the front door. Jess rounded the bar to greet his wife with a kiss, ever so grateful for her timing.

"Absolutely," Alessandra replied as she hopped off the barstool, recognizing the relief in Jess's face and heading for the front door with Lyra.

Too afraid to approach Alessandra with an apology and worried what he might say would anger her again, Orion hid around the corner of the bar, out of Jess and Alessandra's view as they talked at the other end of the bar. He wanted to make the woman smile just like he had witnessed his brother-in-law do. A slight pang of jealousy hit Orion, but he brushed it away, knowing how much Jess loved his sister and how happy he was for the two of them. Orion had always known he wouldn't have the type of home both his brother, Crux, and sister, Lyra, had found. One that allowed for a family and a place to call home. Yet knowing those things had never been in the cards for him, Alessandra was the type of woman that made him think about having both. *Why not?* he thought. Orion jumped when he heard Iker. "Need you to move out of the way, bro!" He moved aside sure he heard his friend give a low snicker. Orion grabbed a beer before heading back into the office, embarrassed his friend caught him hiding around the corner.

The sun was shining over the blanket of snow that covered the scenic mountain town of Hideaway Canyon, as Lyra and Alessandra headed down the mountain into town for lunch and a day of shopping. Alessandra's excitement was revealed on her face by a wide smile. As they reached the spot in the road where Alessandra's jeep had gone off the road, Alessandra asked, "Lyra, do you mind pulling off the side of the road?"

Looking at the woman, Lyra smiled and said, "Of course not." Lyra left her truck running as they sat, looking down toward the deep ravine, and at the spot, Alessandra's jeep had landed off the road. Both women could see the damaged aspen and pine trees that marked the spot so clearly. Remnants of tire tracks and footprints, still remained covered by more recent inches of snow, making it impossible to miss. Lyra reached across the seat and touched Alessandra's hand, "Are you okay?"

Alessandra sighed, "Yes. I guess I just had hope seeing the sight again would trigger my memory. When Orion took me to the hospital for my tests, he pointed the spot out, but I just can't remember that night."

"You will in time," Lyra encouraged Alessandra. "Shall we continue?"

With a laugh, "Yes, let's get shopping!"

It wasn't long before the women were engulfed in the allure of restaurants, boutiques, and gift shops that lined the main street. Lyra and Alessandra browsed through shop after shop of clothes, shoes and boots, and jewelry, modeling outfits for one another. "Alessandra, you have to try this on!" She glanced up from the clothing rack to see the shimmering sequined top Lyra was holding up. "This would look amazing on you," Lyra told her.

She nodded. "It's beautiful but I don't have any place to wear it." She looked at the price tag. "And it's too expensive!" Relentless in her efforts to talk Alessandra into trying the garment on, she plucked an identical top in the color turquoise from the rack. "Okay. Okay, if you try one on, so will I." The women smiled at each other and headed into their dressing room.

Alessandra swirled around, looking into the mirror as Lyra looked on. Despite the ugly scar revealed on Alessandra's shoulder, she looked beautiful in the sequined top. "You have to get it!" Lyra said, suspecting the scar was a remnant of a gunshot wound. The two women laughed and played dress-up, trying on everything in the store, eventually making a decision on what they would purchase.

"You can wear it tonight!" Lyra began explaining.

"Tonight?" Alessandra questioned.

"A local band is performing at The Rip tonight. At the end of every ski season, we sponsor a fundraiser, along with other Hideaway Canyon businesses, supporting a local adoption agency called Creating Canyon Families. All the money raised goes to support adoptive parents and their children."

Alessandra decided to buy it. "You talked me into buying it, but only if you find something too!" With a sly smile, Lyra held up the matching top in a different color. Understanding, Alessandra nodded with a great big smile. Alessandra turned away so Lyra wouldn't see the sadness in her eyes. She was having so much fun and wished the woman was her sister. She wished they could be friends. She remembered the other photo she found of the two little girls. She wondered if she ever had a sister or was the photo of a friend. As the women continued to shop and try on clothes, Alessandra listened as Lyra told the story of how she was found by Oaklin Grey and how the entire Grey family; Oaklin, Abel, Crux, and Orion cared for her, while searching for her biological parents. She was eventually adopted by the Grey family. Lyra told Alessandra how the Grey Foundation continued to fund the Creating Canyon Families organization, which was originally founded by Oaklin and Abel Grey to help and encourage other families to adopt.

"It's our family legacy, to build families and provide a home, however that might look. Families come in all shapes and sizes, and absolutely everyone needs a place to call home," Lyra explained proudly, holding up a pair of boots, "Look at these boots, which one of us is buying them!"

The women giggled at their arms filled with shopping bags, as they walked a couple of blocks on snow shoveled sidewalks to the Main Street Diner for lunch.

Finding a booth by the front window, depositing their bags on the seats beside them, Lyra and Alessandra scrutinized the menu. Before long, a waitress approached with two glasses of water. "Lyra Grey, what brings you to town?" Charlee Anderson asked.

"Hi, Charlee." Lyra looked up, immediately knowing whose voice she was hearing, seeing the woman's focus on Alessandra. "Charlee, this is my friend, Alessandra. Alessandra, Charlee Anderson."

"Nice to meet you," Alessandra greeted the woman.

"Nice to meet you, too. You're not from around here, are you?" Charlee inquired.

Alessandra answered, "No," not knowing how to explain her situation and how she arrived at Hideaway Canyon.

Lyra rescued Alessandra. "She's visiting our family from out of town." Then she redirected the conversation away from Alessandra, "We've been shopping all morning. We've had so much fun." Lyra knew the woman well and changing the subject to shopping and fashion would occupy the waitress's mind and move her thoughts away from quizzing Alessandra.

"It's sure different from when we grew up, isn't it? What did we have, three stores?" the waitress responded, not waiting for an answer to her question from Lyra. "So how's that gorgeous brother of yours?"

Lyra knew, for years, Charlee had tried to deceive her way into becoming part of the Grey family; it didn't seem to matter how she accomplished it. The Greys were friends with the Andersons, and Lyra loved Mr. and Mrs. Anderson, almost like her own parents. Lyra never could understand how two, such wonderful people, had produced a child like Charlee. The Anderson ranch bordered on the east side of Grey's ranch, with a river separating the two properties. Throughout the years, Lyra had witnessed both her brothers vie for Charlee's affections at one time or other; fortunately, the stars didn't align. *Luckily*, she thought, *that didn't happen.* Lyra admitted Charlee was an attractive woman; however, she wasn't convinced the woman's heart was in the right place. "Which one?" Lyra asked mischievously, reminding the waitress she tried to get her hooks into both of the Grey brothers.

"You know Orion and I have always had a special relationship," Charlee scolded in fun. "I heard he was back in town. I can't believe he hasn't come to see me."

"We've all been busy," Lyra looked at Alessandra, sensing her discomfort. Alessandra sat quietly, listening to the women talk. She didn't like Charlee. Her feelings for the woman really weren't fair. She had just met her and didn't even know the woman. Alessandra could see why any man would find her attractive. She was beautiful. She had no right to judge the woman and silently told herself so. That didn't change her feelings. Alessandra writhed with jealousy as the woman talked with Lyra about her brother and as she thought about the woman in Orion's arms.

"He doesn't have a date now, does he? Charlee baited Lyra for information as her eyes lingered on Alessandra. "Let him know I'll be at the fundraiser tonight. I'm sure he'll want to see me. And he can buy me a drink." She laughed, knowing the event was open bar. "I'll save a dance, especially for him." She winked. "Now, do you ladies know what you want to order?"

"I'll take today's soup and salad special, with an ice tea," Alessandra ordered quickly, wanting to give the woman a reason to leave.

"I'll have the same," Lyra added, feeling the same way. After the waitress had gone, Lyra apologized, "I'm sorry about Charlee. Our families have been friends for years, and our ranches are divided by the river." Not sure her explanation had offered Alessandra any comfort, she continued, "And Charlee's been trying to become a member of the Grey family since high school—unsuccessfully, of course."

Struggling with her feelings of jealousy, Alessandra changed the subject, "So do you need any help in the bar tonight?"

"Absolutely not. Tonight's our night to have fun! All the businesses in town help with part of the event. The Rip provides the venue and the band, and food is catered by the Green Bean & Bistro. There's even a cleaning crew that comes in afterward and preps the bar for the next day's business." Lyra paused as she explained the importance of the evening. "Tonight, you and I are guests, as are all the Greys and our staff. Oaklin and Abel planned it that way many years ago, and we've kept the tradition. Our parents always called it one of their 'date nights.'"

It didn't take long before Charlee served the dishes they had ordered, and the women indulged. "This is delicious. Thank you so much for inviting me, Lyra," Alessandra said.

"Don't thank me. I should be thanking you." Lyra stopped eating, meeting Alessandra's eyes. "Alessandra, can we be friends?"

As tears began to gather in Alessandra's eyes, she replied, "I am so touched. I was thinking the same thing earlier. I would love to be your friend," Alessandra said as she felt Lyra's hand touch hers, "I don't know if I've ever had a friend," Alessandra said out loud.

"Well, you have one now…for life," Lyra replied.

"The day's been wonderful. I don't know how I will ever repay your kindness. I would be honored to call you my friend."

"Your friendship is payment enough. Now, let's finish our lunches and head home. I want to pamper myself before the evening begins, and you should too. It will be a late night, but I guarantee one that will be fun." Lyra laughed. "And we're going to own the dance floor in our new outfits!"

Charlee returned to the booth to check on the two women. When the women declined to order anything else, she handed Alessandra the check. "I'll see you tonight." Charlee solidified her intent to monopolize Orion's time at the fundraiser. Hearing the door open and seeing an attractive man scrutinize the restaurant, before finding a seat at the diner's counter, the waitress slithered away.

After paying for lunch, Lyra and Alessandra walked to the truck to stow their packages and head home to Hideaway Canyon. On the return trip, Lyra suggested Alessandra come to her house to get ready for the party. She explained that the women could continue with their "girl" time, relax, and enjoy a preparty glass of wine, thinking to herself the time together was good for Alessandra. The women would have fun getting dressed for the party, and Lyra would help Alessandra put her hair in an updo, which she could style and would look great with her new purchase. Jess, Orion, and Iker would be busy directing traffic at The Rip, getting everything set up. And she'd call Jess and tell him to shower at Orion's. "You know men, it takes them five minutes to shower." Lyra explained to Alessandra that Josie would bring Skye, along with her twins, to the bar, and before the bar became too loud and the crowd wild, Doc Sterling and his wife would take the little ones to their home for a sleepover. The Sterling's loved their role in Hideaway Canyon as surrogate grandparents in their community. And Doc had delivered almost all the little ones in the small village.

Passing The Rip, on their way to Lyra's home, Alessandra recognized her jeep sitting in the parking lot beside the stairway leading up to Orion's apartment, the apartment she had been staying in for over a week. "That's my jeep," Alessandra mentioned out loud.

"Wonderful. Jess and I ran into Rob Taylor and his wife yesterday. Rob told us the parts came in a few days ago, and he would have the work done by sometime today. Jess must have sent Orion over to pick it up for you," Lyra stated. As Lyra continued to chat about Rob's family and their friendship with the Greys on the final leg of their drive to Lyra's house, Alessandra knew she didn't have any other reason to remain at Hideaway Canyon. She had healed; besides her wrapped wrist and the small scar on her forehead, no evidence was left behind that she had been in an accident. Where would she go? What would she do? Alessandra had no idea where her home was, or if she even had one. From the looks of what had been packed in her car, she had been moving. If only she could remember, she would know what to do. What Alessandra did know was that Hideaway Canyon wasn't her home? It was home to someone else. It was home to the Greys. Alessandra knew it was time for her to pack her jeep and drive away.

The truck came to a stop at Lyra's home. Alessandra stepped out of the vehicle onto a ground covered with a blanket of soft white snow. She looked up to see the beautiful cottage, storybook perfect. "Your home is beautiful," she exclaimed, as she helped Lyra gather their shopping bags and carefully maneuver the slippery sidewalk leading to the home.

Lyra opened the door inviting Alessandra in and telling her to make herself comfortable. "Let's take our coats off, and we can drop your packages off in the spare room. It has a bath attached where you can shower and get ready for the party. I'll give you a quick tour and make us a cup of hot tea. We've got plenty of time to sit and relax by the fireplace, if you'd like, before we need to start getting ready." Alessandra nodded, knowing there was nothing she would like to do more than just that. Lyra led her down the hall and into a beautiful bedroom furnished with warm tones of brown, blue, and gray so Alessandra could drop her packages off. A quick tour of the home ended in the kitchen, where Lyra prepared two cups of tea. At the direction of Lyra, Alessandra wandered into the home's great room, where she lingered in front of the fireplace, enjoying the warmth from the fire as she scanned the photos along the mantle. As she entered the room, Lyra saw Alessandra looking at the family pictures. "Some of my favorite photos," she said, handing one of the cups to Alessandra. "The first one on your right is of my family—my parents, Oaklin and Abel, and that's Crux, the oldest, who you'll meet tonight, with Orion and me. The next one, my boys, Jess, Orion, Crux, and Iker, taken about two years ago. They have an inseparable bond, built from years on the job together, more than that though, an unbreakable friendship filled with loyalty and love." She laughed. "Of course, it's difficult to recognize their love for one another, the way they argue. The rest you probably recognize, our little Skye."

Alessandra picked up the silver-framed photo of the little girl with the golden curls. She stared at Skye dressed in a pink tutu. Alessandra's legs became weak, and her body trembled. Alessandra's eyes began to water as she cradled the photo in her hands and pressed it into her heart. "I love the ballet. I remember going to the ballet with my parents. My mother was a ballerina." Lyra jumped up from the overstuffed chair she sat in, gathering her friend in her arms, understanding the emotions that Alessandra must be feeling as the memory returned.

"Alessandra, you had another memory. What a wonderful thing to remember, ballet." Lyra held her friend. "I know Jess, Orion, and Iker will be able to help you find your parents and your home."

Leading Alessandra into the spare bedroom, Lyra suggested, "Why don't you take a short nap? If you aren't up in an hour, I'll wake you so you can get ready for the party. I think a nap and a party is just what you need. We should celebrate. Your memory is returning!"

Alessandra agreed as she thanked Lyra and watched her walk out the door. She moved toward the four-poster bed calling her name. Emotionally exhausted, she found sleep.

While Alessandra napped, Lyra called Jess at The Rip. She checked with her husband on the progress they were making, setting up for the fundraiser, and asked if he needed any help while filling him in on their shopping trip and Alessandra's memory flashback. She suggested tomorrow might be a good time to meet with Alessandra again to help her connect the bits and pieces of her memory. "And tomorrow, Jess, I think it's time you and the boys come clean with everything you know or suspect about Alessandra's family. She's a strong woman, and I know she can handle the truth." Jess listened proudly to his wife's suggestion, knowing she was right; it was time Alessandra found out who she was. Lyra hung up, knowing all was well at The Rip and wanting to make a quick call to Josie to check on Skye before waking Alessandra to get dressed for the party.

The libidinous woman in the diner had no idea she'd assisted the man in finding the woman he thought to be Alessandra Petrovich. He needed to find Alessandra before anyone else did. Charlee Anderson had made it clear to the attractive man that she was game for anything. He smiled, thinking of the beautiful woman; however, he knew it was imperative that his focus remain on finding Alessandra. Unfortunately, he didn't have time for a liaison with the seductive woman from the diner, but he was wise enough to use her tonight to complete his mission. Charlee had given the Creating Canyon Families fundraiser flyer to the attractive man, suggesting to him it was the event of the year, something he must attend. Everyone from the community and tourists alike would show up in the village of Hideaway Canyon, for this event. He knew if Alessandra was living in the mountain town and he had any chance of finding her soon, tonight would be the best opportunity. The man settled into a room at The Inn at Hideaway Canyon, propping his legs up to relax and enjoy the bottle of vodka and cigar he had purchased. He dressed in his usual dark Armani suit having no need to hurry. He wanted the bar to be crowded. He wanted to maintain his anonymity. Tonight, he wanted to blend in, hoping to find Alessandra.

Alessandra woke to the faint sound of water running, knowing Lyra must be in the shower. She peered around the room from under the warm, soft covers, appreciating the comfort she found. Everything about Lyra—and her family, this house, the village of Hideaway Canyon—reminded Alessandra of a deep desire for a home, a forever home, one she felt safe in, one with a family, and one she'd never have to leave. Alessandra knew her memory was coming back. Although most of the memories confused her, she had a feeling inside her telling her that her presence in Hideaway Canyon brought danger to her new friends and people she now loved. Alessandra resigned herself to the fact that she needed to leave, but not tonight. Tonight, just this one night, she would forget her worries and enjoy the evening with her friends!

The night was a special night for Alessandra. She thought how much she wanted Orion to notice her, she hadn't told Lyra and barely admitted it to herself. The only clothes Alessandra had with her were the ones she'd purchased during their shopping trip earlier in the day, luckily Lyra had convinced her to buy a new outfit, including lingerie and new shoes. Lyra had assured her friend, whatever she didn't have with her Lyra owned and she could borrow. As they dressed for the party, the two women sauntered from one room to the others, like sisters, appreciating their purchases and assisting each other when needed. Lyra chose to wear her hair down for the evening, but she insisted Alessandra let her style hers in an updo for the evening. Watching Alessandra in the mirror, Lyra said, "Orion already likes you, but he's going to be stunned by your beauty tonight—just you wait and see!" She held up a pair of diamond earrings. "These were my mother's…and they will look perfect with your outfit."

"Oh, no, Lyra, I can't possibly wear them. You should put them on."

Lyra moved her hair behind her ears to display a dazzling pair of aquamarine and diamond earrings. "Jess bought these for me for our anniversary last year. Now you know why I grabbed the turquoise top," she said and smiled, "hope you don't mind twinning!"

"Not at all," Alessandra said with a laugh. "And thank you for letting me borrow the earrings."

By the time Lyra and Alessandra pulled up to the front door of The Rip guests had already begun to arrive. The women could hear the music vibrate their sounds through the walls as they parked. Lyra saw Alessandra's hesitation to get out of the truck. She looked at her friend, "It's going to be all right, just have fun tonight. You're among friends." Lyra sat with Alessandra as they watched a stream of men and women walk through the front door. "Ready?"

With a big smile, Alessandra opened the truck door. "Yes, I'm ready!" she said laughing.

Alessandra held the door for Lyra to enter the bar, following close behind. The band decided to take a break just as the women entered. As Alessandra walked through the entranceway, she was halted by what felt like hundreds of eyes staring at her. The music had stopped. She turned around to see who stood behind her, but no one was there. Feeling sick, she was struck with panic as the room started to whirl. Where was Lyra? Before Alessandra could faint, Lyra stepped forward to rescue her new friend, wrapping their arms together and leading them deeper into the crowd. Alessandra could only follow, as Lyra guided her to the bar where she saw the four men waiting. A loud, deep laughter resonating from the back corner of the bar catching Alessandra's attention. She tried peering through the crowd to see who the sound came from but saw nothing. She turned back to her new friends. The man in the dark Armani suit knew Alessandra Petrovich had arrived.

Jess embraced his wife with a sensual kiss on the lips and wrapped his other arm around Alessandra, pulling both women close. "Ladies, you made quite an entrance," he chuckled. Looking at the three other men with a smirk on his face. "I don't know about you guys, but I've got what I want. Ladies, follow me." He turned the ladies away from the other three men at the bar, leading the two beautiful women to a large table, by the stage, reserved for the Greys. By the time they sat down, the cocktail waitress had arrived with a couple of beers, a bottle of wine, and two glasses for the women. After drinking her first glass of wine, quite quickly Jess and Lyra noticed, Alessandra's head had stopped spinning, and she relaxed to find herself immersed in conversation with the couple. Jess and Lyra introduced her to scores of guests, one by one, as they approached their table to chat. Alessandra had no idea how she would remember all the names, but she was enjoying herself. Even though she was having a good time, she wondered why Orion hadn't joined them. Alessandra hadn't talked to Orion since morning, and he didn't say a word to her when she and Lyra arrived. Of course, Jess swept them to their table rather quickly. There hadn't even been time for introductions. She recognized Crux from one of the photos on Lyra's fireplace mantle.

Iker and Crux chuckled as they looked at each other, watching Orion sulk standing at the end of the bar. Lyra had called Crux and told him the story of Orion finding the woman on the side of the road. However, she'd never mentioned how beautiful the woman was. After hearing about the woman's accident, Crux offered his assistance, if they needed him. He'd been assured everything was handled, and with the weather conditions, the ranch needed him more. Now, seeing the woman, he wished he had insisted on leaving the ranch. Crux had listened to his little sister on the phone as she suggested the stars were aligning for Orion, insinuating the woman had arrived for Orion. He could only laugh thinking of Oaklin and how much Lyra reminded him of his mother. Glancing at Iker, he said, "I'm not a fool," then turning to his brother and holding a gaze on Orion. "I'm going to introduce myself to the beautiful lady." He sauntered to the Grey table knowing if Lyra's suggestion was true, and it often was, his brother would be fuming with anger. If Orion had no interest in the woman, Crux had every intention of making his known.

Knowing Crux's words and action had raised the level of anger building in Orion's body, Iker made his escape. "Me too, bro. I'm joining the fun. Are you coming?" Tapping his friend on the back, Iker didn't wait for an answer. He wanted no part of the receiving end of the man's anger. He had a feeling the "Grey brothers' rivalry" would rear its ugly head tonight. And he wasn't going to miss the show. He looked forward to sitting back and enjoy every minute of it.

Arriving at the table, in his usual fashion, Crux kissed his sister and told her how beautiful she looked, then turned to Alessandra and introduced himself. As Jess saw the eldest Grey brother introduce himself to Alessandra, he smiled, recognizing how interesting the night had become. After the brief introductory interlude, Crux gestured toward the chair, asking if he could sit down next to Alessandra. Alessandra nodded as she watched the man confidently seat himself in the chair next to her. She smiled at Iker as he approached the table, glancing behind the man, only to be disappointed Orion hadn't followed. An empty chair remained between Jess and Iker, across from Alessandra. Catching Alessandra's glance across the table, Lyra gave her husband a look, one he knew well. Jess stood up, asked anyone if they needed a refill, and excused himself. It was his job to find out what corner Orion chose to brood in. Lyra wanted to thump her youngest brother on the head.

The band's break ended, and the music began. Josie arrived with Skye and the twins, and the children played around the table. Doc Sterling joined the Grey table, introducing his wife, Jacinta, to Alessandra. Everyone was dancing, eating, and enjoying the party. Guests were talking about the silent auction and placing their bids.

Jess found Orion sulking in the same spot he had left him. He sidestepped his friend to grab a couple of beers from the refrigeration unit behind the bar. After Jess twisted off the tops, he handed one to Orion before taking a long drag on his own.

"Thanks." Orion nodded.

"You going to join the party?" Jess asked.

"Yeah, sure," Orion said without moving. "I made a fool out of myself, didn't I?" Orion knew the answer. Jess didn't respond. "When Alessandra walked through the door, I was stunned. I couldn't speak. I've never seen her look like that." Jess only listen as Orion stumbled through his thoughts. "I mean, I thought she was beautiful before. She's just never worn makeup or dressed like that…that top…her hair." Orion chugged his beer as he choked out the words, trying to describe his feelings to his friend.

Jess wanted to laugh; however, he knew it would only provoke his friend, and also he understood. He'd been in Orion's shoes. "I remember a time when I was being stupid with your sister. You threatened to kill me if I hurt her. But you know what, brother. You followed up, telling me not to miss out on the best opportunity I would ever have in my lifetime." Jess smiled at his friend, giving him a slap on the back. "You were right. So don't mess up your opportunity. You deserve something great too, and you'd be a fool not to go for that!" Jess picked up the tray to walk to their table. "I like her, and I know you do too. I think she'd be good for you." Jess walked away, knowing Orion would join them.

"I've been waiting for a dance," Lyra said as her husband returned to the table and set the tray of drinks on it. Jess offered a hand to his wife, sweeping her off toward the dance floor.

"Daddy, Daddy," Jess heard a little voice calling behind him, as he turned and hauled his daughter up and into his other arm. Jess smiled while he danced, holding his wife and daughter, appreciating the best thing that ever happened to him.

"Do you dance?" Crux asked Alessandra.

"I don't know," Alessandra responded. Seeing his puzzled look, Alessandra pointed to her head with a giggle. "I really truly don't know."

Catching her meaning, Crux laughed too, extending his hand. "Let's find out!"

"Let's," Alessandra giggled as she stood up. As Crux ushered her to the dance floor in front of them, Alessandra saw Charlee Anderson as she emerged from the crowd. Alessandra's eyes followed the beautiful woman as she hustled toward Orion, who was on a direct path to join their table. Alessandra couldn't take her eyes off the woman as she seemed to devour Orion. Crux gently placed his hand on Alessandra's shoulders, witnessing the same greeting Charlee gave his brother. He distracted Alessandra and headed her onto the dance floor, not before seeing the hurt in the woman's eyes. This Grey was not a fool, and he had every intention of making sure Alessandra had a good time.

Alessandra was having a wonderful time. In addition to actually being a great dancer, Crux kept the conversation light. He talked about the family ranch and his love for ranching and his family. He was charming and almost as attractive as his brother. Orion and Crux could have passed as twins. Crux was clean-cut; he had a polished and professional look. He expressed his surprise that Orion hadn't already invited her out to see the ranch, and he extended the invitation saying he wouldn't take no for an answer. During her second dance with Orion's brother, Alessandra saw Charlee lead Orion onto the dance floor. Her heart sunk as she witnessed the scene. Deciding she wouldn't let the woman's actions ruin her night, she returned her attention to Crux. She liked him. In some ways, he reminded her of his brother; in others, they seemed so different. After three dances, Alessandra pleaded exhaustion and the need for a drink in order to convince Crux to return her to their table.

It didn't take long before Skye, who was playing around the table with Josie's twins, made her way onto her Uncle Crux's lap. The little girl really was adorable. The night continued, everyone taking turns dancing. Alessandra, wondering where Orion, had disappeared too. She hadn't seen him since his dance with Charlee. Iker interrupted Alessandra's thoughts, asking her to dance, admitting he wasn't as smooth as Crux. As she rose from the table, she heard Jess and Lyra warning their daughter, that it was almost time to leave with the Sterlings. Even the little girl didn't want to leave the party, she was having so much fun.

After her dance with Iker, Alessandra saw their drinks had been refreshed, and Crux was joining Doc Sterling's wife on the dance floor. Doc Sterling was shuffling the children to the front, near the door, knowing his wife would join them after her dance. It wasn't late, but Doc teased, "It's time for the children and old folks to head to home." Alessandra offered to help Doc corral the children to the front door, where they would wait for Jacinta to finish her dance with Crux.

The Grey men leaned up against the bar. The fundraiser had drawn the usual crowd, locals and tourists. Everyone seemed to be having a wonderful time. Iker was the first to talk. "Two in the front corner of the bar, keeping an eye on everyone entering and leaving, just like last night, vodka and cigars, they're the two from last night, we saved the video." The other three men acquiesced as he continued, "Number three, sitting in the back corner, near the back door. Seems like he's having a good time. Never seen him in here before." Iker shared what he saw. "It seems Charlee Anderson knows the man, or she wants to know him. They seem rather cozy."

"We'll keep watch, but none of them have done anything wrong," Jess instructed. "Anything back from facial rec?"

"Nothing yet. I'll grab a couple still shots of our third guy off the video tonight and run him too," Iker responded.

Not wanting to alarm the guests or Lyra and Alessandra, Jess said, "Let's get back and enjoy the party."

The men approached their table to find Lyra sitting by herself. "Where's Alessandra?" Orion asked uneasily.

Frustrated that Orion hadn't paid more attention to Alessandra, Lyra didn't respond.

"Lyra, where's Alessandra?" he asked again with a curious look.

"If you'd asked her to dance, you would know."

"That's why I'm here," he said, realizing Lyra was trying to make a point.

"She's helping Doc Sterling corral the children. Doc and Jacinta are getting ready to leave."

Orion looked around the bar, locating Alessandra and Doc at the entrance. On a mission, he headed to the front door, not letting anyone interrupt him. Doc saw Orion approach, "Great party.

Alessandra is helping me keep the children corralled until my wife finishes her goodbyes." He laughed.

Hardly able to keep his focus on Doc's words, he said, "Thanks, glad you could make it." Orion watched Alessandra turn to face him. Keeping Alessandra's gaze, he heard Jacinta speak to him.

"Another wonderful party, Orion," Jacinta said as she hugged him. "Like each year, the event helps a wonderful cause. We've got to get the children home and in bed. They're all wound up like usual. With Doc's special hot chocolate and a bedtime story, I think we'll manage." She and Doc hustled the children out the front door, leaving Orion and Alessandra standing together.

As she stood face-to-face with Orion, Alessandra thought about how she had waited all day for this party. She wore the outfit she purchased while shopping with Lyra, hoping it would impress Orion. She dressed methodically, wanting everything to look perfect. She wanted Orion to notice her. Why hadn't he? Why had he seemed to avoid her? "I suppose we should get back to the others," Alessandra said, breaking the uncomfortable moment as she turned and took a step toward the table upfront.

Orion stopped her motion, gently reaching for her hand and refusing to let go. "I apologize. I mean I should apologize to you. The moment you walked through the door, I...I was stunned, you look. You look beautiful tonight, Alessandra." Orion refused to take his eyes off her even though his words weren't coming outright. "I mean...I didn't mean. You've always looked beautiful since the first day I saw you." A slow smile appeared on Alessandra's face. Orion noticed. She had hoped all day, to hear those words come from Orion. Orion saw a twinkle in Alessandra's eyes and the slightest of an upturn on her lips. He tightened his grip on her hand and led her, willingly, toward the dance floor. Alessandra had no intention of letting go.

Orion led Alessandra into the middle of the crowded dance floor just as the beat of the music slowed. When the couple reached the center of the floor, Orion turned slowly toward Alessandra, knowing exactly where he wanted to place his hands, gracefully slipping his arm around her waist and pulling her gently toward him.

Alessandra could feel the heat rise in Orion's body, or was it her own, as she slipped her hand around his back and rested her bandaged wrist on his chest, tilting her head slightly to meet his eyes. As she watched Orion, from eyes hidden under her long brown lashes, she saw passion in his dark eyes. She held his gaze as they rocked to the rhythm of the music, neither needing to speak, refusing to break the sensations erupting within the embrace. Orion held Alessandra as close as his body would allow, maintaining a measured distance, afraid his desire would be revealed. Not realizing how much time had passed, Orion felt a swift tap on his shoulder, looking over to see Lyra and Crux moving off the dance floor. "Bro, the music stopped," Crux said with a wide smile, "at least for some of us." With a wink to Alessandra, Crux guided his sister to their table where Jess and Iker waited. Embarrassed, Orion and Alessandra followed. Jess and Iker smiled at each other as they watched the couple approach, Orion holding Alessandra's chair, immediately sitting down next to her claiming his territory.

The band announced they would return for their last set, after taking a fifteen-minute break. Jess took the opportunity to signal a waitress to take the table's order for their last round. Crux decided to use the opportunity to find out more about the beautiful woman who mysteriously arrived at Hideaway Canyon and captivated not only his brother's heart but seemingly his entire table of friends. Crux didn't think of himself as a cynic; however, it was his job to look out for his family, and he couldn't help but wonder if this woman was too good to be true. Clearly, she was attractive. She had a beautiful smile and an easy laugh and seemed forthright and genuine during their conversation while dancing. It just didn't hold well with him, that someone wasn't looking for her.

"I'd like to propose a toast." Crux held up his glass as the rest of the table joined in. "To Oaklin and Abel Grey and another success-ful Creating Canyon Families fundraiser." With huge smiles across everyone's face, the group raised their glasses for the tribute. "To fam-ily"—Crux looked toward Alessandra—"even our new members."

Lyra raised her glass with warmth in her eyes. "To Alessandra." Alessandra returned a smile to Lyra, hiding a need to cry. How could she ever leave these people? Yet she knew she had no choice. This wasn't her home. The Greys embodied everything she knew she wanted—love from a family and a home.

"So, Alessandra, I hope you'll have an opportunity to visit the ranch before you leave." Crux surprised everyone by asking. Orion and Lyra stared at their older brother. Had Alessandra told Crux she was leaving?

"Yes, I've…I would like to see it," she stuttered as she faced Orion's brother, "I'm so grateful, so grateful to all of you for everything you've done." Alessandra continued, "I'm healed. I'm so sorry for overstaying my welcome."

"You have not overstayed your welcome. You are welcome in our home for as long as you would like," Lyra stated, using a voice they all knew too well. "We love having you. You are my friend. You have become part of our family."

"I know it's time for me to leave. I was only stopping for one night. I wanted to enjoy the mountains. But then the officer told me the road was closed…the snowstorm…I had to find a hotel… and then the deer." Alessandra stopped talking, shocked at her own words. She looked at Lyra, and then one by one, at each person sitting around the table, until she arrived at Orion, sitting next to her. Alessandra's eyes met Orion, and she began to talk. "I remember. I was moving to California." She continued slowly, her eyes starting to water. "I love the mountains and planned to spend the night. To go hiking. But the storm came. It was bad. The road was closed, and an officer directed me off the highway onto a side road. I was looking for a hotel when the deer jumped out onto the road, and she had a baby with her. I swerved to miss them." She touched Orion's hand and said, "I remember." Alessandra was grateful to hear the band started its last set.

Lyra moved swiftly, kneeling beside Alessandra's chair, cradling the woman in her arms. "It's wonderful, Alessandra, another memory has returned."

Alessandra looked up with a smile, not feeling happy. "Yes, it is." She excused herself and went to the lady's room. Lyra followed.

The four men stayed sitting at the table, looking from one to the other, not sure what to say. All of them had wanted Alessandra to regain her memory; they'd even tried to help. Today, she'd been able to recall a large chunk of her memory from the accident. It would be easier for her to piece her life together. Wasn't that a good thing? Why was the mood rather somber at the table? Why did Lyra seem angry at them again?

"Looks like we have more to celebrate tonight, Alessandra getting more of her memory back," Crux stated, feeling proud for instigating the memory and watching his brother's reaction.

Orion glared at Crux. "Not the part about her leaving." Angry, he told the men at the table, "I don't want her to leave."

Satisfied with Orion's realization, Crux stood up and asked if anyone else needed a beer. Knowing the elder Grey brother had goaded Orion into admitting his feelings about Alessandra, Iker laughed. He stood up and joined Crux as he headed to the bar with a pat on the back he said. "I always knew the old man was full of tricks."

Jess stayed at the table with Orion, listening to the music and wondering when his brother-in-law would talk. Lyra returned to the table. "I want both of you to know that Alessandra is my friend, and she is welcome to stay here as long as she wants. Remember, she has nowhere to go. However, I think she now feels obligated to leave, and that's her choice, but please stop encouraging her to do so. If she wants to visit or ever return, she is welcome."

"Of course, I like her." Jess understood. "How about one more dance with your husband?" Lyra accepted too angry to want to be around her brothers.

Before his sister left the table with her husband, Orion said, "Talk to your other brother. I don't want her to go."

Wondering why her brother seemed so dense, she said, "You'd better tell her before it's too late. Tell her you don't want her to go." Jess grabbed his wife and swirled her onto the dance floor.

Orion waited for Alessandra to return to the table. Where was she? he thought. Iker and Crux returned to the table with a beer for Orion. He took a long draw before checking his watch for the second time. He scanned the dance floor as he saw Lyra and Jess return.

Lyra questioned, "She's not back?" Orion shook his head. The band finished their last song and began to pack up. The bar cleared quickly after the music stopped. Where was she?

"I'll go check on her," Lyra looked worried.

As she looked toward the ladies' room, she saw Alessandra appear from the dark hallway followed by a large man in the Armani suit. Lyra sat down as the four men at the Grey table stood up on alert, watching Alessandra walk slowly toward them with a look of shock on her face, followed closely by the man. They knew he was packing but, so were they. Who was the man, and what did he want with Alessandra? Adrenaline pumped through Orion's veins. Anger mounted. He remained calm.

The Grey men already knew the bar had emptied quickly, and only four cleaning crew remained. Earlier, they had seen the two suspicious men, who had shown up for the second night, leave after the band began to break up. Although suspicious that all three men were together, now they weren't sure. Orion took a step forward as Alessandra approached with the man. Her eyes darted nervously at him. "Alessandra, is everything all right?" Orion asked the question, reaching out to her. The man in the Armani suit stood directly behind Alessandra and said nothing.

"This man...he said he's been looking for me," Alessandra answered Orion. Moving in unison to a defensive position. Jess stepped in front of Lyra, while Crux and Iker moved beside Orion, preparing to protect both women.

"Does the man have a name?" Orion asked Alessandra cautiously, never taking his eyes off her, nor the man's hands.

"He says his name is Koysta Ulanova. He says he's my uncle," she answered nervously.

The name sounded familiar to Iker. He wasn't sure why. "You have an ID?" he asked the man.

The man raised his hands and pointed to the top pocket of his expensive suit. The Grey men watched as the man slowly pull his wallet out, making no abrupt move. He opened the wallet and handed his ID to Iker when he stepped forward to take it. Iker studied the identification, looking back and forth from the photo to the man. Where had he heard the name? he thought.

Iker asked the man, "Do you mind if I check this out?"

"I'd expect nothing less, Mr. Stiel." The man's booming laugh resonated throughout the room as he saw Iker's surprise. Looking from man to man, "Mr. Kincaid, Mr. Crux Grey, and Mr. Orion Grey, of course, I've checked you out. I don't trust just anyone with my niece."

Lyra stepped around her husband to take Alessandra's hand and usher her into the chair next to where she was standing and then sat down, joining her. While doing so, she directed a question to the man. "Would you care to join us at our table? It seems we have something to discuss."

"That would be nice, Mrs. Kincaid, and your men are okay with this?" the man said hesitantly, in a deep voice with a thick, seemingly Eastern European accent. The man cautiously looked from Jess to Crux and then Iker. His gaze ended on Orion, standing closest, knowing from the lack of expression on Orion's face, the man meant him harm.

"Of course, can we get you something to drink, sir?" Lyra said as Iker walked toward the office, never turning his back on the table, while the other three men carefully made way for the man who said he was Alessandra's uncle to sit across the table from Alessandra. Crux positioned himself next to Lyra, while Orion moved himself next to Alessandra, inserting the two women between them. Koysta chuckled to himself as he witnessed their move. He liked these American men, protecting the two women. The Grey men knew Iker would run a check through The Firm's computers, which would provide considerable information about the man within a manner of minutes. They also knew Iker would use the hidden door in the office to survey the outside perimeter, checking for the two unidentified men and to make sure the property was secure. The men had worked together far too many years, not to have established security protocols for situations like this. They were never caught off guard.

"Please, call me Koysta. And yes, a vodka would be nice," the big man said as Jess walked away from the table. Like all the Grey men, Jess was good at his job. Using the excuse to play bartender, Jess would make sure all weapon stations along the bar were unlocked and ready if needed. None of the Grey men trusted the man who called himself Koysta.

Alessandra watched the man claiming to be her uncle. Why didn't he look familiar? Why didn't she remember him? Sensing Alessandra's uneasiness, Orion placed his hand over hers to offer comfort. Jess arrived at the table with beers and a bottle of vodka. Too worried, both women declined a drink. Koysta poured a shot of vodka and downed it in one gulp. He poured his second shot and said to the table, "I'd like to take my niece home." He paused to look at Alessandra. "However, she seems to have made new friends she's not sure she wants to leave." They all knew Alessandra had just announced her intentions to leave Hideaway Canyon; however, she was not inclined to tell the man so.

"If you're her uncle, how come she doesn't know you?" Orion challenged having no intention of allowing Alessandra to leave with this man.

Koysta downed his second vodka as everyone watched and waited for him to speak. His gaze met the eyes of the man demanding an answer, "As you already know, Alessandra has lost her memory." His gaze moved from Orion to Alessandra. "I am the one that can give her memory back." Orion, held his composure, knowing the entire village knew of Alessandra and her accident, so the information was easy to come by. It was never a secret. Orion and his family had wanted to help the young woman, notifying everyone, asking around to see if anyone in the community was expecting a guest. Orion took a long draw on his beer as he scanned his family sitting at the table; he still didn't trust the man.

Alessandra looked at Koysta knowing if he was her uncle, he was right. He was someone that could give her memory back and wasn't he someone she could trust. He should be able to tell her about her family. She desperately wanted the bits and pieces of her memory put back together. She wanted the puzzle solved. Earlier tonight, she realized that it was time for her to leave Hideaway Canyon, yet she didn't know where to go. Where were my parents? Where was home? And why was my jeep packed, as if I had been moving somewhere? Alessandra slowly reached into the pockets of her jeans and pulled out one of the two old photos she had found—the photo of the man, woman, and child that she'd kept hidden in her pocket every day since finding it. Without telling anyone, she placed the two photos in her pocket each day, feeling comforted knowing they were there. One of the photos, she'd already shared with the Greys, the other photo she'd hidden. Maybe she had a family somewhere, a family filled with love, like the Greys. Alessandra looked at the photo before extending her arm across the table and handing the photo to the man. "Do you know who this is?" she asked.

While everyone's eyes at the table remained on the man, Koysta studied the photo in his hands. "Yes, I know this photo. The child is you. You were nine or ten years old." He looked at his niece. His eyes returned to the old photo, "And the woman, she is your mother. My sister, Alina Ulanova Petrovich, she was prima ballerina, until she met your father." He turned away from watching the tears flow from his niece's eyes. "She was so beautiful. Everyone loved to watch her dance." Koysta looked up into Alessandra's eyes. "You look like her. You always have."

"Where is my mother? Is my mother in Paris?" Alessandra blurted out.

Koysta patiently answered the woman's questions, as everyone else sat silently and listened, "No, she is not in Paris. Your mother is safe. She is being protected by my men."

"Why does she need to be protected?" Alessandra continued to want answers.

"It is a very long story, one I am not sure you want to share with these people," Koysta replied as he looked at everyone seated at the table. "No disrespect intended. A family issue."

Lyra was unable to keep quiet. "Why does Alessandra believe her mother is in Paris?"

"I'm not sure. A memory perhaps. Her mother is not in Paris. As I said, she is safe with my men. Alessandra has been to Paris. She was there, with her mother, for three or four months many years ago." Without seeming willing to go into further details, Koysta finished his answer by saying, "Paris is part of the long story I speak of."

"The man in the picture…is my father?" Alessandra asked the question, knowing the answer.

"Yes, Anton Petrovich, he is your father." Koysta stopped talking before continuing as a grim look took over his face, unsure of what to say. His eyes roamed the table, stopping at his niece. "I liked this young officer in the picture." He continued to search for words, "I no longer feel that way. He is the reason you and your mother need protection." Koysta felt the tension rise at the table. He poured a third shot of vodka before landing his gaze on Orion, as if knowing what the man was thinking. "Part of the long story." Koysta downed the shot he had poured without taking his eyes off Orion. "I would never harm Alessandra, or her mother, they are my family. I am here to see that they remain safe." Orion felt the hairs stand on the back of his neck.

Interrupting the stare between Koysta and Orion, Alessandra pulled out a second photo, to everyone's surprise. She shyly glanced at Lyra and then to Orion. "I found a second photo." She held the photo for Orion to see. "I didn't really think it meant much, just two little girls playing." Alessandra turned to her uncle and handed him the second photo.

He smiled. "This is you, with Milena. She was your best friend. You were inseparable as children." Koysta abruptly handed both photos back to Alessandra. "She is dead."

Shock resonated through Alessandra. "Why?" Tears filled her eyes.

"Part of the long story," Koysta said in a cold stare.

Iker entered the room, handing Koysta's his identification card. The Grey men could tell, by the lack of alarm in his demeanor, Koysta checked out. The man was who he said he was, Alessandra's uncle.

Crux, Jess, and Lyra watched Orion closely. Orion didn't feel relieved by the news. "Micah Rollins sends his regards," Iker extended his hand to Koysta, who stood up.

"I believe we've met briefly, years ago in Kosovo. You were with Micah," Koysta said.

"Yes, it was on one of my first assignments. I thought your name was familiar," Iker said as he began to reminisce.

"I was a much younger man," he added jovially, then looked at Alessandra as tears continued to run down her cheeks. "I think it's time I take Alessandra home."

"No!" Orion refused.

Koysta stepped back from the table, not used to being refused. Crux moved stealthily to Orion's side, worried that the man meant to harm his brother.

"It's late. I think we all need a good night's sleep," Lyra jumped in to defuse the situation. "You can't possibly want to travel so late at night."

"No, I have a room at The Inn. Alessandra can join me there. After a good night's sleep and a healthy breakfast, we will leave in the morning," Koysta revealed his thinking.

Lyra knew Orion would have to let Alessandra go, but was sure he'd put up a fight. She could see Crux was prepared to stand by his brother. Lyra also wasn't convinced that Alessandra wanted to accompany her uncle to the Inn for the night. "Couldn't she stay with us for the night?" she asked. "You must understand that all of this is so much for her to absorb tonight. We're all she's known for the past week. She's become part of our family since her accident, and none of us are prepared to let her go." Lyra hoped her gentle persuasion would convince the man.

Alessandra moved from the protection of Orion and his family and took several steps toward her uncle. "I'm not a scared child anymore," Alessandra said. "I make my own choices." Koysta listened proudly as Alessandra spoke. "Uncle, if you love me, you will understand my wish to stay here for the night." Koysta only listened as Alessandra spoke. She wiped a lone tear that ran down her cheek. "We can have breakfast and talk more in the morning. Lyra is right.

I need sleep. We all need sleep." Alessandra took a step closer to her uncle, taking his hand and looked in the large man's eyes, "Please?"

Koysta had never been able to deny his niece anything, but she probably didn't remember that. He gently placed his hands on her cheeks, brushing both sides with a quick kiss. "Yes, Kroshka." He stepped away from Alessandra and moved within two feet of Orion, and their eyes met. "Do not dishonor my Alessandra." Koysta walked away, knowing Orion had received his message.

After Koysta left, Iker addressed Alessandra directly as the others looked on. "He is your uncle." He waited for her to respond.

"I know." She looked down at her hands in her lap. "I knew the moment he called me kroshka. I have memories of a man saying those words to me." She looked up into Orion's questioning eyes. "I wasn't sure until I heard that word. It means 'little one.' I remember."

Iker filled Alessandra and his friends in on what he knew. Koysta was a well-respected member of the Russian Special Services, Iker had thought the name seemed familiar. He'd only met the man once, when both were much younger, on assignment with Micah in Kosovo. He hadn't had enough contact with the man to recognize him, other than remembering his size. Micah knew the man well and said to cooperate fully with anything that Koysta would need. Micah made it clear to Iker that The Firm's services were available to Koysta, should he need them. Iker continued talking to Orion, Jess, and Crux, telling them nothing had come back on the two other men. Micah suggested showing the video to Koysta to see if he knew them. If Koysta couldn't identify the men as his or part of the RSS, he might know where the men came from.

"I'll have breakfast ready here, at ten o'clock, if everyone agrees," Iker asked for consensus. "I'll send a message to the Inn for Koysta, asking him to join us," Crux agreed, exiting The Rip to check the perimeter of the building before heading back to the ranch. Iker said good night and indicated he would see everyone in the morning.

"Agreed," Jess said as he looked at his wife.

"Agreed," Orion answered for him and Alessandra.

Cautiously, Lyra broached the subject. "Alessandra, would you feel more comfortable staying in our spare bedroom?" She looked to Jess, hoping for his support, but he said nothing.

"No, she's been staying in my apartment, and there's no reason for that to change," Orion grumbled, not willing to concede on any other option.

His sister offered an explanation to Alessandra and Orion, "I've never had any doubts about Alessandra staying at your apartment. I like the two of you together. However, Koysta's warning and your safety, does concern me."

Softening his stance, Orion hugged his sister. "Sorry." He felt like he was losing control, he was losing Alessandra, but he didn't need to take it out on his sister, he knew she was only trying to help.

"We'll be fine." Understanding Lyra's concern and knowing what she said to be true, Alessandra interceded, "Koysta respects my decision to stay at Orion's tonight, you have nothing to worry about."

As the two women embraced and the men exchanged good nights, Crux stuck his head in the front door, "Perimeter's secure. Heading back to the ranch, I'll catch you in the morning," and waved good night. Jess locked the front door as he and Lyra headed to their truck. Orion took Alessandra's hand to cross the room, turn out the light, and head up the stairs.

Orion followed Alessandra up the stairs and into the apartment. She excused herself and went into his bedroom and closed the door. She hadn't even said good night. He looked at the couch, wishing he would be sleeping somewhere else. He wanted to sleep in his own bed with Alessandra. Orion told himself he should feel grateful she remained in his apartment. He didn't want to remember his other option. He walked out onto the deck and grabbed a load of wood to stoke the fire. The sky was clear, and millions of stars lined the sky. Orion paused to find the Milky Way, thinking how beautiful it was and wondering what Oaklin Grey would think about Alessandra. Warmth rushed through his body, giving him the answer he sought. He opened the door and walked back into his apartment to stoke the fire for the night. Orion looked at his watch and saw it was almost two o'clock. He didn't blame Alessandra for being tired. He should be too, but he knew sleep wouldn't come easy for him tonight. After making his bed on the couch, he stripped his shirt off. He reached to turn off the small light on the end table and began to lie down, just as he heard the bedroom door open.

Alessandra stood in the doorway leading from his bedroom to the living room. She hadn't expected him to be going to bed. She stopped, realizing he was going to sleep. She had let her hair down and changed into his pajamas. Heat raced through his body when he saw her. He moaned. Someone needed to tell the woman there wasn't a piece of lingerie in existence that was sexier than how she looked to him in his old, worn-out flannel pajamas. His eyes were drawn to a sparkle reflected from her ears, telling him she wore the diamond earrings Lyra had lent her for the night. Neither woman had told him, but he recognized the earrings as those that had belonged to his mother. As he saw Alessandra take a step backward to return to his bedroom, he stood up, signaling to her he didn't want her to go. Orion walked slowly toward the woman, worried he would scare her if he moved too quickly, but Alessandra's citrine eyes remained constant, unafraid, as if reading his soul. "I can't sleep," she whispered to him as he arrived at the doorway. He picked her up and carried her to his bed. She tucked her head under his chin and wrapped her arms around him. He felt safe. He felt like home. As he lay Alessandra gently on the bed, he took care lowering himself alongside her. Orion wanted to make love to Alessandra, but he wouldn't. He remembered Koysta's words. Orion would always be an honorable man. He held her in his arms, knowing it would have to be enough for both of them now. They both fell asleep, Orion knowing he was in love.

Hideaway Canyon, April 26, 2013

Orion woke early in the morning, finding Alessandra, peacefully lying in his arms. He knew he wanted to wake up like this every day for the rest of his life. He couldn't remember a time he felt so much warmth and contentment holding another person in his arms. Orion lay still, listening to the soft, slow rhythm of her breaths and appreciating the feeling of her body, relaxed and pressed gently against him. He had no idea Alessandra's nights had been so sleepless until last night. No wonder she had shot him, he thought. She tossed and turned and cried out during the night. Her restless dreams and frightening memories woke him three times throughout the night. He wondered why Alessandra hadn't said anything to him about them. Her childhood memories must be awful? Didn't Koysta elude to that fact when he used the words "it's a very long story"?

Orion had experience with nightmares. His last mission had left him with sleepless nights of his own. He knew to wait patiently until the worst of the cries subsided, before reaching for her, cradling her in his arms, knowing there was nothing else he could do. For days he had wished Alessandra would regain her memory, he wanted to know everything about her; however, now he wasn't so sure. Maybe it would have been better for her memories to stay wiped clean. It was hard for him to imagine a childhood filled with such terror when his had been nothing short of a dream. He knew her past didn't matter to him; he liked everything about her. But he never told her. Somehow it hadn't seemed right to pursue a relationship with a woman who didn't know who she was. He had convinced himself to wait. Now, as he lay quietly next to Alessandra, fear engulfed him. Time had run out. She was planning to leave.

Looking at the clock, Orion carefully slid out of bed, not wanting to disrupt Alessandra's sleep. He quietly found a pair of jeans and headed to the bathroom for a shower. It didn't take long for Orion to shower. He ran his hands through his wet hair. He wasn't much for shaving if he could put it off until the next day. He went into the kitchen and started a pot of coffee before heading out onto the deck to bring in wood for the stove.

As he began to stoke the fire, he heard the cold pipes from the bathroom groan and the faint sound of water running, indicating Alessandra was awake and in the shower. There was no need for either to be in a hurry, Iker wouldn't have breakfast prepared for everyone downstairs until ten o'clock. Orion knew this would be his last morning, with Alessandra waking up in his apartment, unless he did something. But what could he do?

"Good morning," Alessandra found Orion sitting at the kitchen table, enjoying a cup of coffee immersed in thought.

He looked up with a smile. "Good morning," he said, wishing he could hear Alessandra gentle greeting every morning. "Would you like a cup of coffee, fresh pot, and we have plenty of time?

"Yes, thank you." Alessandra sat down at the table with Orion watching him pour her a cup of coffee. She took a sip. "Orion, thank you." She paused. "Not for the coffee. Well, yes, for the coffee, but I want to thank you for last night." Orion smiled at Alessandra's words. "I had a wonderful evening. You have such a special family. I only wish the night had lasted longer. I wanted to dance with you all night."

"Me too," he answered. Sitting quietly for a moment, both caught up in their own thoughts, Orion remembered the silver star necklace he bought for Alessandra with the citrine stone that had reminded him of her eyes. He stood up. "I'll be right back." When he returned, he sat down at the table with Alessandra and handed her the little black velvet box. "This is for you."

Apprehensively, she took it from his hand. "What is this? You didn't need to get me anything." He watched her. She opened his gift, struck by the beauty of the thought, as well as the gift. "Orion, it's beautiful." Alessandra looked at Orion questioningly. "I don't understand, what is it for?"

"It's for you. When I took you to the hospital, I saw it. It reminded me of you." He paused. "A star to watch over you, and the stone reminded me of your beautiful eyes." Orion took the necklace from her hands and stood up, helping her put it on. She rose to meet him, wrapping her arms around him, not wanting to leave.

"Thank you," she said, with tears in her eyes. "I will cherish it...always." She knew she would never take it off. The couple savored the pleasure of their embrace, neither wanting to think about Alessandra's departure.

Alessandra broke their silence first. "Even with Koysta filling in some of the gaps in my memory, I still feel like something's missing," she said, looking at Orion. "I need to find out. I need to resolve my past before I can know what I want in the future."

Orion's thoughts swirled in his head. *What is she saying? She is confirming that she is leaving. She can't go. I can't let her go. She's still in danger.* He finally spoke out loud, "Alessandra, I don't want you to leave. I think you are in danger."

"Orion, I don't want to go either. This feels so much like home. I love your family and…I have feelings for you. I have deep feelings for you." She stopped pleading with Orion and reached for his hand. "I love you, Orion, but I have to go. I have to know what happened. What brought me here? Where was I going? Why did I leave my home?"

Unable to look into Alessandra's eyes, Orion relented, "I understand." Orion did understand; however, his understanding her need didn't mean he wanted to let her go.

Orion and Alessandra finished their coffee without talking further. Both had so much to say, yet remaining silent, not knowing where to start. Orion didn't blame Alessandra for wanting her memory back or for wanting to leave to find out where she came from. He was more afraid than he'd ever been on any mission before, afraid to let her go. He sensed Alessandra was in danger. Not from Koysta, but from an awareness he'd always had, an intuition that made him good at his job. He needed to protect Alessandra, and he couldn't do it if she left, and he didn't trust anyone else to do it.

While Alessandra went back into the bedroom and finished packing her things, Orion kept himself busy straightening his apartment. He didn't know what else to do. He knew within a couple of hours, the woman he fell in love with would walk out the door. He worried he would never see her again.

By the time Orion and Alessandra descended the stairs to join everyone for a last breakfast at The Rip, Orion had thought up a number of reasons to prevent Alessandra from leaving. He hadn't thought that Koysta would anticipate Orion's plans to derail Alessandra's departure and come up with his own. Alessandra and Orion looked at each other surprised by the cheerful voices and laughter coming from the bar. It almost sounded like a party was going on. When they entered the room, Orion saw Koysta talking with Iker and sampling food. Orion suspected the fit man had to be in his early seventies and wondered if the man owned any other type of clothes beside Armani suits. Orion could see someone sitting in a chair, talking to Jess and his siblings, blocking his view, as Koysta's approach distracted the couple. Koysta embraced his niece. "Good morning." He extended his arm to shake Orion's hand. The man seemed much friendlier and more relaxed today. "I have a surprise for you, kroshka." Orion didn't like surprises.

"Oh," Alessandra said, not knowing what to expect.

All eyes followed Koysta's arm as it extended toward the table where Orion's siblings stood. Jess and Lyra moved aside to reveal Crux, assisting a frail woman to her feet. The years had not destroyed the woman's beauty and grace as the woman stood and moved toward Alessandra. Koysta urged his niece forward, holding her arm to steady her as he felt her knees begin to buckle. As Alessandra's eyes filled with tears, Koysta told his niece, "Your mother wanted to see you."

As the emotional reunion took place, Lyra's eyes tracked to Orion, who stood paralyzed. He knew none of the reasons he'd devised would keep Alessandra at Hideaway Canyon. He had to let the woman he loved go.

Jess signaled to each of the men to join him in the office, while the women visited with one another. Koysta joined Iker, Crux, Orion, and Jess at the conference table. "I've asked Koysta to disclose information that leads up to Alina and Alessandra's exile from Kosovo and arrival into the United States. I've assured him, any information he shares with us will be confidential and remain confidential for the protection of both women," Jess said, observing each man as he signaled his understanding and acceptance of the agreement. All eyes moved to Koysta.

Koysta began, "I understand that my niece has little, if any, recollection of her father. Without betraying my niece, I would like to explain the importance of Alessandra's return to her country."

Every man in the room continued to listen. "It is correct to surmise that Alessandra's father, Anton Petrovich is a very dangerous man. As Iker has informed me, you know Petrovich is first in command of the Yugoslav People's Army, tasked with carrying out the direct orders of Mikozavich, president of Kosovo, who has deliberately created ethnic conflict between Serbs, Croatians, and Muslim Bosniaks for years. As a young man, he showed promise. However, his desire to rise in power has led to oppressive tactics and violence toward the people in Kosovo. Petrovich destroyed villages and forced hundreds of thousands of people to flee their homes. During a two-year period, over one million people fled Kosovo and became refugees in other countries." Koysta paused for a moment as the men remained silent. "Alessandra loved her father and wept each time he left home to fulfill his duty as commander of his army. Petrovich could be gone for weeks and months at a time. One day Alessandra and Milena were out horseback riding when they saw Petrovich leave the house. They followed him to a small village, hiding in the woods, as he met up with some of his men. Alessandra witnessed her father order the village burned to the ground and the massacre of innocent people refusing to leave their homes. Before the girls were able to run away and hide, some of Petrovich's men spied them."

Koysta stopped and took a drink, knowing it would be difficult to continue his story, anger rose in his eyes. "Petrovich ordered his men to pursue and kill the witnesses, initially not knowing one of them was his daughter. The pursuit led to Milena's death and Alessandra being shot. The young soldier who shot Alessandra found her alive and hid her in the tall grasses. He thought she was too beautiful to kill. The young man told Petrovich the girl had escaped."

Koysta looked at Orion and continued his story. "The young officer was shot by Petrovich when the soldier identified the girl that escaped as his daughter." Koysta took another deep breath. "Alessandra survived with the help of an old farmer and his wife, who found her half-dead in the field. They didn't know who she was, but they hid the girl in their dug-out home, nursing her back to life. Alina was devastated, not knowing if her daughter was dead or alive, or if her husband was responsible. There had been rumors of

Petrovich's part in the country's violence, but Alina refused to believe the man she loved would be part of such atrocities." He continued, "Anton kept guard over Alina, knowing if Alessandra was alive, she would find a way to return to her mother, she had nowhere else to go. Petrovich feigned desperation to find the daughter he loved, searching the country offering a reward for her return. Without Petrovich's knowledge, I sent several of my best men to search for Alessandra. By the time we found Alessandra, I had already received word that Anton ordered the deaths of my sister and his daughter. I arranged for their escape." Orion's stomach lurched at the thought of Alessandra's father ordering her killed. He wanted to kill the man himself.

Koysta finished his story of the two women's flight from their country. "Alina and Alessandra had to travel hundreds of miles on foot hidden among thousands of refugees to the border, where I met them and transported them by car to a ship crossing the Adriatic Sea into Italy. One of my contacts drove them to Rome, where they caught a flight to Paris. For three months, Alina and Alessandra hid in Paris at the apartment of one of Alina's friends from her time with the ballet. After I was able to secure false identities for them, they flew from Paris Charles de Gaulle Airport to Montreal, Canada, where they were met by one of my men who drove them to Sault Ste. Marie. They were able to cross the border by car, entering the United States illegally from Canada, through Michigan and into Illinois." Koysta looked around the table after providing the information, expecting a reaction. The men continued to listen without asking any questions.

"As Iker may have already told you, I reviewed the video of the two men who showed up here the past couple of nights. As you suspected, the men belong to Petrovich. If I was able to track Alessandra here, so can they. Petrovich would only have old photos of Alessandra to share with his men. She's changed in the last fifteen years. However, if they have a photo of Alina as a young woman, it would be an easy connection for them to identify Alessandra, she looks so much like her mother." Koysta stopped talking when the office phone rang.

"Kincaid here," Jess said, answering the phone. The men sat quietly as Jess listened to the person on the other end of the phone.

"Yes, he's with us. Let me put you on speakerphone." Looking at the men sitting at the conference table, Jess said, "It's Micah."

"Koysta, my Russian friend, I hope my team is treating you well." Micah laughed as his voice could be heard on the speaker.

"Yes, they have become much friendlier, although I see no vodka sitting at our table." He laughed as he filled Micah in on what had already been discussed. "You must fill your men in on our custom." Iker stood up and walked out the door, returning shortly with a large bottle of the best vodka in the house and shot glasses for the men. Everyone looked at Orion as he reached for the bottle, poured a shot, drank it, and poured another. This time, he filled the other shot glasses, offering them to all the men at the table.

"I have some news all of you need to know," Micah stated to the group.

"Let's hear it, my friend," Koysta replied as he downed the vodka in his shot glass.

"The State Department has notified us that a warrant will be issued by the International Criminal Court for the arrest of Anton Petrovich for war crimes and engaging in acts with the intent to ethnically cleanse the country of Kosovo against political opponents and ethnic minorities. The charges include rape and murder." Micah paused to see if anyone would ask questions. When no one spoke, he continued, "You might want to check with Marco. I know the man's eighty-three years old now, but he's sharp. Other than Koysta, he's known Petrovich the longest, and he'll know the man inside and out."

"The old man is still alive?" Koysta chuckled as he asked.

Iker was the first to respond, "Yeah, he's like a cat. Nine lives and always lands on his feet!" Micah joined the men in a laugh, knowing Marco was given the highest respect from everyone in the room.

"What about Alessandra?" Orion said, already knowing the answer.

Responding sullenly, Micah's voice was heard through the speaker. "Petrovich loved Alessandra. However, he will choose to save his own neck. He has every reason to need his daughter dead."

"She doesn't even remember her father, let alone what she's lived through," Orion answered in defense.

"Very true, my friend. But Alessandra's memory has been returning, there is no reason to believe her memory won't return in full," Koysta calmly said to Orion, knowing the pain that lay inside the man.

"You're right, Alessandra's memory lapse is a problem. It is rumored that Alessandra is the one person that can offer undeniable testimony, and the prosecution is expected to seek her cooperation at trial. She is in danger," Micah said.

Crux added, "If she makes it to trial. Petrovich doesn't know she's lost her memory. He needs her dead."

"Koysta has verified the two men we captured on our video, are Petrovich's men. They have already tracked her to the area," Iker said.

"The more reason for us to get Alessandra away from here," Koysta said, knowing his words would alarm Orion.

Orion knew Koysta was right, although he didn't like it. The men continued their meeting, devising a way to get Alessandra safely off the mountain and to a safe house. Alina would remain in hiding with Alessandra to answer any questions she had, as her memory returned, and Koysta, along with his men, would cover security detail. Micah would make arrangements for the three to stay in a hotel in Denver for the night. Early in the morning, a private plane was hired to take them to a safe house in New York. After the men agreed on the plan, they left the office to join the women.

The rest of breakfast was a blur for Orion. Alessandra's mother was charming, and he could see the deep love between mother, daughter, and Koysta. As they ate, Alina stayed by her daughter's side, answering her questions and filling in bits and pieces to assist her daughter's memory. Orion stayed close to Alessandra, not wanting to leave her side. His heart sunk as she graciously hugged his family and friends, thanking them for their kindness and generosity. When his eyes met hers, he could only look away, not wanting to reveal the pain he was feeling. He knew the woman he loved would soon be driven away.

Anyone witnessing the scene would have thought the gathering was that of two families who'd shared a lifetime, reminiscing and enjoying a meal together. No one would have suspected the reason for their recent meeting. As everyone enjoyed themselves, all too soon for Orion, the conversation changed to Alessandra's departure with her family.

Orion felt like he'd been swimming endlessly in a lake as he listened to quiet conversations and watched Koysta's man carry Alessandra's property from Orion's bedroom, down the stairs and pack it into Koysta's car. Each time the man carried another load down the stairs, Orion felt like he was being pulled under, soon to drown. As the last of Alessandra's personal items were carried to the car, Orion remembered the guns in his safe. Accompanying Orion upstairs to secure the guns, Orion told Koysta the story of how Alessandra had shot him the first night she regained consciousness. Koysta laughed and laughed as Orion relayed the story of the shooting, telling Orion how he had trained his niece from the time she was a child, to use a gun and protect herself. She may not remember the training, but her instinct had kicked in. Koysta told Orion that he provided Alessandra and her mother with the two guns for protection, once they arrived in the United States, confident that Alessandra could use them should Petrovich find them. He also told Orion he was lucky to be alive, Alessandra's skills were among the best, even better than many of his men. As much, Orion didn't want Alessandra to leave with her uncle, he had begun to trust, maybe even like Koysta. The two men joined the rest of their families' downstairs at the front door for goodbyes. Crux and Orion had agreed to hide Alessandra's jeep at the ranch until further arrangements could be determined.

Lyra and Jess walked up to Alessandra and Orion to say their goodbyes. Lyra embraced the woman and made her promise to get in touch as soon as it was safe. As the two couples stood together, Alessandra started to remove the diamond-studded earrings she was wearing, the ones Lyra had loaned her the night before, for the fundraiser. Alessandra said, "I felt like I was wearing stars from the sky last night. They are so beautiful. Thank you for letting me borrow them," she said. With a wink from Lyra, Orion reached his hand up, stopping Alessandra from removing the earrings, "Please keep them," he said.

Confused, Alessandra looked from sister to brother, "I can't possibly keep these. They belong to your mother."

As Lyra wrapped her arm around her brother's waist, the two looked at Alessandra, and Lyra replied, "It will make us feel better knowing the same stars that watch over us, are watching over you." Lyra and Jess walked away.

"Oh, Orion, I can't," Alessandra said, understanding the earrings sentimental value.

"Please," he said, without giving her an option, and directed his attention to Alessandra's mother.

Alina approached Orion to bid her farewell. "Mr. Grey," she said, reaching for his hand as her daughter looked on.

"Please, it only feels right that you call me Orion."

"Orion, I want to thank you for rescuing my daughter. Your kindness, and that of your family's, can never be repaid, nor will it ever be forgotten," Alina stated with poise and grace as she looked into the man's eyes.

He bent down as he raised the frail woman's hand to his lips and gave her a gentle kiss, "I believe you are the one I should be thanking, it has been my honor getting to know Alessandra." Orion's eyes moved from mother to daughter as he released the woman's hand. Alina walked away, giving Orion and her daughter some privacy, joining the rest of the group as she entered Koysta's car.

Tears welled in Alessandra's eyes as she reached to hold Orion's hands. "I don't know what to say, Orion. You own my heart." She started to talk but was interrupted by Orion pulling her into his body, wrapping his strong arms around her in the warmest of embraces.

"And you, have mine," he said softly while holding on to her tight. He thought about saying, *I'm in love with you. I will be your family. I will provide you a home.* But he willed himself to remain quiet. Hadn't he and his family wanted her to regain her memory, wanted her to find her family and find her home. Didn't she have that right? What kind of man would he be if he tried to deny Alessandra? He knew it would be selfish of him. It was obvious to him. Her mother loved her. He couldn't help but think of his own mother. Hadn't the stars aligned? If Oaklin were here, what would she tell him to do?

The accident had caused her to lose part of her life. He had watched her struggle with her memory, to find her family, to find her home. Now that she knew, how could he ask her not to go. Orion also thought of the impact Alessandra's testimony would have at her father's trial. He knew it would be critical to the conviction and incarceration of Anton Petrovich, a man who had claimed the lives of hundreds of thousands of people, in his effort to gain power. After a few minutes, Orion loosened his hold long enough to lure Alessandra's lips into a long and passionate kiss with his.

Seeming like no time had passed, Orion looked up to see Koysta and his family as they stood silently waiting by the man's car. Breaking his embrace, he held onto Alessandra's hand as he led her into Koysta's car. Orion leaned over, brushing his lips across Alessandra's cheeks one more time, as tears streamed down her face. Orion stepped away from the car to shut the door. Koysta stepped toward Orion, extending his arm in a warm handshake. "I will take care of her. Like you, I am an honorable man." Tears were streaming down Lyra's face as she watched her brother and Alessandra. The passion the couple had for each other was obvious to not only her but everyone else. She didn't understand how this passion and love, that lie smoldering within these two people, could go unrequited. She secretly pleaded with Oaklin to help her understand. How could the stars have aligned and this happen? Lyra held Jess's hand as she walked to Orion and stood on his right side. Crux and Iker followed suit on Orion's left. The Grey family stood silently and watched as Koysta's man drove Alessandra away. Without speaking to his family, Orion turned and ascended the stairway to his apartment, not wanting anyone to see the tears that began to stream down his face.

Koysta had to make one stop at the bottom of the mountain to deliver a bouquet to the beautiful woman he had met at the Main Street Diner. If circumstances had been different, he would have enjoyed more time around Hideaway Canyon, seducing the woman called Charlee, with his charms. Koysta understood why it would be difficult for Alessandra to leave the beautiful community, not only because of her feelings for Orion, but he, too, enjoyed the short time he'd spent in the mountain community. As his driver pulled up to the diner, Koysta said he would be right back. He opened the car door, bouquet in hand, and entered the diner, looking for the woman. Charlee smiled as she glanced up from serving two men at the counter when she saw Koysta open the front door. After checking to see that the men she'd been serving had everything they needed, Charlee walked around the counter to greet the man.

"For you, beautiful Charlee," Koysta handed the waitress the flowers. "I must leave town." The two men at the counter concealed their interest in the waitress's conversation without turning around.

"Oh, Koysta, they are beautiful," Charlee cooed. "Will I ever see you again?"

Koysta smiled at the woman, "Should Russia ever get too cold, this is the first place I'll come to get warm." He kissed the waitress on the cheek and walked out the door. Koysta had only allowed himself to be extricated from retirement to secure the safety of his family. He thought, *Duty is not always convenient when meeting a beautiful woman.*

When they heard the door shut, the two men stood up without delay, hastily making their way to the front of the diner. As one man threw some cash on the counter, the other grabbed coats, pausing for a moment to peer out the diner's window to see what direction the man went.

Surprised by their quick movement, Charlee took her face from the flowers. "Was something wrong with your meal?" Neither man looked at her, seeing the coast was clear, they opened the door, intent on following Koysta Ulanova. As they hurried to their car, the men smiled at each other, realizing just how lucky they had been.

Orion sat alone in his apartment, stoking the fire and drinking beer. The weatherman had predicted another cold night, freezing temperatures but no snow. His phone rang for the fourth time. He let the answering machine pick up the call. As he sat, drinking his beer, he listened to the message being left by his friend, as Iker described how he would come over to kill him in his apartment, if he didn't let one of his siblings know he was alive. Orion had already received messages from Lyra, Jess, and Crux. He didn't feel like talking to anyone, but he knew Iker would be at his doorstep if he didn't return someone's call. The man had often served as intermediary in the family. He knew his best bet was to return Iker's call, knowing the man wouldn't want to offer his advice. He picked up the phone and dialed.

"Christ," Iker said, answering the phone, knowing it would be Orion, "can't you just answer your phone!"

"I'm all right. I want to be left alone," Orion grumbled.

Irritated, Iker responded, "I know, but you'd better tell your sister."

"You tell her," Orion said as he hung up. Similar to Orion's first arrival in Hideaway Canyon, Iker served as the family relay station. Like always, Iker served his duty as the middleman, contacting Lyra and Crux, assuring them he'd heard the man's voice, and Orion was all right and needed some time alone.

Koysta's man drove the family for almost three hours before arriving at the hotel where they would stay for the night. The men moved Alina and Alessandra into the hotel hastily, not suspecting they had been followed, but not wanting to be seen or to take any chances. In his meeting with Micah and the Grey men, it was decided that Petrovich's men probably couldn't identify Alessandra, but Koysta knew not to risk the women being seen any more than necessary. Tonight, they would eat dinner in their hotel room, and leave early in the morning for the airport and their flight to safety. Koysta's man did a perimeter check, reporting all was clear at the hotel. Koysta made a quick call to Micah, informing him they had arrived safely at the hotel, and he would check in before their departure in the morning. Micah sent word to the team that all was good.

Alessandra and her mother, and Koysta and his man, settled into their adjoining rooms for the night. After eating dinner ordered through room service, Koysta and his man took turns standing watch and checking the perimeter. After showering, Alina and Alessandra wished the men goodnight and closed the door between their adjoining rooms. They were expected to be up early the following morning, dressed for breakfast, and packed for an early flight to safety. As she lay awake in the darkness of the hotel room, in the bed not occupied by her daughter, Alina could hear muffled cries under the blankets covering her daughter's head. Alessandra's mother thought how painful love could be.

Undisclosed location, Denver, April 27, 2013

The call never came from the hotel. By six o'clock, Micah put his team on alert and placed a chopper on standby, concerned he hadn't heard from Koysta. He'd notified Jess, who would follow procedures and ready his team. Jess was able to talk with Iker and Crux but knew Orion would still be immersed in self-pity, refusing to answer his phone. Jess knew it wouldn't be long before a call would come from Orion's apartment, knowing Iker and Crux were on their way to his apartment, not above breaking down the door if necessary. Crux rarely activated for missions since taking over the family ranch; however, in this case, family was involved, and nothing could keep him away.

Orion's head pounded as he lay face-planted in his bed. Feeling a chill and refusing to get out of bed to stoke the fire, he pulled the blankets from the bed further over his head. He'd had a right to wallow in his own self-pity. He'd sacrificed. He'd done the right thing by letting Alessandra go, but he refused to leave the bed that smelled like Alessandra, an aroma of honey, lemon, and mint, the only thing he thought he had left of her. He couldn't remember how many beers he had consumed throughout the night. It was early morning before he rallied himself with courage and drank enough beer to crawl into his own bed. *Christ, this pounding won't stop*, he thought. Last night, he decided that if he remained on the couch, by some miracle, Alessandra would appear sleeping in his bed. He'd stood on his deck looking at the stars for hours, promising he'd forever love the woman if the gods would only grant him this one wish—just return her to his bed.

With time running out, Iker and Crux kicked Orion's front door in, moments before the startled man, head pounding, was awaken by the noise and grabbed his gun. The three men met in the middle of the man's apartment, ready for battle, Orion instantaneously seeing the men standing in the middle of the room. "I should still shoot you!" he yelled angrily, removing the chambered bullet and setting the gun down on the end table, angrily turning to go back to bed.

"Get dressed," Crux commanded as Iker watched on.

"Screw you, get out of my house," Orion shouted at the men.

"No contact was made this morning," Iker said in a low, calm voice.

Orion eyes met those of the men who had intruded into his home, instantly sobering, knowing what the words meant. He walked into his bedroom, coming out in minutes, dressed and ready to board a chopper he knew would be waiting. The team would fly to Denver to breach the hotel rooms and secure the safety of the parties involved. Somehow their routine operation didn't go according to plan; the call hadn't been made. Orion knew, like all the others, that the party could have simply overslept. Take off was in fifteen minutes, and soon they would have their answer. Orion looked at his brother and Iker. "Thanks," he said without embarrassment, as he grabbed his gun and walked over his front door as it lay on the floor, not worried about anything else but Alessandra. He needed to be sure she was safe.

Jess, Iker, and the Grey brothers boarded the helicopter bound for the undisclosed hotel in Denver with a plan to meet Micah on location. During the few minutes it took for their flight, Orion's anger mounted. Mistakes like this could cost lives. Like clockwork, the men executed their entry into the adjoining hotel rooms to find Alina and Alessandra missing.

Checking on the adjoining room where the women had slept, Orion shouted, "Clear!" He returned to the room with three men lying on the floor, shot. "Koysta?" he asked.

"Alive, but it doesn't look good," Jess replied, leaning over the man, checking for a pulse and applying pressure to a bleeding wound.

Paramedics arrived moments later to treat the two critically injured men with multiple gunshot wounds, taking them away by ambulance, while the third man was transported to the morgue.

Micah's forensic team had already arrived on scene and began filtering through evidence. "Our mission to breach the hotel room has now changed," Micah said to his team with a long look at Orion, "to one of search and rescue. I'd say we have less than a twenty-four-hour window before it becomes a recovery."

Iker continued, "Hotel video confirmed it was Petrovich's men. They'll have orders to keep the women alive. Petrovich is sadistic enough to want to kill Alessandra and her mother himself. He's got money, as well as military and political resources at his fingertips. We know he's already made bail."

"If Petrovich wants the ladies returned to him, the only way would be by airplane. Everything else is too slow." Iker had already begun tapping The Firm's resources. "No shows at the airport this morning. I was thinking they might try to commandeer the prearranged flight that Koysta was supposed to be on. Since that didn't pan out, I've got two of our men monitoring all public and private flight plans and passenger manifest, looking for two men with Alessandra and Alina." He continued, "I sent recent photos out to all TSA agents." Iker read, questioning looks in his team's eyes. "I pulled photos from video at The Rip. Most likely, they'd be traveling under assumed names, so facial recognition will come into play." The men appreciated how good Iker was at his job.

Needing to be involved, Orion added details from the confidential file he read previously. "Petrovich was known to be possessive of his wife and daughter, almost to a point of obsession. That could buy us some time. He may hesitate to kill them. If Alessandra's memory hasn't returned, he might feel safe. And Alina would say anything to protect her daughter."

"What we don't know for sure is whether Petrovich would try to enter the United States illegally or not. The question is, would he come here himself? He's more recognizable in Eastern Europe; however, here, he could travel almost anonymously," Jess added another possibility.

"Once they are out of our country, our search and rescue operation would be unsanctioned, which adds a whole other layer of problems finding the women," Micah said. "Right now, we have no leads. Let's get two pair of eyes on every flight plan, passenger manifest, and TSA facial recognition check." He issued orders. "Crux, you and Jess head to the hospital to see if we can get any information from the two surviving men when they get out of surgery." He paused. "Orion, Iker, you check rental car and hotel records. Alessandra and Alina are being held somewhere. The men are waiting for instructions from Petrovich. We need something to go on. We need it now."

The members of the Firm searched for several hours, looking for the smallest of clues that would lead them to the women. By nine o'clock that morning, the men regrouped in their temporary command center to go over the information they collected and see if anything could point them in a direction leading to the location of Alessandra and her mother.

"It looks like the waiter was collateral damage. According to the food service staff, Koysta ordered breakfast the night before, to be delivered at five-thirty in the morning for a party of four. No one was seen at his party, other than Koysta. It's my guess until it can be confirmed, but it looks like Petrovich's men hid, forcing their way into the room when the door was opened. The waiter had a hundred-dollar bill in his pocket. Possibly he was paid; however, we'll never know because the man's dead. One hundred dollars for your life…kind of sad" Micah stated.

Iker jumped in providing additional information, "We found a rental car receipt, leading us to the car used by Petrovich's men in Hideaway Canyon, while they were searching for Alessandra. We placed an APB on the vehicle, it was found by the local police abandoned at the bus stop. The forensic team was sent out to take photos and collect fingerprints and evidence. Right now, they are working to identify hair fibers and blood found in both the hotel and car. It hasn't been confirmed yet, but the hair fibers in the car could belong to Alina and Alessandra. The lab is also sorting through multiple blood samples. We know some belong to the waiter, Koysta and his man. Possibly someone else has been injured." Iker glanced at Orion, knowing the information would hit him hard; the blood could be Alessandra's.

"The crime lab is running tests on the bullets collected in the walls at the hotel, and those recovered from the men's bodies. Residue was found on Koysta and his man's hands, so we know they were able to get some shots off. If anyone was hit, we don't know. Both men are out of surgery and in ICU. It's touch and go, but at this time, we have no witness testimony," Crux said, providing information he and Jess had gathered from the hospital and labs. When he finished, he handed an evidence bag to Orion. He knew his brother would recognize the contents. "This was found in the car," he said.

Looking at the contents closely, Orion recognized the necklace in the clear plastic bag, the silver star-shaped necklace with a citrine stone he had given Alessandra, irrefutable evidence she was alive. "Alessandra was in that car. She was wearing this when she left yesterday." Without having a need to explain to the team, he knew she had left it for him to find.

Worried Orion's personal involvement would interfere with his professional judgment, Micah said, "Right now we have no reason to believe the women have been harmed. Nor do we know the condition of Petrovich's men, we know Koysta and his man got some shots off. We just don't know if they hit their target. We will continue to operate on the assumption that Petrovich wants Alina, and Alessandra returned to him as soon as possible. Therefore, our mission remains one of rescue. Any questions?"

Simultaneously, the five men heard the sound signal from the computer screen and looked over to see the list of bus ticket purchases made in the last two hours. One purchase stood out. Within the past hour, four tickets had been purchased at the same time, telling the men this group of passengers was traveling together. The bus was headed to Sault Ste. Marie and the Canadian border, the same route used by Alessandra and her mother fifteen years ago as they sought asylum from Anton Petrovich.

"That's them. They are traveling by bus across the border," Orion offered.

"Doesn't make sense. Petrovich would move them out of the country as soon as possible," Iker responded.

"He's smart. He knows we'd check all the airports first, and that's exactly what he wants us to do. Put all our resources into checking airports and flight plans while he has them driven out," Orion had a keen sense of the way Alessandra's father thought.

"What if it's not them?" Crux stated out loud, wanting his brother to think about the repercussions if his call was wrong.

Orion was sure, "It's them. I know it."

Crux asked, "If you're right, he's hired someone to file a flight plan out of Canada."

"Check all private and commercial flights out of Toronto and Montreal. Those are the two largest airports across the border from the bus stop," Micah commanded. "If we miss them coming off the bus, we can ask the Canadian mounted police to be on the lookout as they make their way to the airport. I've got a couple of friends I can call. They must be renting a car from the border to the airport. We'll check rental too."

"We need to stop them before they reach the border," Orion said, knowing he could never let the two women leave the country. The men planned their operation, coordinating with all government stakeholders in a plan of action. Now, all they had to do was wait until early morning to activate.

En route to the Canadian border, April 28, 2013

Wheels were up in thirty minutes, as the five men worked to activate the plan to rescue the two women at the border. By the time the men landed an hour later, local and state police had set up a command post and surrounded and set up surveillance of the bus stop. The FBI was onsite to monitor the Firm's operation under the command of Micah. The Canadian Justice Department contacted multiple Canadian law enforcement agencies, all placed on standby, ready to act if the fugitives made it across the border.

Micah called for a joint operations meeting to determine a course of action. They had two hours to coordinate their efforts, before a bus filled with fifty-eight people, would arrive. Fifty-eight potential hostages or victims if their operation didn't go as planned. The plan of action was to get everyone off the bus before trying to make an arrest. It would be too easy for Petrovich's men to use Alessandra, Alina, and the other passengers as hostages. Orion changed into a bus driver's uniform, entering the bus upon its stop at the station, making a usual shift change with the bus's driver. The two women would immediately recognize him and know a plan was in place for their rescue. He insisted his position be in closest proximity to the women when the operation was executed. Like Orion, Crux changed into a uniform identifying him as a bus driver, giving him access to the passenger unloading area, while Jess concealed his identity with a security officer uniform. Iker took a sniper position on the roof of the station, prepared to shoot when commanded. Uniformed police officers had closed the block down; however, they remained hidden, waiting for orders to advance. Micah would handle any necessary negotiations. Once the plan was agreed upon, and everyone was in place, there was nothing to do but wait. The bus's ETA was fifteen minutes away.

As Orion waited the longest fifteen minutes of his life, he thought about his feelings for Alessandra. He was in love with the woman he'd known less than two weeks, unconcerned about her past. He just knew, the stars in the sky had sent her for him. He smiled, thinking about his mother, knowing Oaklin had been a part of the plan all along. The stars did align. He had been guided to the right place, at the right time, so Alessandra could rescue him. Orion never thought it was possible for him to desire the peace and contentment only a wife and family could provide. He thought he'd been destined to be alone. He knew now, he was wrong. As he saw the bus slowing to enter the open parking spot at the station, he knew he couldn't live without Alessandra.

"On my command." Orion heard Micah's voice through his earpiece. Iker sighted the closed door of the bus at six foot two and waited. He'd make any adjustments to the height on the spot. After the bus came to a complete stop, the doors open slowly to a man wearing a bus line uniform. He stepped off the bus, turning to greet passengers as they disembarked. Orion made his way to the driver.

Acting his part, he said, "How's the trip?"

The bus driver turned to him, smiling as he recognized the uniform. "Good, all systems working." Giving him a second glance, he said, "New to the job?"

"Yeah, just hired on. From out of state. Joe sent me over to relieve you, said you've had a long drive," Orion said, hoping to encourage the man to leave the area without causing alarm. Passengers continued to file off and grab their luggage. The bus driver walked away, relieved of his duty. Orion could hear Micah counting passengers as they left the bus. He glanced over his shoulders, sighting Crux and Iker, confident he had backup. Still, there was no sight of Alessandra or her mother.

Orion heard Micah's count, "Forty-nine." Then he saw Alessandra's mother appear on the first of two steps leading off the bus. He said nothing, not sure she had recognized him, but he offered her his hand, like any bus driver would. One of Petrovich's men appeared behind her. Orion kept calm, hoping the man wouldn't recognize him as he wondered where Alessandra and the other man were. He cautiously watched as the two proceeded to the luggage compartment. A woman carrying a baby with two small children in tow was next in line to disembark the bus. Again, Orion played his part as a bus driver, assisting the woman with the small children. Tension began to rise in the team. Had Petrovich outsmarted them by breaking the foursome up? Orion heard Micah's voice again. "Alina and suspect one identified...fifty-six." Micah's count continued. Alina and Petrovich's man made their way to the luggage compartment collecting their belongings as the woman holding the baby with two small children joined them. The woman struggled as she collected her luggage and managed her three small children, not knowing the danger she was in. "Suspect one, armed and looking nervous," Micah warned his team recognizing the bulge underneath the man's coat. "Op two and three, move into position." Micah's words moved Crux and Jess into position. They couldn't afford, having the woman and three children taken hostage or become victims. Crux played his part, wiping down the adjacent bus as if prepping it for passengers. He positioned himself as close to Alina as possible without arousing suspicion. Representing the bus depot's security, Jess moved over to help the woman with the three small children, intent on moving them out of danger.

"Hold, we've got two to go," Micah said quietly over coms. As if commanding Alessandra to appear, the woman descended the two steps leading her off the bus, followed closely by Petrovich's second man. Alessandra's eyes met the familiar dark gaze of the bus driver. Anger rose in Orion as he saw the man callously push Alessandra forward toward the luggage compartment, her mother, and the other man. It took all Orion's willpower to hold back, waiting for Micah's command. The entire team watched as Jess corralled the woman and her three children to safety. Iker's finger itched in anticipation. He had one of Petrovich's men in his crosshairs. With a quick survey of the area, intent on saving innocent lives and those of Alessandra and her mother, Micah gave the order. "Take 'em out."

Both men dropped. From his rooftop perch, Iker took out Petrovich's man standing closest to Alina, while Orion grabbed Alessandra, pulling her to safety on the ground as Iker took his second shot. Neither of Petrovich's men had time to pull their gun. Chaos ensued. Tears ran down Alessandra's face as she clung to Orion, refusing to let go as he led her to the awaiting ambulance and her mother. Only after seeing her mother was Alessandra able to release her grip on Orion so he could return to his team and to assist in securing the area. Until the forensic team arrived, Micah called out orders assisting in the confusion. Before long, order was restored at the bus depot. Micah ordered members of the joint operations to stand down. The rescue mission was deemed a success, and local law enforcement took over.

A Gulfstream G650 was waiting on standby to take the team, and Alessandra and her mother, back to Denver where they would check on Koysta's status before heading home. The time on the flight would allow Micah to debrief his men, deciding to hold off interviewing Alessandra and her mother until the next day. Both women had been traumatized enough for the day. As their plane descended, Micah saw four black SUVs parked on the tarmac. Without alarming the two women, he alerted his men. Micah had arranged for two SUVs to transport the group; however, he was concerned with the appearance of the additional two vehicles with tinted windows. Did Petrovich send more men?

As the ramp extended from the plane, Orion saw four men step from the two vehicles with the word ICE written across their backs. "Stay here," Orion ordered Alessandra and Alina, as he drew his gun and charged down the ramp. "Who the hell informed ICE about our arrival?" he said angrily. The four agents approached cautiously when sighting the visibly displayed gun as the angry man descended the stairs, followed by four others. Orion stopped walking, standing his ground, flanked by his teammates, two on each side. Agent Ed Barnes pulled out his badge, thinking, *I don't get paid enough for this job.*

The agent flashed his badge at the men and pulled out some papers. "Ed Barnes, Immigration & Customs Enforcement," the man's extended hand was met with deaf ears.

"Orion Grey."

"Mr. Grey, I have an immigration hold issued for Alina Ulanova Petrovich and Alessandra Petrovich. It is our understanding that these two women boarded this plane," Agent Barnes stated.

Micah stepped forward, "What do you want with these women?"

"The women have illegally entered this country, and we have been ordered to return them to their country," the customs official said. "May we search the plane?"

"You have a search warrant?" Orion asked.

Agent Barnes stared from one man to the next, "No, but if you don't cooperate, I can return in the next twenty-four hours with one." Micah's refusal to allow the search presented Agent Barnes with no other choice. Barnes and his men drove away.

Iker said, "Petrovich isn't giving up."

The men waited until the SUVs had disappeared from their sight before going back on the plane to escort Alessandra and Alina to their waiting vehicles.

The party's first stop was the hospital, where Koysta had regained consciousness. Still in critical condition, his doctors allowed Alessandra and Alina a few minutes with Koysta, before sending them home, indicating the man needed rest. The doctor assured the two women, Koysta was receiving the best care money could buy. Micah increased the number of men on hospital watch, uncertain of any actions Petrovich might take. He called his contacts at the State Department, as well as the Firm's attorney, to see what legal action they could take to block any warrant for Alessandra and Alina's arrest.

It had been a long day, and the helicopter powered up for the short flight from Denver to Hideaway Canyon, where Alessandra and Alina would be safe. Jess had phoned Lyra to let her know they would have additional house guests. Alessandra and Alina would be staying with them. Orion didn't have room in his apartment for both women, so he was coming too. He refused to leave Alessandra's sight, or to trust anyone with her protection.

Lyra waited up for her husband, brother, and the two women. She had put Skye to bed hours ago and readied the extra bedrooms for their guests. When they arrived, she threw the door open, shuffling everyone into the warmth of their home. Lyra showed Alina to her room after the woman excused herself, exclaiming exhaustion. She grabbed a bottle of wine and beers, joining her husband and Orion and Alessandra, as they sat warming themselves by the fire. They talked for an hour before Orion reached into his pocket, remembering the star-shaped necklace. "Alessandra, this is yours," Orion said as he held out his hands.

Seeing the necklace Orion had given her, tears began to form in Alessandra's eyes. "I hated leaving it in the car, but I wanted to leave some kind of sign or trail. I wanted you to know we had been in the car and we were alive."

Orion pulled her close as they sat on Lyra's couch, "I know. It was like a beacon in the sky. I knew you had left it for me to find." He kissed the top of Alessandra's head as he watched Jess and Lyra rise.

"We're going to bed. Catch you in the morning," Lyra said.

Jess turned to his wife. "I'll be right there. I need to get some more wood from the porch, it's going to be another cold night in these mountains."

"No, go to bed with your wife. I'll take care of the wood," Orion volunteered.

Knowing he and Alessandra needed sleep too, he stood up and headed to the porch for wood. Alessandra followed. Surprised to see that she had followed him, he wrapped his arms around her, hoping to keep her warm. They stood embraced as they watched the stars in the sky. "I'll never let you leave me again, Alessandra," Orion said quietly.

"Orion, I'm here illegally. My mother and I saw the ICE officers at the airport. I know what that means. I remember. My mother and I have been hiding for years from my father and from your government. We knew claiming citizenship would lend a trail for my father." Alessandra looked up at Orion, wanting him to understand. "I don't want to hide anymore. I don't want to run. I want a home. I want a family, just like everyone else. I want a forever home," Alessandra said softly, wrapped in Orion's warm embrace, both deep in thought.

Orion knew he had to do something. He'd meant it when he told Alessandra he would never let her leave him again. Orion gave Alessandra a tight squeeze. "I know. I do too. We'll find a way to work things out." He'd wait until tomorrow when Micah would have more information for the team. If Micah's contacts didn't come through, he knew what actions to take to remain with the woman he loved. He would give everything up for her. It was getting cold, and Orion had volunteered to get more wood for Jess's fire. With a chuckle, he bent over and picked up a log, handing it too Alessandra and said, "It's nice having help." He continued to fill his own arms. Not long after the fire was blazing, Orion walked Alessandra to the guest room. With a soft, warm kiss, he said good night. Remembering he was an honorable man, he headed to Lyra's couch.

Hideaway Canyon, April 29, 2013

Jess and Orion slipped out of the house early in the morning to meet with the team at The Rip. Micah had good and bad news to share with the men. He began, "Koysta and his man are both out of intensive care and are expected to make a full recovery. Local police are providing armed guards on both men at all times until Petrovich has been located." He continued, "After hearing about the kidnapping of Alessandra and her mother, and the death of the young waiter and the attempted murder of Koysta and his man, the International Criminal Court issued a second warrant for Petrovich's arrest. Unfortunately, Petrovich had enough warning to go into hiding, he remains at large."

"Any indication where he might be hiding?" Orion asked.

"Not at this time. There's no reason to believe he's in the United States or would attempt to come here, even for Alessandra," Micah said, knowing Orion remained worried about the woman. "Word is that he's staying deep, There's a lot of people that would like to see the man dead. We'll let the International Court handle the search for Petrovich. If their government asks for our assistance, we'll activate."

"So what's next?" Iker asked.

Micah looked around the table at his men, stopping at Orion. "My contact tells me that Agent Ed Barnes has secured warrants for the arrest of Alina and Alessandra." He paused, expecting Orion to have something to say. When Orion sat quietly, he continued, "Barnes is on his way to take the women into ICE custody. The documents are not for the usual forty-eight-hour hold. They will not be detained in the United States. The warrants authorize the immediate deportation of the two women, back to Kosovo and potentially, into the hands of Petrovich."

"Barnes must be dirty," Jess said, suspicious of the agent's persistence in securing Alina and Alessandra's deportation. "Petrovich is offering a reward for their return."

"What you need to know is the search warrants are for Orion's apartment and The Rip," Micah said.

Jess replied, "She's not there."

Micah held up his hand to stop any further discussion of the ladies' location and said with a big smile across his face, "I don't need to know where the ladies are," knowing his men could buy time hiding Alessandra and her mother. "I've got every source I have working with the State Department and the International Criminal Court trying to find a way to keep the women here. As soon as I get word, you'll be the first to know. You know where to find me." He walked out the door. After Micah was out of hearing range, the men continued their conversation.

"They're safe. Both are at my place," Jess said.

"That will be the next place they look," Iker added.

"True, but it will buy us a little more time. He'll have to get a judge to sign off on the warrant to search my house." The four men looked from one to the other, knowing that wouldn't be buying a lot of time.

"Take her to the ranch," Crux suggested. "Jess's place is surely the next place to be searched. It could buy us another twenty-four hours if we took the women to the ranch."

The men nodded in agreement, except for Orion, "I'll marry her."

The men were speechless, not sure they had heard Orion correctly. Watching his brother closely, Crux was the first to ask, "Did you say, you would marry her?"

"Sure, why not?" Orion said with a look that dared any of the men to argue. The marriage would save Alessandra from deportation; however, it wouldn't protect the woman's mother. Crux was the first to respond to his brother's suggestion.

"Great idea!" Crux didn't have a problem supporting his brother's happiness, but he wanted to bring it to Orion's attention that it took two people to agree to get married. Matter-of-factly, Crux continued, "So have you asked Alessandra if she'll marry you?" He was sure he already knew the answer.

"No, but I will," Orion said. After an uncomfortable silence, the men started making plans. Knowing Orion like they did, the man was serious.

Standing up, Crux took control. "I'll head out to the ranch and start getting things set up. Jess, you and Orion head to your house to pack up the women and drive them to the ranch." He stopped and looked at Iker. "Iker, you want to contact Preacher, and put him on standby. Maybe give Micah a call and invite him." Thinking the team had done some crazy things, this topped them all. Who was he to say, what would make Orion happy? Jess, Iker, and Orion agreed they needed to be back at Hideaway Canyon by two o'clock, working at the bar when Agent Barnes arrived. They wanted the agent to think he had caught them off guard.

On the way to Jess's, Orion said, "I'd rather not say anything to the women about my plan to propose, not yet." Jess waited for Orion to speak. "For now, I'd like the women to know we're hiding them at the ranch?"

Jess shook his head yes, wondering if Orion was starting to have some doubts about volunteering to marry Alessandra.

"I'd rather talk to Alessandra tonight, alone."

"Totally understand," Jess jumped in, "we're just getting them to a safe place and buying some time for Micah to work his magic with the State Department, which is true." Jess knew he couldn't be dishonest with Lyra; he was always truthful with his wife.

The Firm's plan worked, and Alina and Alessandra's deportation would be delayed another day. By late afternoon, Agent Barnes's men had served two warrants with no luck finding the women. After threatening to arrest Jess, Iker, and Orion for obstruction of justice and interference in the apprehension of the two fugitives, Barnes finally conceded for the night. The ICE agent and his men drove away more determined now than ever to see Alina, and Alessandra deported and placed within reach of Petrovich. Barnes was close to retirement, and his pension just wouldn't cover the lifestyle he and his wife wanted to live. The reward Petrovich offered would have them set for life.

By six o'clock, the Greys all convened at the ranch, while Iker and Josie covered at The Rip, prepared to close for the night. There had been no word from the State Department or the Firm's attorney, and Orion knew he needed to talk to Alessandra tonight. It was clear to everyone Agent Barnes, and his men would invade the ranch within the next twenty-four hours with search warrants, and there was no place else for the women to hide.

The atmosphere at the ranch reminded Orion of the days when Oaklin and Abel were alive, giving reason for celebration tonight. Their plan worked, and Alessandra and Alina were safe for the night. The evening offered everyone a moment of reprieve after a stressful day under ICE agents' scrutiny. Putting aside their fears for what tomorrow would bring, the Grey family sat down to a meal as a family, giving thanks for their blessings. After feasting on a dinner prepared by Lyra, Alina, and Alessandra, the family retired to the great room to play games and visit. Alina, already feeling like she held a place in the hearts of the Grey family, fell in love with Skye, as though she'd always been a grandmother to the little girl with golden curls. Crux laughed and shared funny stories about his younger siblings and life on the ranch. Lyra shared stories of their parents. Orion talked about riding horseback for miles and miles, checking the fences and cattle with his father. The three siblings talked of sharing campfire nights, sleeping in bedrolls under the stars with their parents, and Oaklin's unending stories about the gods in Greek mythology and how bright stars formed the beautiful constellations. The Grey children grew up knowing they were loved and that Oaklin and Abel would be forever in the sky, watching over them.

Orion's mind wandered away from his sibling's stories and their guests, to the proposal he had planned. Jess and Crux were aware of his plans to propose to Alessandra and suspected Lyra knew by now, too, although throughout the evening she hadn't revealed to him, her knowledge of his secret plan. Orion had managed to slip into town to visit the jewelry store and purchase a ring for Alessandra. He knew his decision would seem rushed, serving only as a means to protect the woman, yet Orion knew in his own heart, he'd fallen in love with Alessandra. He wanted his proposal to be special, regardless of the circumstances. As everyone in the family settled into their conversations after dinner, Orion leaned over to Alessandra and said, "Would you take a walk with me?"

Alessandra gladly accepted Orion's offering, wanting to spend some time alone with him, "I'd like that."

Excusing themselves from the group and helping Alessandra into her coat, Orion opened the back door to the cold mountain air. "How about walking to the stables? I guess it's a little colder than I thought for a walk outside, but the stables will be warm inside. We'll be warm while we talk."

It was a beautiful evening as the man and woman walked arm in arm deep in their own thoughts. The moon was full, and stars covered the skies. As she looked at the stars in the sky, Alessandra found little consolation, knowing she would forever share the same stars in the sky with the man she loved, yet unable to be comforted by his warm embrace. Alessandra wondered if Orion, like she, was thinking about tomorrow. She had reconciled in her own mind she and her mother would surrender themselves to the ICE agents the next day. She also realized, upon that surrender, they would immediately be transported from the United States, never to see Orion again. Alessandra struggled to keep tears from collecting in her eyes, knowing she may never see Orion again, the man who rescued and cared for her, the man she grew to love.

When they reached the stables, Orion took Alessandra from stall to stall, proudly showing her the beautiful horses that were stabled at the ranch, promising he'd take her riding one day. They lingered at the stall of a young foal, watching the animal struggle with its new legs before Orion led Alessandra into the tack room. Her eyes roamed the room, landing on a plaid blanket covering the bundled hay, as her eyes adjusted to a soft glow coming from a small lantern. She saw a single red rose, lying in the middle of the blanket. Orion was nervous, feeling like he was a young man asking a girl on a first date, as he watched Alessandra for her reaction.

With soft eyes smiling as she turned to Orion, she said, "For us?" He nodded yes.

Leading Alessandra to the blanket where the couple sat down, Orion held her hand as he began by telling her he had never met anyone like her before. He told her, once again, what a wonderful childhood he had; however, he had always been skeptical of his mother's stories of how their lives were written in the stars, stories that were only fairy tales. He told Alessandra he never felt he was meant to have a wife and family, like his mother or sister. The career he chose had been a dangerous one that took him to dark places around the world, places he found difficult to crawl out from. However, since meeting her, he found hope, he found strength to try. He wanted a home. He wanted a home forever with Alessandra. Orion took the small box out that he had been hiding in his pocket and opened it, saying, "When I look at the stars, I think of you, Alessandra. I always think of you." Orion, struggling to think of the right words, said, "Alessandra, will you marry me?"

Alessandra stared at the beautiful diamond ring in the box, sparkling like a star in the sky. Her eyes began to water. She was in love with Orion and wanted nothing more than to spend the rest of her life with the man. How could she make him understand? Her memories had returned, and she knew Anton Petrovich would stop at nothing to kill her. He would kill anyone that stood in his way.

Tears filled Alessandra's eyes as she began to talk. "Orion, I love you. There is nothing I would like better than to spend the rest of my life with you."

"Then marry me. Crux started making arrangements for a wedding at the ranch yesterday. We can marry before ICE agents arrive. I love you Alessandra. I can't bear to let you leave again," Orion said.

She paused. "But it can't be. My marrying you would make me happy for a lifetime and protect me from ICE, but it won't protect me from my father. It also won't protect my mother. My father will kill anyone that gets in his way. I would never be able to live with myself, leaving my mother to fend for herself against my father."

"Then I'll go with you. I will protect you and your mother from Petrovich. I would be happy with you anywhere. Alessandra, I will not lose you again!"

"I don't want to lose you either, Orion," Alessandra said, looking at her finger. He took the ring out of its box and slid it on her finger. He kissed her gently on the lips.

He pleaded softly, "Don't give me your answer now. Please, for me tonight, wear the ring? Think about it, Alessandra. It makes no difference to me where we live. We will take care of your mother together, you and me. Please, don't make me live without you." Alessandra felt the warm embrace of the man she loved. For tonight, she would sleep with the ring on her finger and dream of a life with the man she loved. However, deep down she knew the danger she would bring to him and his family and to the beautiful mountain town that had become her home. Realizing it was late, the couple returned to the house, walking under a starlit sky, to find everyone had gone to bed. Like the evening before, Orion walked Alessandra to her room and, with a passionate kiss, said good night. As he returned to Lyra's couch fearful of what could happen the next day, he thought of his mother's promise to her children. The stars would align when you find your true love. Orion listened to the quiet sounds offered by the night until he sacrificed himself to exhaustion.

Grey's Ranch, April 30, 2013

Unable to sleep any longer, and seeing Alessandra's door was still closed, Orion went outside to start the ranch chores. He owed Crux that much. He hadn't helped much since returning to Hideaway Canyon. It only seemed right to do so now that the whole family was staying on the ranch. He also needed to burn off some energy. He could see wedding preparations getting underway at the house, from where he was standing working in the barn. He was the only one that knew Alessandra hadn't accepted his proposal the night before. She hadn't declined him either, waiting for an answer was harder than he thought it would be.

By nine o'clock, the wedding preparations made by Crux were well underway. Caterers had taken over the kitchen, and the florists were setting up flower arrangements and chairs for the intimate wedding scheduled to take place at noon. Crux, with the help of his assistant, had planned carefully, wanting to make the ceremony special for both Alessandra and his brother, regardless of the situation. Since everyone went to bed before Alessandra and Orion returned from their walk the night before, the outcome of Orion's proposal wasn't known. Micah called to say he was on his way, wanting to be at the ranch when the ICE agents arrived. He was expecting a phone call by early afternoon from the Firm's attorney, who was working diligently on a deal with the State Department and the International Criminal Court, pooling their resources to secure an injunction to keep Alessandra and Alina in the United States.

Hearing all the commotion, Alessandra got out of bed. She dressed quickly, wanting to be a part of the festive sounds coming from the other rooms. As she walked down the hallway past the great room and into the kitchen, she saw the preparations underway. Immediately recognizing them for what they were, she sank into a chair at the kitchen table across from her mother and Lyra. None of the men were around. Alina and Lyra saw the ring on Alessandra's hand as the woman sat down at the table and burst into tears. Immediately, Lyra and Alina moved to be by her side.

"Are these happy tears?" Lyra asked as she stroked her friend's back.

"Yes…no," Alessandra answered honestly. "Orion asked me to marry him last night." The two women waited. "I love him."

"Then why the tears?" Alina asked as she stroked her daughter's hair as she smiled.

"I love Orion and want to marry him. But it's impossible. Marrying Orion may allow me to stay in the United States, but it will put all of us in danger. Father wants me, and he will harm anyone that gets in his way. Marrying Orion won't protect either of us from father. You will still be deported. I cannot live knowing you are not safe, nor can I live with the fact that I put so many people I love in danger," Alessandra answered, looking from one woman to the next.

Alina wrapped her arms around her daughter and began to talk to her. "Listen to me. There is nothing a mother wants more than to see her child happy. And I know Orion Grey makes you happy. I can see that he is a good man." Lyra watched and listened as Alina continued, "Koysta will keep me safe. I do not fear Petrovich for myself. I only fear him for you, what you witnessed, and what he would do to you to protect himself. I have many friends and family in Russia, so returning makes no difference to me. What does matter, my dear daughter, is knowing that you are happy with the man you love."

"I know my brother loves you, Alessandra, and I know he would do anything to make you happy," Lyra tried to offer her friend comfort. "You will have the family's protection."

Crux and Jess found Orion in the stables mucking out stalls. It was obvious something was on the man's mind. Both suspected the response Orion received from Alessandra for his proposal hadn't gone as planned. Trying not to startle his brother, Crux gave warning from the doorway to the stables. "You're up early this morning." Orion looked up from his work to see Crux and Jess walk in.

"Yeah, couldn't sleep," Orion replied as he stopped working. He knew the men wouldn't go away until they heard the information they were after. "Alessandra hasn't given me an answer. She's worried that she's brought danger to all of us. She knows her father will do anything to protect himself. He'll kill anyone that gets in his way."

"Did you tell her that doesn't worry us?" Jess asked. "Did you tell her that's kind of our business?"

Orion looked at Jess with disgust, "Killing people, I didn't think that information was appropriate during a proposal! And our business isn't killing people, sometimes it just happens."

"Well, little brother. Now's as good a time as any. Let's go find out her answer. And if it isn't the one you want to hear, we'll help you change her mind," Crux said as he took the shovel from his brother's hand and led him out the door toward the house and Alessandra. The Grey family stuck together, especially when one needed help.

The three men walked into the kitchen to find the women at the table. "Good morning, ladies." Crux was the first to speak.

"Morning," Lyra responded.

"Good morning, gentlemen." Alina smiled at the three handsome men. She suspected something was on their mind.

Alessandra stood, turning to face the men, offering a smile, as she let her eyes drift to Orion.

Feeling more confident with the help of Crux and Jess, Orion reached deep within himself, knowing he was strong enough to endure anything Alessandra might say to him. Orion couldn't stand the suspense. He believed in ripping off the Band-Aid. He'd never been known for patience; he was a man of action. Taking one more deep breath, he asked, "In front of all these people, Alessandra. I love you. Please tell me you will marry me."

"Please, Alessandra. Marry him," Crux added. "We won't be able to live with him if you don't," he said with a wide smile.

"Yeah, he'll make us miserable," Jess added.

Lyra smiled as her family came together to help Orion, "No pressure. But we all love you."

Alina took a step forward to wrap her arms around her daughter, thinking her daughter couldn't find a better family to marry within and said, "It's all right. We'll figure something out."

That was all it took; Alessandra was melting in emotion as she stood looking at her new family. She reached for Orion's hand and, with a big smile, said, "Yes, I love you too." Not able to hold himself back, Orion engulfed his fiancé with a warm embrace. "Petrovich will—" Orion stopped Alessandra's words with a passionate kiss. At that moment, no one was worried about Petrovich. The Firm knew how to handle a man like him. Alessandra and Alina would be protected.

The women hurried off to get ready for the wedding, while the men were put in charge of handling the final details. The men suspected Agent Barnes and his men would arrive early afternoon, like they had the day before, so the ceremony was on for noon. Jess placed a call to Micah to see if he and Iker were on their way. Micah's phone went to voice mail. The preacher had arrived, and all final preparations were in place. The men waited patiently in the beautifully decorated great room for the arrival of the bride, Lyra, and Alina.

At eleven forty-five o'clock, four black SUVs drove up the mile-long blacktop driveway leading to the Grey family ranch home. Although cold outside, the sunshine spread warmth onto the valley, as snow-capped mountains seemed to protect everything they surrounded. Already dressed for the wedding, the four Grey men met their guests on the veranda with weapons concealed in their jackets. Agent Barnes had arrived earlier than expected, accompanied by his driver and twelve armed ICE agents. Jess slipped into the house to place another call to Micah. Still no answer. There was nothing they could do. The men watched as Agent Barnes approached them with a warrant to search the property and arrest Alessandra and Alina Petrovich.

Crux walked down the steps to meet Barnes and take the papers from him. "As you can see, everything's in order," Barnes said as he handed over the documents.

Crux nodded. "As Alessandra Petrovich and Alina Ulanova Petrovich's attorney, you understand I have the right to review these documents in their entirety to assure they are in order before allowing your search to take place?"

"Of course, you will find everything in order," Agent Barnes fumed at another tactic to stall what he saw as inevitable. Crux returned to the veranda where Orion and Jess stood, waiting. As the two men watched their guests, Crux took his time reviewing the documents.

After completing his review, Crux turned to Jess and Orion. "They're in order. There's nothing we can do." Jess and Crux could see Orion's body tense, worried the man was readying himself for a standoff.

"You interrupted my wedding, Alessandra and I are getting married," Orion called out trying to delay the inevitable.

"Let me see the marriage license," Barnes demanded.

The preacher joined the men on the porch, standing beside Orion. "The ceremony was just about to start," Preacher explained.

"Then I take it, you have no license?" Agent Barnes's patience was getting thin. He signaled to his men to approach the ranch house. Crux and Jess kept their eyes on Orion, anticipating his response.

Orion adjusted his stance and drew his gun. Barnes and his men stopped in their tracks. With one swift motion, Agent Barnes signaled the thirteen men that escorted him to answer Orion's movement by drawing their own weapons.

"Please stop!" Alessandra's cry came from behind Orion and the men on the veranda, and she and her mother slowly walked out the door, toward the steps, with small luggage in hand. "You can at least let us say our goodbyes without guns pointed at anyone's head!" Lyra joined the men on the porch.

Orion watched Alessandra, unable to move or speak. He knew he must be dreaming. How could this be possible? Alessandra led her mother carefully down the steps, sitting their luggage on the ground. She turned to Jess and Lyra. "Thank you for everything. I can never repay your kindness." She embraced the husband and wife as tears flowed from both women's eyes, no one knowing what else to say. They walked down the steps to Alina as Alessandra moved toward Crux.

Crux wrapped his arms around Alessandra in a big bear hug. "We'll take care of this. Don't worry, we'll find you." He released the woman that didn't need a piece of paper to make her part of the family, and with a big smile, he said, "I'm looking forward to our next dance, partner!"

Hearing a familiar sound off in a distance, Jess and Orion simultaneously glanced toward the sky, unable to see the sound's source.

Without realizing it, Orion had holstered his gun. He couldn't believe what he was hearing and seeing. He was being forced to say goodbye to Alessandra again. The woman he loved stood in front of him, tears streaming down her cheeks. Orion watched as she began to fidget with the ring he had given her. "No." He stopped her from removing the ring from her finger. "It's yours. It will always be yours." He grabbed Alessandra forcefully, wrapping her in his arms, unable to let her go or stop the tears from forming in his own eyes. "I love you. I will find you," he said before searching through dust he saw swirling from the ground around the agents standing guard, as the wind seemed to pick up. The roar of helicopter blades made his head pound as he looked up to see Jess and Crux shelter Lyra and Alina from the dust and loud noise. His eyes panned toward the stables as he saw Marines armed with AK-47s unload from two Chinook helicopters that had landed one hundred yards away, surrounding the ICE agents. Alessandra turned to see where the noise was coming from, unable to leave Orion's firm grasp. Orion watched as Micah and Iker evacuated one of the helicopters, followed by four men in black suits.

Micah and Iker advanced to the front veranda, followed by the men in suits. As they got closer, Koysta and his man appeared from behind. Orion didn't recognize the two other men. As Iker took the frail hand of Alessandra's mother and picked up one of the small suitcases to lead her back toward the veranda, Micah spoke, "Agent Barnes, I'd like to introduce you to Director Joseph Thomas of the State Department and Attorney Devlin Marsden, representing Alessandra Petrovich and Alina Ulanova Petrovich." Micah kept his eye on Barnes as he commanded the ICE agents to put their guns down. Each complied without further question.

Barnes's face turned red with anger, making eye contact with the men he'd been introduced to, fearing what he might say if he spoke. He knew the status of his retirement had just changed. Micah extended his hand to Barnes, offering a stack of papers for his review. "If you would like to review these documents, you will see that the two women are under the protection of the United States government, specifically under the protection of the members of The Firm. Judge Isaac Grimaldi from the International Criminal Court has signed the order of protection, due to Ms. Petrovich's agreement to testify at the criminal trial of her father, Anton Petrovich."

As Agent Barnes glanced at the papers, Koysta walked from behind Micah and embraced his sister, giving her a big hug. Orion kissed the top of Alessandra's head before releasing her to join her mother and uncle.

"I take it everything is in order?" Micah asked the agent. With a signal to his men to load up, Agent Barnes gave Micah a nod. "I assume we won't be seeing you again?"

Agent Barnes replied, "No."

"As a warning, if we do, you will be the man under arrest." Micah's warning was received. Agent Barnes walked to his car and led his team of agents back out the mile-long blacktop entrance to the Grey ranch, never looking back.

Orion left the veranda to join Alessandra, Alina, and Koysta. "Kroshka," Koysta announced, "I am here for your wedding!" With a laugh, he grabbed Orion in a big bear hug as everyone headed into the ranch house to celebrate Orion and Alessandra's wedding. "I brought good vodka." Koysta smiled. The small family affair was witnessed by Director Joseph Thomas of the State Department, Attorney Devlin Marsden, and half the residents of Hideaway Canyon. After securing their weapons, Crux even invited the Marines to join the party. The party lasted into the early morning. The ranch house, with its guests and bunkhouses, had plenty of room to accommodate overnight guests.

Early morning, Grey's Ranch, May 1, 2013

"Mrs. Grey, would you take a walk with me?" Orion asked his new bride with a smile as he swept her into his arms.

"I'd like that," Alessandra answered her husband with a questioning look, about to grab a coat.

"You're not going to need that. I promise to keep you warm." Orion winked.

The new couple walked out into the dark mountain night, unaware of the cool breeze blowing through the trees. Before they entered the stables, where Orion had once again prepared a special spot in the tack room, Orion warmed Alessandra with his embrace as he pointed to the sky. He searched for the seven bright stars that made up the hourglass pattern for the constellation, Orion, pointing out his findings to Alessandra. After locating the three stars in the center of the rectangular shape, he saw how the stars aligned. Oaklin Grey was watching over him.

Orion walked his new wife into the stables, where they found their special spot in the tack room. This time the single red rose was replaced with a huge bouquet of roses. Alessandra hugged Orion. "Thank you. They are beautiful." Orion gently kissed his new wife as he listened to her continue. "I have always wanted a home, one I'd never have to run from, one I could stay at forever."

His eyes met hers as he said, "Alessandra, wherever we are, whatever we choose to do. I will always be your forever home." He lowered his lips to his new brides for a warm, intimate kiss.

Epilogue, May 2014

Three months after her wedding and remaining in protective custody in the United States, Alessandra, accompanied by Orion, traveled to Kosovo to testify as a witness against Anton Petrovich, the father who had ordered her execution. Petrovich was given the maximum sentence of life in prison without the possibility of parole for the role he played in an attempt to ethnically cleanse a geographic region, a crime against humanity, the Kosovo War. A war that forced over a million people to be displaced from their homes, seeking refuge in other countries.

At the end of the trial, Alessandra and Orion took a late honeymoon, accompanied by Alina and Koysta, who acted as tour guides for the young couple. Alessandra and Orion visited the grave of her best friend, Milena, and the small village, Gjakova, where Alessandra grew up. She and Orion rode horseback through the tall-grass plains and pine-tree-filled mountains, a beautiful place that would always own a part of Alessandra's heart. After their whirlwind trip through Eastern Europe, the couple boarded a plane and retraced Alessandra and Alina's flight to safety, through Paris and Canada and on to their final destination in Hideaway Canyon.

As Orion sat next to his wife in the helicopter, he thought about how much his life had changed in the past year. Never believing the fairy tales he was told as a child or forgetting the darkest moments of his job, he had been able to find peace and contentment in his role as a husband to the beautiful woman who sat next to him, a woman he found unconscious along the road. He was proud of the strength Alessandra showed, facing her father at trial, rectifying her past with the journey she and her mother were forced to travel that led her to the small village near Orion's family ranch. Orion glanced at the large man and frail woman who sat in the seats in front of him, thinking how proud he was to call them his family. He knew the United States government had granted residency status to Alessandra and her mother for their cooperation with the International Criminal Court's prosecuting attorney. The surprise would be waiting for them at the ranch.

In the distance, he could see the ranch buildings of his family's property as the helicopter approached Grey's Ranch. Orion tightened his arm around his sleeping wife and leaned over to kiss the top of her head, gently waking her. After spending the past nine months out of the United States, Orion was anxious to bring his new family back to the valley he grew up in, the mountain community where he planned to add to his family, a family who knew they had a forever home.

Lyra could hear the helicopter's arrival from a distance as she glanced toward the riding arena where Jess, Crux, and Iker stood guarding over her daughter. Skye was riding the pony Crux had given his niece for her birthday, practicing for Orion and Alessandra's arrival. Lyra patted her growing belly, reminded of how lucky she was. When the dirt stopped swirling as the engines were turned off and the helicopter blades came to a standstill, Lyra looked up into the bright sunlit sky, knowing her parents were watching over them. The Grey family celebrated through the evening, catching up on the news and sharing stories. As the night sky took over in darkness, Orion leaned over to his wife and asked her, "Would you take a walk with me?"

With a smile, Alessandra answered, "I'd like that." She knew Orion wanted her alone in their special place. The couple walked arm in arm to the stables, stopping before entering to look at the stars. Like many evenings before, the stars were aligned, this time, Alessandra pointing out her husband's namesake constellation with a smile.

Before seeking out their special spot in the tack room, Orion turned his wife into his warm embrace. "We're home," he said, holding her tight.

She looked up into his eyes. "Yes, you are my forever home."

About the Author

With a career exposing her many talents, Pamela J. Roe finds herself accorded the opportunity to pursue a lifelong dream of writing. Presently living in Arizona, Pamela considers the world her home. When she's not writing, she and her husband travel as often as possible, visiting Colorado, Iowa, and Michigan, where their children and family reside. Always game for a trip to the beautiful state of California, Pamela and her husband enjoy the sunshine and being outdoors; running, reading, hiking, and taking long walks on the beach count as some of her favorite times. She holds a Bachelor's degree in Economics from the University of Colorado at Colorado Springs and a Master's degree in Educational Leadership from Northcentral University in Arizona.

Readers:

Watch for the upcoming release of *Crux Grey* and *Celestial Wishes*, books two & three of the series, *Grey's Ranch Trilogy* by Pamela J. Roe

CPSIA information can be obtained
at www.ICGtesting.com
Printed in the USA
BVHW030644070821
613910BV00006B/44